LAST RESORT

ANTHONY M. STRONG

**WEST STREET
PUBLISHING**

ALSO BY ANTHONY M. STRONG

JOHN DECKER THRILLER SERIES

What Vengeance Comes

Cold Sanctuary

Crimson Deep

Grendel's Labyrinth

Whitechapel Rising

Black Tide

Ghost Canyon

Cryptid Quest

Last Resort

Dark Force

JOHN DECKER SERIES PREQUEL

Soul Catcher

THE REMNANTS SERIES

The Remnants of Yesterday

The Silence of Tomorrow

STANDALONE BOOKS AND NOVELLAS

The Haunting of Willow House

Crow Song

WRITING AS A.M. STRONG

Mystery Crime Thrillers

THE PATTERSON BLAKE SERIES

Never Lie to Me

Sister Where Are You

Is She Really Gone

West Street Publishing

Cover art and interior design by Bad Dog Media, LLC.

ISBN: 978-1-942207-23-8

This book is dedicated to
Valerie Wilfred of Mt. Isa.
I'm so glad you read my books and enjoy them.
Keep on reading.

CLASSIFIED UNIVERSAL SPECIAL PROJECTS

VERUM CONQUISITOR

LAST RESORT

PROLOGUE

THE BAHAMAS—SEPTEMBER, 1912

CELINE LYDIA ROTHMAN, one of the wealthiest women in the world, walked through the packed ballroom of the Grand Fairmont Hotel as if she owned it. And in a way, she did. At least, since she'd married Howard Rothman III, heir to the Rothman merchant shipping fortune, at a beach-front ceremony earlier that day on the tropical island paradise of Singer Cay in the Bahamas.

It was evening now, and a storm was rolling in. She could hear the distant rumble of thunder even over the ragtime stylings of Irving Berlin being played by the orchestra her husband had shipped in specifically for the wedding.

Howard Rothman himself had given her one dance shortly after they arrived at the ballroom, then left Celine to her own devices and surrounded himself with a cadre of wealthy investment bankers, railroad tycoons, and Washington politicians. These men—drinking whiskey from cut glass tumblers and smoking fat smelly cigars—had been invited to the wedding not because of their enduring friendship, but so Rothman could show off his new luxury resort hotel and make deals. Even on his wedding night, Howard Rothman couldn't bear to let an opportunity slip away.

"My dear, you look positively ravishing."

Celine turned to find Clarence Rothman, Howard's younger brother, leaning against a marble pillar with a martini clutched in one hand and a cigarette in the other. He was everything her new husband was not. Tall and handsome with thick dark hair and sparkling blue eyes, Clarence had won the gene pool lottery at the expense of his sibling, who was shorter, mildly overweight, and already balding despite being only a few years into his thirties. Because of his bohemian lifestyle and lack of interest in big business, he also held the dubious honor of being the family's black sheep.

"I see my brother has abandoned you to kneel at the altar of capitalism," Clarence said, a slight smile touching his lips. "If you had married me today, I would not take my eyes off you the entire evening."

"But I didn't marry you," Celine replied, suddenly defensive despite her irritation at being ignored on what should be the happiest night of her life. "I knew what Howard was like when we started courting. I would expect nothing less of him."

"Fair enough." Clarence sipped his drink and watched the new bride over the rim of his glass. "I only hope you don't find a fat banker sitting between the two of you in bed when you retire to the bridal suite."

"Your concern for my welfare is admirable if a little crass." Celine glanced over her shoulder toward Howard, hoping he was done with his business cronies. She was disappointed to find him still holding court and briefly wondered what life would have been like had she married Clarence instead. Granted, there would be less money. The man survived on a meager trust fund, having been otherwise cut off from the family fortune when they discovered he had no intention of entering into the business. But what he lacked in wealth, he made up for in temperament. Clarence was a free spirit who liked to mix with artists, poets, and musicians. He kept rooms at the Hotel Albert in New York's Greenwich Village and lived unencumbered by the expectations of class. Life with Clarence would have been fun, for sure. An avant-garde whirlwind to delight the senses. But Howard offered stability, social standing, and more money than she had ever dreamed of. If given a choice, she would pick Howard every time. Having decided she'd made the right selection in her new husband, Celine smiled politely and gestured toward the throng of revelers crowded into the ballroom. "It's been a pleasure talking with you, as always. But if you don't mind, Clarence, I have other guests to attend to."

"As you wish." Clarence shrugged and downed the last of his martini. He observed the glass for a moment, then picked up the olive and popped it into his mouth before glancing toward the bar. "My glass is dry, anyway. Enjoy your evening, Celine."

"Thank you," Celine responded, before turning and making her way further into the ballroom toward the grand staircase at the far end. She had every intention of mingling and accepted the congratulations of several guests as she went, but her heavy wedding dress was uncomfortable. She would feel more relaxed once she'd changed into the evening gown that waited in their suite of rooms at the top of the hotel. She ascended the stairs to the second floor, walked to a private elevator that only went to the penthouse, then stepped inside and pulled the grill closed. As it rose, the sound of the party grew faint, and by the time she'd reached their rooms, she could barely hear it at all.

But she could still hear the storm.

It was raging outside, peals of angry thunder shaking the

very building itself. She crossed to a set of French doors at the other side of the spacious lounge area and pulled them open, recoiling at the sudden onslaught of stinging rain driven into the room by a mighty gust of howling wind.

Beyond the doors, a covered balcony overlooked a sandy cove and the roiling ocean beyond. She dared not step out, but even so, she could see giant waves building far out to sea and rushing toward shore with the storm's full force at their back. The night was darker than any she'd ever seen. She and Howard had stood on this very balcony and looked up at the waxing moon only the night before, but now it was obscured behind thick clouds veined with creeping fingers of lightning.

She felt a knot of apprehension twist in her stomach.

The storm was magnificent in its ferocity. It raged and crashed with a power she'd never before seen. It scared her.

A sudden bolt of lightning ruptured the sky, lancing down and hitting the beach with a resounding crack close enough that she felt the hairs on her arms prickle.

She took a nervous step backward, deciding she'd seen enough, but before Celine could close the doors, another bolt erupted from the heavens, and this time it didn't strike the beach.

Celine opened her mouth to scream, but at that moment, her world disappeared in a sudden flash of blinding light. The air inside the penthouse tore itself apart with a deafening bang. And then Celine found herself falling into a void of merciful darkness.

———

"Celine, my love, why aren't you enjoying the party?" Howard Rothman said, entering the penthouse suite from the private elevator. More than an hour had passed since he noticed his wife leaving the ballroom and making her way upstairs. He had assumed she would soon reappear in the evening gown purchased for this very occasion. When she didn't, he decided to go and look for her.

Now he found the penthouse suite empty and silent. Or at least it would have been silent if not for the storm that raged outside and the balcony doors that banged in the wind.

He mumbled a curse and walked to close the doors.

Why were they even open in the first place?

As he drew close, the carpet squished underfoot, soaked by the rain blowing into the room.

"Celine, what in the devil is going on here?" He shouted over the melee, assuming his wife was in the bedroom. "The carpet is ruined."

When he still received no answer, Howard stopped. He turned toward the bedchamber, noticing how that door too stood open.

"Celine?" He shouted again, overcome by a sense of foreboding. Something was not right.

The French doors banged back against the wall, a pane of glass breaking with an audible crack.

"Damn it all, woman," Howard bellowed, making a clumsy grab for one of the wild swinging doors, and grunting in pain when he missed, and it smacked into his knuckles instead.

He cast another glance toward the bedroom. Wedding night or not, there would be hell to pay when he found her.

Howard made another grab for the doors, managed to catch them this time. But closing them would be no easy matter. The wind was a force to be reckoned with. Practically a gale. It pushed against him, fighting back like it did not wish to be excluded from the room. And then, just when he was winning the battle, he caught sight of something that sent a chill up his spine.

A white piece of sheer lacy fabric caught on the balcony's iron railings flapped in the wind. Celine's wedding veil.

Howard released the doors in terror, letting the wind smash them back against the wall. More glass tinkled, but he didn't care.

Howard stepped onto the balcony, ignoring the stinging rain that lashed his face like a thousand needles and the wind that tore at his tuxedo. He grabbed the wedding veil and held it in one hand as he stared over the balcony toward the sliver of beach and frothing water below. If his wife was down there somewhere, he could not see her.

A choking sob of despair replaced Howard's anger.

He looked out at the churning ocean and cried his lost wife's name into the tempest.

His only answer was another ominous rumble of thunder.

ONE

JOHN DECKER STOOD on the steps of La Casa de Playa and watched the sleek black limousine glide up the tropical road toward him under a canopy of palm and gumbo limbo trees. He wiped a bead of sweat from his forehead and waited as the vehicle sliced through shafts of early evening sunlight and approached the expansive portico.

Behind Decker, the building's façade towered four stories high, its colorful Moorish architecture giving the hotel the appearance of a structure much older than its actual age. No, not so much a hotel, but more an exclusive corporate retreat on the Bahamian island of Singer Cay. The island was owned by his employer, Classified Universal Special Projects, more commonly referred to as CUSP by its management and operatives. Outside of this small circle, the organization was barely known, except to those in friendly governments on both sides of the Atlantic with the required security clearance. La Casa de Playa had welcomed more than one world leader through its doors and played host to top-secret conferences that had shaped the globe. Now it would serve as a backdrop to one of the most important events in John Decker's life. His wedding.

The limousine came to a stop. Its driver hurried to open the back door, then stood there, not even breaking a sweat, while the car's occupants emerged.

"There he is. John Decker. The condemned man," roared Colum O'Shea, ex-Irish Special Forces Ranger, and current CUSP operative.

"Good to see you, Colum," Decker said, shaking the big guy's hand as he mounted the steps. "I was worried you wouldn't be able to make it."

"Are you kidding me? I wouldn't miss this for the world."

"He practically threatened to quit if I didn't give him the time off," said a familiar voice from behind the Irishman. This was the other occupant of the limousine. Their boss, Adam Hunt. "And the last thing we need is Colum O'Shea turning his talents upon the world as an independent contractor."

"Independent contractor?" Colum turned to look at Hunt. "Are you implying I'd become a mercenary if you weren't cutting my paychecks?"

"Would you?" Hunt raised an eyebrow.

"I think I'll plead the Fifth on that one, as you Americans like to say."

"It looks like we have our answer," Decker said with a grin.

"Where's the wife to be?" Colum asked, peering past Decker into the building's expansive lobby.

"She's hanging with the girls for the evening up in the presidential suite. You'll meet her soon enough." Decker led the two men into the building while a pair of porters scurried the other way to collect their luggage from the car.

"Are you telling me all the women are locked away and won't be joining us?" Colum looked disappointed.

"It's the night before the wedding," Hunt said. "Bad luck to see the bride."

"I'm not worried about the bride," Colum retorted. "It's the bridesmaids I'm more interested in."

"You never change, do you?" Decker asked, smirking.

"Absolutely not. I lay my life on the line every day, saving the world from shady secret organizations—no offense to CUSP—and chasing monsters most people stopped believing in centuries ago. I need something to look forward to when I finish work. And right now, that thing is bridesmaids."

"Fair enough," Decker said. "Actually, you already know one of the bridesmaids."

"Really?" Colum perked up. "Who?"

"Mina."

"The cute blond from London who almost got herself killed by Jack the Ripper?"

"One and the same."

"John was adamant we fly her in," Hunt said. "I would have sent the private jet, but she insisted on traveling commercial. And in economy, at that. Said she didn't want to be indebted to CUSP. It was all I could do to get her on a private charter from the mainland. For a moment, I thought she was going to insist I let her swim over here."

"Good for her." Colum clapped his hands together. He watched the porters bring their bags in and ascend the sweeping central staircase that dominated the lobby.

A young woman in a black skirt and crisp white shirt with a name tag attached approached them with a smile frozen on her face. She greeted Hunt and then handed the new arrivals their room keys, which were white plastic cards with magnetic stripes on the back. Their room numbers were written in black marker on a paper sleeve.

"I'm surprised there are so many staff on the island,"

Decker said as the woman beat a hasty retreat and disappeared into an office behind the check-in counter.

"We only keep a skeleton staff here when the island isn't in use," Hunt replied. "A couple of handymen, gardeners, and security who rotate out on a monthly basis. We fly the rest of the staff in when required."

"Where are they the rest of the time?" Colum asked.

"We have various other facilities on the mainland. Many of them work at our headquarters in Maine."

"Makes sense." Colum glanced around before his gaze settled upon Decker. "What's the plan tonight, my man? Since it's just the guys, I assume there will be a bachelor party?"

"Everyone's meeting for drinks out by the pool bar at seven," Decker replied.

"There's a pool bar?" Colum grinned. "I like this place more and more with each passing minute. Can't wait to get the party started."

"It's just going to be a pleasant evening with friends before the wedding," Decker said. "I'm warning you; there aren't going to be any hijinks."

"Whatever you say." Colum's attention shifted to Hunt. "That bar had better be well-stocked."

"I think we'll manage," Hunt said. "I even ordered in a bottle or two of Irish single malt just for you."

"Now we're talking. I assume there's going to be food at this little shindig, too?"

"I've ordered up a full buffet," Hunt replied. "We're not going to starve."

"Brilliant." Colum tapped his key card. "Guess I'd better crack on up to my room and make myself presentable, then. We've got some drinking to do."

"I concur with that sentiment," Hunt said. "Settling into my room, that is. Not the drinking part."

"Goodness, man. We're on a tropical island for a mate's wedding. Lighten up."

"This is me lightening up," Hunt replied without breaking a smile. Then he stepped around the other two men and started up the stairs without looking back.

"He's going to be a barrel of laughs, I can tell," Colum muttered, watching their boss turn at the top of the staircase and disappear from view.

"Hunt gave us the use of this island for my wedding. He's picking up the food and bar tab. The man can be as stiff as he wants so far as I'm concerned."

"Yeah. You say that now." Colum grimaced. "But nothing's free with Adam Hunt. Just you wait until he uses this as leverage to get you risking your life on some god-awful assignment in the middle of nowhere."

"I'm sure that's not going to happen." Decker shook his head.

"Perfect. You keep telling yourself that." Colum slapped Decker on the back and chuckled. He glanced at his watch and then started toward the stairs. "See you out by the pool in a couple of hours."

TWO

COLUM WAS ALREADY PROPPED at the bar when Decker arrived at the pool deck a little after seven. He was in the company of Adam Hunt, who looked more relaxed now with a drink in his hand. Rory stood on the other side of the big Irishman, looking the least nerdy Decker had ever seen him. His hair was neatly styled, he wore a shirt that fit his wiry frame well, and he wasn't even wearing glasses. It was a marked difference to the fashion-challenged geek Decker had spent several days with a few months ago in the Amazon Forest.

Decker recognized several other wedding guests, mostly his fiancé's relatives, standing at the bar or sitting with drinks near the pool. Nancy's cousin—he vaguely recalled the man's name was Pete—was talking loudly to an older gentleman who was either Nancy's great uncle or her godfather. Decker didn't remember which.

"Rory. You're looking good," Decker said, focusing on the group from CUSP as he approached the bar.

"Isn't he, though?" Colum agreed, giving the diminutive

archaeologist an approving once over. "Are you wearing contacts?"

"Sure am," Rory replied. "Cassie said I should get them."

"Cassie?" Decker raised an eyebrow. "The biologist we rescued in Brazil?"

"I'm not sure she'd agree that you actually rescued her. It was more of a team effort to get out of that pyramid. But yes!"

"I don't believe this." Colum gave the archaeologist a quizzical look. "Are you telling me you have a girlfriend?"

"I guess that's what she is." A wide grin broke out on Rory's face. "We've been seeing each other since we got back to the States. It was virtual at first. Emails and a couple of Zoom calls. But the last few months, we've been spending more time together."

"Nancy said you were bringing a plus one," Decker said. "I assume . . ."

In answer, Rory's grin grew even wider.

"Good for you," Colum said. He picked up his glass and downed the last of his beer. "Time for another round. We have some celebrating to do."

"We do, indeed," Hunt said. "This time tomorrow, John will be a married man."

"And let's not forget my man, here." Colum gave Rory a hearty slap on the back. "With any luck, there will be another wedding in the near future."

"Let's not get ahead of ourselves." Rory looked aghast. "She only met my family for the first time a few weeks ago."

"Already met the parents." Colum was in fine form. "I give it six months before we're all back here."

"I thought you didn't believe in marriage." Decker ordered a drink and leaned against the bar.

"I don't if I'm the one having to do it," Colum replied. "I

have no problem with anyone else tying the knot. Kind of like it, to tell the truth."

"Bridesmaids?" Decker asked.

"Exactly. Women get all romantic at weddings. They get this itch to pair up. Must be all the love in the air. Works out great for me."

"You're a regular Romeo; you know that?"

"Damned right I am." Colum nodded.

"More like a hard-drinking fly-by-night Casanova," Hunt said.

"Guys. You're flattering me."

"That wasn't the intention," Hunt shot back.

"I'm taking it anyway." Colum glanced around. "This is a pretty small party."

"I told you," Decker said. "Small wedding. I don't have much family, and neither does Nancy."

"But even so, just the four of us?" Colum asked.

"There are other people here." Decker nodded toward Cousin Pete, who was gesturing wildly as he talked, almost spilling his drink in the process.

"Most of whom you barely know," Colum said. "What about friends? You must have some of those."

"I do. You're right here."

"Not us. Other friends."

"Well, there was my old partner in New York back when I was a detective."

"Why isn't he here?"

"Prison. He stole a priceless statue from our evidence locker, then lured me to an abandoned warehouse where he tried to kill me."

"I can see how that would put a crimp in your relationship. Anyone else?"

"My deputy in Wolf Haven. Chad. He threw me under the

bus after I saved the town from a Loup Garou hell-bent on revenge."

"I don't think I know that particular beastie," Colum said.

"A Cajun werewolf," Rory answered before Decker got the chance.

"Very good." Decker shot Rory a surprised look.

"I've been reading up on my monsters. Cassie has her own Cryptozoology TV show now she knows they're real. Darren Yates wasn't too pleased, I can tell you."

"And his show?"

"Cryptid Quest got canceled. He's doing a podcast out of his house with a couple of conspiracy theory types, but I don't think it's going very well."

"Shame. He was such a nice guy," Decker said sarcastically.

"Yeah. Not! But it worked out for Cassie. Turns out she was a more popular presenter than him anyway. She's really excited about the show. First episode airs in the fall."

"Good for her." Decker was pleased Rory had someone in his life. "Let me know when the show airs. I'll be sure to watch."

Rory nodded. "Naturally."

"Isn't that a conflict of interest?" Colum asked. "Dating a woman who has a TV show about monsters while you work for an organization that keeps the world safe from them?"

"I don't think so," Rory said. "It's hard not to set her straight sometimes, though. When she gets it wrong I have to bite my lip."

"I bet." Colum grinned. "Imagine what she'd say if she knew you helped catch Grendel and his mother."

"Imagine what she'd say if she knew they were currently residing on an island in Maine," Decker said.

"Right?" Rory laughed. "Would she ever get a kick out of The Zoo."

"Which she is *never* going to see," Hunt said. "Or even know about. As far as Cassie Locke is concerned, you work for a boring government organization that was as surprised as anyone else to find Cyclops living in the Amazon."

"Don't forget the Hydra," Decker said. "That one was worse. Almost ate us for dinner."

"I'll never forget the Hydra," Rory replied with a shudder. He looked at Hunt. "Don't worry. I won't spill CUSP's secrets. At least until we're married."

"You won't spill them even then." Hunt glared at Rory.

"You're thinking about marriage," Colum said. "I knew it."

"Not seriously."

"Yeah, right. You're not the love 'em and leave 'em type."

"I could be," Rory protested.

"No, you couldn't. You—"

"Guys," Decker cut in. "Can we get back to the matter at hand? My bachelor party, small as it is?"

"Sure." Colum shrugged. "But answer me one question."

"What?"

"Aren't bachelor parties supposed to be for the men?"

"That is the tradition," Decker said.

"Then perhaps you could explain why Mina is heading this way like she's on a mission." Colum pointed toward the doors leading into the hotel. "And she's brought a friend with her."

THREE

MINA BARRELED across the pool deck toward Decker with a determined look on her face. Behind her, rushing to keep up, was Nancy's daughter, Taylor.

"You know this is a bachelor party, right?" Colum asked as she arrived at the bar.

"Which is why we're here," Mina said. "We're not leaving. Do you have any idea how boring that party upstairs is?"

"No. We're not up there," Decker said. He looked at Taylor. "What's all this about?"

"Beats me. I already told her not to come down here." Taylor looked winded.

"And yet here you both are."

"Well. I kind of agree with Mina. They're gossiping about their high school boyfriends and drinking prosecco. It's not exactly rocking."

"It's not a rave down here either," Colum said. "In case you hadn't noticed."

"At least you have a real bar." Mina pushed her way past the men and motioned the bartender. "Jack and Coke, please."

"Me too." Taylor's eyes glinted with mischief.

"Not sure your mother would agree to that," Decker said. He fixed Mina with a disapproving stare. "And you shouldn't be drinking liquor either."

"You really want to go there?" Mina spun to face Decker. "After everything that happened in London. I almost died saving your butt. I got abducted and stabbed by Jack the Ripper. You forget that?"

"I'm well aware—"

"Jack the freaking Ripper." Mina's eyes flew wide.

"Okay. Fine. Have at it." Decker knew when he was beaten.

Mina huffed with satisfaction. "Besides, I'm twenty-one now. You can't stop me."

"Me either." Taylor reached past Mina and took her drink.

"Oh boy." Hunt watched the proceedings with arms folded. "That put you in your place."

"Yeah." Decker swigged his beer. "I know."

―――――

Later that evening, as the alcohol flowed freely and the moon slid low behind the palm trees lining the pool deck, Decker noticed Mina sitting alone on a sunbed cradling her drink and staring off into the distance.

Taylor was deep in conversation with Colum, listening with rapt awe as the Irishman regaled her with his war stories.

Decker excused himself, made his way over to the pool, and sat on a sunbed next to the glum young woman. "You look like the weight of the world is on your shoulders."

"Maybe it is." Mina glanced sideways at Decker.

"Want to talk about it?"

"Not really."

"You sure?"

"No." Mina sighed. "But it's the night before your wedding. I don't want to ruin the vibe."

"Duly noted." Decker nodded. "Tell me what's on your mind."

"You can't guess?"

"Abraham Turner?"

Mina nodded.

The previous year Decker had gone up against Jack the Ripper, AKA Abraham Turner, a vampire who had survived across the centuries by draining the life force of his victims and stealing their remaining years. Decker had defeated him, but not before Turner almost killed Mina. When Turner died, he was still in the process of psychically draining her lifeforce, and the process got thrown in reverse. His lifeforce, and those of all his victims, had flowed back into her. It had saved the young woman from certain death and healed her wounds but transformed her into something more than human at the same time. Neither of them knew what that thing was and how it would affect Mina long term.

"I almost didn't come to the wedding," Mina said. "After what happened I wasn't sure it was a good idea. What if I'm like him? Abraham Turner?"

"You're not a monster." Decker reached out and touched her arm.

"We don't know that." Mina looked down at her drink. "I still have nightmares. They're so real. It's like I'm there. I see the things that man did, the pain he inflicted. It's so . . ." Her voice trailed off.

"I wish you'd let me tell Hunt what you're going through. He might be able to help."

"He can't fix this. I don't want him to know." Mina pulled her arm away, briefly revealing the symbol burned into her wrist. Another gift from Jack the Ripper. The mark of a vampire. "Promise me you won't tell him."

"I already did, and I won't. Not if you don't want me to."

"Thanks." Mina looked relieved. "It's not just the bad dreams, though. I get these terrible urges. I want to do things. Horrible things."

"But you haven't, right?" Now Decker was concerned.

"No." Mina shook her head. "It wouldn't do me any good even if I wanted to. You took Turner's watch."

"It's safe. Tucked away in a shielded vault where it can't do any more damage."

"I know. At first, I could sense the medallion hidden inside the watch calling to me, just like Turner was able to. But now . . ."

"As I said, we have it locked away. You won't sense it again, I promise."

"That's good to know."

"These urges you mentioned . . ." Decker wondered if he should be keeping Mina's struggles from Hunt. CUSP had access to all kinds of technology and over a century of knowledge with such things. He wondered if they really could help her. "Should I be worried?"

"No more than I already am." Mina downed her drink. She looked at Decker, her eyes catching the light from a string of bulbs looped across the pool deck. "They are nothing I can't handle."

"You sure about that?"

"As sure as I can be," Mina said in a low voice. Her glass was empty now. She glanced back toward the bar, no doubt wishing to change the subject. "I need a refill, and you need to get back to the party. This is your night."

"I think Colum is enjoying it more than me," Decker replied, glancing back toward the Irishman.

"Even so . . ." Mina stood up.

"Mina, I need you to know something." Decker grabbed her arm. "I'm here for you whenever you need me. Day or night. Understand?"

"I know." Mina met his gaze. "I appreciate that."

"You can talk to me any time."

Mina nodded, slipped her arm from his grip, and started toward the bar. "Come on, Mr. Monster Hunter. I'll buy you a drink."

FOUR

LATER THAT NIGHT, a little woozy from the alcohol he had imbibed at the bar with Colum and the others, Decker wandered up to La Casa de Playa's third floor. It was late, and everyone else had retired for the night. Even Colum, who had tried to convince Decker they should stay longer by the pool to take advantage of the free bar. The building was eerily quiet.

Decker left the grand staircase behind and made his way down a wide corridor toward a door at the end. This was the presidential suite. More world leaders than Decker could list had stayed here over the past forty years since CUSP had built this island retreat. For the next few days, it belonged to himself and Nancy.

But not the night before the wedding.

Tonight, it was Nancy's alone. Decker's accommodations were one floor below, at least until they tied the knot the following afternoon. Even so, he couldn't see the harm in saying good night.

He took his key card out, was about to hold it against the

lock, when he changed his mind and knocked instead. It didn't seem right to barge in unannounced, even if it was only his soon-to-be wife on the other side of the door.

When Nancy answered, her eyes flew wide. "John. You're not supposed to be here. It's bad luck."

"I'm not coming in. I just want to see you one last time before we get married."

"Why?" Nancy must've been in bed already. She was wearing a white négligée underneath a dressing gown she now pulled closed with a shiver. "It's not like I'm going to suddenly turn into an old hag at two o'clock tomorrow afternoon."

"I know that." Decker was now second-guessing his decision to pay an unannounced visit to the presidential suite. He had a feeling the copious amounts of alcohol foisted on him by the big Irishman had clouded his judgment. "I shouldn't have come up here."

"No. You shouldn't. It's bad luck to see the bride the night before the wedding."

"That's just superstition," Decker said, realizing as soon as he spoke that he was wading into dangerous waters.

"You, of all people, should believe in superstition," Nancy countered. "Remind me again what you do for a job?"

"Point taken. But in my defense, it isn't the night before the wedding anymore. It's gone midnight, so technically, this is our wedding day."

"Still bad luck." Nancy shooed him away. "Go to bed, John. See you tomorrow."

"Okay. I'm going. But not before I get a kiss."

"Oh, for heaven's sake." Nancy stepped close and wrapped her arms around him, planted a lingering kiss on his lips. "Good enough?"

"For now," Decker said with a grin.

"Good." Nancy stepped back into the room, unable to stop herself from smiling despite her obvious annoyance. "Get some sleep. You're buzzed, and we have a big day tomorrow." Then she closed the door without waiting for his reply, leaving Decker alone in the hallway.

FIVE

AT 10 AM the following day, Decker stood on the front balcony of La Casa De Playa and looked out over the lush tropical landscape that sloped to the ocean beyond. In his hand was a mug of coffee, which he sipped gratefully.

The door opened behind him, and Colum stepped out, breaking the solitude.

"There you are." The Irishman joined Decker at the railing, cradling his own mug of Joe.

"Hangover?" Decker asked. Colum had made quick work of the free bar the evening before, and even though he appeared to be in control of his faculties when they retired to bed, Decker found it hard to believe he wasn't at least a little soused.

Colum shook his head. "I've had worse nights than that."

"I believe you." Decker glanced toward the horizon, where dark clouds were gathering.

Colum followed his gaze. "Looks like we're in for some nasty weather."

"And on my wedding day, too." Decker and Nancy had discussed holding an outdoor ceremony, but in the end they had opted to use the small wedding chapel converted from a rustic barn behind the main building. Apparently, CUSP had held nuptials here before, no doubt lending the island out to high-ranking officials and powerful world leaders looking for privacy when they got married. And it made sense. Singer Cay was about as secure as you can get. Despite its laid-back island atmosphere, state-of-the-art security features guarded the small spit of sun-drenched land, including hidden high-definition surveillance cameras, seismic monitoring systems that could detect movement as light as a footfall, and under-water motion sensors designed to prevent unwanted visitors from getting too close. Not to mention the satellite in a geostationary orbit high above that could detect not just oceangoing vessels, but also incoming aircraft and even other satellites trying to pass over the island. It was, in effect, a tropical fortress. And allowing dignitaries and world leaders to use it provided CUSP with vitally needed goodwill and influence in the top echelons of world government. The very satellite that guarded against incoming hostile craft had picked up the storm when it was still far out at sea and mapped its trajectory over Singer Cay, making Decker glad they had opted for an indoor ceremony. "If we're lucky, the bad weather will hold off until after the wedding."

"I wouldn't count on it." Colum took a large swig of his coffee and smacked his lips with satisfaction. "I spoke to Adam before coming out here. He's been in contact with the ops center back in Maine. Another hour, two at most, and those thunderheads will be right on top of us. It's going to get nasty in a hurry."

"Shame," Decker said, studying the approaching dark clouds. "It's weird. I checked the weather yesterday and there was no mention of a storm. It was supposed to be ninety degrees and sunny all day. Damn thing came out of nowhere."

"That's the tropics for you. Count yourself lucky it's not hurricane season or we might be evacuating instead of having a wedding."

"From where I'm standing, it might as well be a hurricane." The storm had drifted closer now. Angry black clouds tinged with silver roiled out on the ocean. Decker could see the water turning dark under the maelstrom. A demarcation point where the clouds blocked out the sun and rain fell in a torrent.

"It's no cyclone. There isn't a center of rotation. Heck, there's no rotation at all. It's just a bunch of angry clouds and a whole lot of lightning. If we're lucky, it will pass over us by evening."

"I hope you're right." The nuptials might be indoors, but the reception that evening was on the pool deck. If worst came to worst, they could hold it in the hotel's ballroom, but what was the point of a tropical wedding if you couldn't enjoy the tropics?

"Don't let it spoil your day, mate."

"Nothing could do that," Decker said. His mug was empty, and it was about time he got ready for the ceremony. "Guess I'd better head back inside."

"Yeah," Colum agreed, giving Decker a hearty slap on the back as he turned back toward the door. "Come on. We have a wedding to dress for."

SIX

"YOU READY TO DO THIS?" Colum asked, glancing sideways at Decker as they stood in the converted barn chapel on La Casa de Playa's grounds. It was early afternoon and the storm had rolled in like a battering ram with ferocious disregard for the small island beneath it. Outside, rain lashed down in sheets, and the wind howled like an angry banshee. The tropical maelstrom appeared hell-bent on ruining Decker and Nancy's big day. It was all they could do to get the wedding guests from the main hotel to the chapel without getting soaked, even though there was a breezeway connecting the two buildings.

Decker did his best to ignore the inclement and unexpected weather. He could not believe that in less than an hour he would be married to his high school sweetheart and someone he had considered lost to him for so many years before they had reconnected again. It was the one good thing that had come out of Annie Doucet's killing spree in Wolf Haven almost twenty-four months before. Many fine people had died during that dark time, and it still haunted Decker. If he had seen Annie Doucet for what she was earlier, maybe some of them would still be alive. Decker wished he could go back in time and prevent all that from happening, even if it meant he wouldn't be here today marrying the woman he loved. But he couldn't. The past was immutable. The future was a blank canvas, which was where he must now look.

Decker banished the maudlin thoughts from his mind and turned to Colum. "I've been ready for this since high school. I only wish I hadn't waited so long."

"A condemned man's last words," Colum said with a wide grin. When he saw the look on Decker's face, the grin relaxed into an apologetic smile. "Just kidding. I'm happy for you both."

"You'd better be, or I'll find myself a new best man." Decker sensed the eyes of the wedding guests sitting behind them in rows of white folding chairs on his back. A guitarist played soft music, while Adam Hunt, who had agreed to be the officiant, stood with his hands clasped together. It wasn't his first wedding, Decker knew. Hunt had overseen the nuptials of at least two other CUSP operatives. There was, apparently, no end to his talents.

Until now, Hunt had remained silently dignified while they waited for Nancy to make her trip down the aisle, his eyes fixed somewhere beyond Decker and Colum toward the closed barn doors. Now his gaze shifted downward toward his two employees. "Cut it out, the pair of you. This is a wedding, for heaven's sake."

"Sorry, boss," Colum whispered, as the guitarist began to play an arrangement of Johann Sebastian Bach's Baroque masterpiece, Air on a G String.

Decker felt butterflies swarming in his stomach. This was the music Nancy had selected for their bridal march, which meant she must have exited the small side room attached to the barn where she and her bridesmaids had gone to change into their dresses and apply their makeup. They had originally intended to get ready in the presidential suite before making their way to the chapel, but the storm had changed all that. A dripping wet bride would not do at all. The backup plan had obviously worked to perfection, and right now, the future Mrs. Decker was walking down the aisle with all eyes upon her, dry and happy.

"It's now or never, mate," Colum whispered, leaning close to Decker. "I'll distract everyone while you make a run for the hills."

"Not sure I'd get far, this being an island, and all," Decker said. "But thanks for the offer. You got the ring?"

"Right here." Colum tapped the pocket of his tuxedo jacket. "Safe and sound."

Decker nodded and took a deep breath. He could hear footfalls behind him. Nancy drawing closer with her bridesmaids, Taylor and Mina, a step behind. He turned to look at them, unable to help a smile, when his eyes met Nancy's. She looked beautiful in a sleek ivory A-line scoop neck lace wedding dress. Her hair tumbled down over her shoulders in wavy curls. She wore no veil, instead opting for a vintage barrette passed down by her mother. Since both her parents were dead, she had decided not to be given away and just have bridesmaids.

Behind her, Taylor and Mina were resplendent in their own deep green silk dresses. Despite her sour mood the evening before, Mina was doing everything she could to contain an excited grin. Decker noticed that she wore a thick gold bracelet circling her wrist, hiding the mark that had appeared when she survived Abraham Turner's attack in London several months before.

"Whoa." Even Colum was impressed. "I take back everything I said. You hit the jackpot."

"Change your mind about marriage, huh?" Decker replied.

"No. But if I ever do end up getting hitched, I hope my bride is as gorgeous as Nancy."

"I'm sure she will be, the poor thing," Decker said with a chuckle.

"I already told you pair to knock it off," Adam whispered. "It's like dealing with children."

"Sorry, old man." Colum turned back frontward.

Nancy was at the podium now. She took her place next to Decker and looked up at him, blushing a little.

"Shall we begin?" Hunt asked.

"Ready when you are," Decker replied. "Let's make this official."

"Very well." Hunt paused a moment while the music finished playing, then he welcomed everyone to the wedding.

It was a brief ceremony, and ten minutes later, they were approaching the vows. Decker turned to Colum.

The Irishman fumbled in his pocket, then came out with a small box, which he opened. He removed Nancy's ring and handed it to Decker.

The chapel was quiet, all eyes upon the couple. Only the incessant drum of rain on the roof and the whistle of wind through the rafters disturbed the silence.

They had written their own vows. Decker had practiced what he was going to say over and over again, terrified he would trip over the words. Now that the time had come, his mouth was dry, and his mind gone blank. A moment of panic overcame him. He looked down at the ring, then up at Nancy. His heart skipped a beat, and then he remembered what he wanted to say. He clutched the ring tight, ready to slip it on her finger, and opened his mouth to speak . . . Just as the chapel doors burst open.

They banged back on their hinges with a smack. A torrent

of rain and wind howled in through the opening. It was early afternoon, but the sky was so dark outside it might as well be night. And standing in the doorway, bedraggled and confused, a young woman Decker had never seen before. A woman wearing a white wedding dress.

SEVEN

THE STRANGER STUMBLED forward in her rain-soaked wedding dress. She looked dazed. Her eyes were wide with fear. Several wedding guests were already on their feet, hurrying to aid the stricken woman.

Nancy shrank back. She looked at Decker. "What's going on?"

"I don't know," Decker said. He turned to Hunt. "Are there any other weddings taking place on the island?"

"No." Hunt shook his head. He stepped down from the podium and started toward the young woman, his brow creased with concern.

Decker and Colum fell in behind.

When they reached the woman, she was already being guided to a seat by one of the other guests. Her sodden wedding dress clung to her thin frame. Her long hair fell to the sides of her face, matted and limp. Decker wondered how long she'd been out in the storm.

"What is this place?" She asked, looking up at them with imploring eyes. "Where am I?"

"This is La Casa de Playa," Hunt responded.

"Am I still on Singer Cay?" The woman's gaze shifted around the building's interior. "I don't recognize any of this. Who are you people?"

"My name's John," Decker replied, kneeling next to her. "What's your name?"

"Celine." The woman wiped water from her face. Her lips trembled. "Did my husband invite you here?"

Decker could see that Celine was cold. She was shivering. And no wonder. He looked toward Hunt. "We need a blanket. Something to warm her up. Towels too."

"Taylor can go fetch those from the main hotel," Nancy said. She and her bridesmaids had made their way down the aisle and were now standing behind Decker.

"That's a good idea," Hunt said. He turned his attention to Taylor. "Run back to the hotel and find Dayana in house-keeping. She'll probably be making up rooms. Ask her for a warm blanket and towels."

Taylor nodded.

"And bring back a mug of hot coffee, too," Decker said.

"Tea." The newcomer looked up. "I don't drink coffee. Never liked it."

"A mug of tea, then." Decker watched Taylor depart through the barn's open back doors, lifting an arm to shield herself from the driving rain as she went, then turned his attention back to the stranger in the wedding dress. "Can you tell me how you found yourself here?"

"I don't know." Celine shook her head. "One minute I was in my room watching the storm, the next I was out in the forest. You didn't answer my question. Am I still on Singer Cay?"

"Yes. You are." Hunt stood with his arms folded, eyes narrowed.

"Did my husband invite you here for the wedding?" Confusion flashed across Celine's face. "But that can't be. I don't know who any of you are. I don't recognize this place. If you attended the wedding, I would have seen you already."

"We are here for a wedding," Decker said. He felt Nancy's hand on his shoulder. "My wedding."

"That's not possible." Celine tried to stand up. "None of this is right. I have to find my husband. He'll know what's going on."

"Is your husband still out there, in the storm?" Decker asked. "Did you get separated?"

"No. He's back at the hotel with the rest of the wedding party."

"The only hotel on this island is La Casa de Playa, and there's only one wedding taking place," Hunt said. "This one."

"You're wrong. The Grand Fairmont is the only hotel on this island. I know that because my husband and I own this island. He built that hotel. Which means all of you are trespassing."

Decker exchanged a look with Colum. To Colum's left, he saw Adam Hunt stiffen, and his brow furrow. He looked at Nancy. "Will you take over here for a moment?"

"Sure." Nancy hitched her wedding dress up and kneeled beside the other bride as Decker stood and steered Colum and Hunt away from the clustered guests.

"Do you have any idea what's going on here?" Decker asked Hunt in hushed tones.

"About as much as you do." Hunt rubbed his chin. "If this woman was at the Grand Fairmont, it's no wonder she's drenched."

"You've heard of that place?"

Hunt nodded. "It's an old resort hotel on the other side of the island. A millionaire named Howard Rothman built it at the beginning of the last century. He was a shipping magnate who wanted his own private resort to show off his wealth. The hotel was lavish by all accounts. A grand ballroom made entirely of marble and onyx, with a chandelier that was rumored to have once hung in the Palace of Versailles. A private elevator accessed the penthouse suite. It even had a Turkish bath. The cost of transporting the materials here alone would have been a king's ransom."

"So why did CUSP build La Casa de Playa? Why not just use the original hotel?" Colum asked. "It sounds ideal."

"Because Rothman abandoned the resort less than a year after it was built. Left it to rot. It's nothing more than a gutted ruin. It was already falling into the ground when CUSP acquired this island."

"Why would he do that?" Colum asked.

"Grief." Hunt drew in a long breath. "He rushed to complete the resort so that it would be ready in time for his wedding to a young socialite he met not long after purchasing the island. His nuptials would double as the resort's grand opening. But on their wedding night, a terrible storm moved in. It was so violent, apparently, that the wedding guests could hear the thunder's rumble over the band despite being in the hotel's ballroom. At some point in the evening, his young bride went upstairs to change out of her wedding dress and never returned. When he went to look for her, he discovered their suite was empty, the doors to the balcony standing open. And caught on the balcony railing, her wedding veil. For whatever reason, his bride had jumped to her death, flinging herself into the churning ocean, never to be seen again. After that, he wasn't the same. He left the island, and the hotel he'd built upon it, never to return. He died a broken man twenty years later without ever knowing what happened on that fateful night."

"You're kidding me," Decker said. He glanced back

toward the stranger sitting in her soaked wedding dress. "What was the bride's name?"

"Beats me," Hunt said with a shrug.

"You don't think . . ." Colum's voice trailed off as he followed Decker's gaze.

"Only one way to find out." Decker returned to the clustered wedding guests, eased his way through, and kneeled next to the trembling woman again. "Can you tell me what date it is?"

"What? Why?" Celine looked confused.

"Just humor me. What's the date today?"

"It's September ninth."

Decker looked up at Colum. It was still only the middle of April. The Irishman's hunch might be correct. "And the year?"

Celine hesitated a moment, staring at Decker as if he were crazy. Then she said, "Well, it's 1912, of course."

EIGHT

DECKER SAID nothing for a long moment while he absorbed Celine's answer. He could sense Nancy next to him, heard her let out a small sigh of surprise. He was about to press Celine for more information when Adam Hunt laid a hand on his shoulder.

"A word, if you please," Hunt said, motioning for Decker to step away from the group.

Decker stood and followed Hunt and Colum until the rest of the wedding party couldn't overhear them. "What is it?" He asked.

"Look." Colum held his phone out.

Decker glanced at the screen, and a faded black-and-white photograph Colum had found on the Internet. The portrait of an attractive young woman with flowing long hair. The face staring back at him in shades of gray was the same one that had looked at him with wide eyes and proclaimed the date to be 1912 mere moments before.

A caption underneath the photograph identified the subject as Mrs. Celine Rothman. Decker frowned. "That's her."

"There's more, too," Hunt said. "Read the article beneath the photo."

Decker took the phone from Colum's hands. Across the top of the webpage, in bold black type, was an ominous headline.

The mysterious disappearance of millionaire tycoon Howard Rothman's bride on their wedding night in 1912.

Below, in smaller type, was a subhead.

Suicide or something more sinister? Was the beautiful newlywed socialite abducted?

He scrolled down, reading the accompanying article, which was mostly speculation about Celine Rothman's fate, then handed the phone back to Colum.

"If that woman sitting over there really is Celine Rothman, then it wasn't suicide or an abduction. Somehow she ended up a hundred and ten years in the future."

"If it's not her, someone's playing a hell of a trick on us," Colum said, his eyes fixed upon the bedraggled bride.

"It's no trick," Hunt said. "She's real, and she's here. Question is, how?"

"Some kind of dimensional anomaly that trapped her in time?" Decker asked. "Like those German submariners on the U-boat?"

"I don't think so." Hunt shook his head. "Alien technology removed from a foo fighter in World War Two trapped those German sailors. There's nothing like that on this island, I can assure you."

"Come again?" Colum's eyes flew wide with surprise. "I have a feeling I'm missing something here."

"It's a long story," Decker told him.

"And it's classified, too," Hunt said.

"Which means you're not going to tell me." Colum looked disappointed.

"That's exactly what it means." Hunt rubbed his chin. "Besides, there are more pressing concerns. Like finding out how a bride from 1912 ended up spirited across time to gate-crash this wedding."

"We need to find out what else she remembers," Decker said. "And she needs to know where and when she is."

"Are you sure that's wise?" Colum asked. "We don't know how she'll react."

"We have no choice. She's going to find out sooner or later." Decker walked back toward the rest of the group, and their unusual guest. "Celine?"

"Yes?" The soaked woman in the wedding dress looked up, her eyes wide.

"I have something important to tell you, and it might come as a shock."

"What?" A look of alarm spread across Celine's face.

"You said the year is 1912."

"That's correct."

Decker kneeled next to her. "I'm afraid that isn't true. Not anymore."

"What are you talking about?" Celine looked around the assembled group. "Of course it's 1912."

"No." Decker shook his head. "Whatever happened to you when that lightning struck. It did something. Brought you here. Transported you to the future." Decker paused, wishing there was a way to soften the blow but there wasn't. "Celine, the year is 2022."

NINE

WHAT?" Celine jumped up. "No. That's impossible."

"I'm afraid not." Hunt stepped forward. "John's telling the truth."

"I don't believe you. You're lying." Celine looked frantic. "Did my husband's business rivals put you up to this? Oh my God. This is a kidnapping. Yes, that's what's going on. Are you going to blackmail Howard? Hold me to ransom?"

"This is not a kidnapping," Decker said. "I promise. What we're telling you is the truth."

"See?" Colum held his cell phone out for her to view. The date was displayed on the screen. "Look at this."

"That doesn't prove anything." Celine shook her head.

"Have you ever seen a device like the one my friend is holding?" Decker asked. "Look around. Look at the lights. Look at our clothing. Do we look like we're from 1912?"

Celine studied her surroundings. "No."

"That's because we're not. I know it's hard to believe, but this is 2022. I assure you of that."

Celine's shoulders slumped as the fight drained from her. "How?"

"We don't know." Decker wished he could give her answers, but they didn't have any to give.

"But we *are* going to find out," Hunt said.

"That means Howard . . . everyone back at the wedding reception . . . they're all dead."

Decker nodded.

"I'm alone." Celine sank back onto the chair. She began to cry.

"John?" Nancy took Decker's arm. "Can I have a word?"

"Sure." Decker turned to her.

"That young woman is freezing," Nancy said, her gaze drifting to Celine then back to Decker. "And she's in shock."

"Taylor should be back with the blankets soon," Decker replied.

"We need to do more than that. If she doesn't get out of that wet dress she'll catch pneumonia. Goodness knows how long she was out in that storm. We must get her back to the hotel so she can take a hot shower and get into dry clothes. And we need to do it quickly."

"What about the wedding?" Colum asked. "You guys were about to seal the deal."

"It will have to wait." There was a tinge of disappointment in Nancy's voice.

"Understood." Decker knew Nancy was right. Their most pressing concern was to make Celine comfortable. Then, once she was dry and warm, after the shock of Decker's revelation had worn off, she might be able tell them more about her sudden and strange appearance. Something that would allow him to unravel this mystery and put things right. Only then would they be able to think about continuing their own ceremony. But he knew one thing. Their wedding wouldn't be happening today. He met Nancy's gaze. An unspoken communication that they were both on the same page. Then he turned to Hunt. "Let's get everyone back to the main house. Nancy and Taylor can take care of our uninvited guest. Make sure she doesn't catch her death."

"Then we can get some answers," rumbled Colum as another peal of thunder shook the barn. He observed Decker under hooded eyes. "I swear, man, it's like trouble just has a way of finding you."

"Tell me about it," Decker replied with a grimace. "Fate won't cut me a break."

TEN

AN HOUR LATER, Decker stood outside of a room on La Casa de Playa's second floor. Inside, Nancy, Taylor, and Mina were attending to the soaking wet and terrified bride and had so far forbidden anyone else to enter. He paced back and forth, frustrated not just that he couldn't question the woman further, but also because her untimely arrival had delayed his wedding.

"Cut it out, mate," Colum said, leaning against the wall of the corridor door with his hands pushed into his trouser pockets. His tuxedo jacket and necktie were gone. He'd rolled the sleeves of his white shirt up past his elbows. "You're going to wear a track in the carpet at this rate."

"What's taking them so long?" Decker said, more to himself than anyone else. They had already confirmed their strange visitor's identity as Celine Rothman, the bride of a wealthy shipping magnate who vanished on her wedding night a hundred and ten years before, but how she got here, and why, remained a mystery. "If Nancy would just let us in there, we could get to the bottom of this."

"I'm sure she will just as soon as possible." As usual,

Colum's outward demeanor was calm and collected. If anything rattled him, he didn't show it. "You saw the state that poor woman was in. Have a little patience."

"Easy for you to say. It's not your wedding day."

"The timing isn't ideal, I grant you that," Colum admitted. "Maybe Adam will have something for us when he returns."

"Let's hope." Decker stopped pacing and rubbed his temples. Adam Hunt had excused himself moments after returning to the main building and retreated to an office on the ground floor, taking Rory along with him. He wanted to contact CUSP back in Maine to see if there was anything in their records regarding Celine Rothman's strange disappearance all those years ago. Decker wondered if that disappearance had anything to do with their employer's stewardship of the island and he said as much to Colum. "Don't you think it's strange that CUSP just happen to own an island where a woman vanished into thin air over a century ago, only to reappear right now?"

"The coincidence does stretch credibility." The Irishman had clearly been thinking the same thing. "But I can't imagine Hunt knew this was going to happen. Otherwise, why would he suggest you get married on Singer Cay, surrounded by people that aren't aware of what we do for a living?"

"I don't know," Decker admitted.

"And think of the cleanup. We'll need to swear the entire wedding party to secrecy. Not an easy task. I can't imagine how we're going to accomplish that one."

"We have ways of persuading people to keep quiet."

Decker turned to see Adam Hunt striding down the corridor toward them with Rory in tow. "That sounds ominous."

"The sort of thing a supervillain might say right before he shows you his tank full of hungry sharks," Colum said.

"Nothing of the sort," Hunt replied, apparently missing

the sarcasm in Colum's remark. "I can assure you that CUSP has nothing like that."

Colum snorted. "If you don't count the secret prison hidden under an island in Maine where you hide terrifying creatures from the general population."

"I think we're getting a little off track here, gentlemen." Hunt stopped outside the closed hotel room door and glanced toward it. "Any luck, yet?"

"Not so much as a peep," Colum said. "How long can it take to dry someone off and give them some clean clothes?"

"Apparently, more than an hour." Decker looked at Hunt. "What did you find out?"

"Zip. There's no file in CUSP's archives on Howard Rothman or his bride."

"Are you sure about that?" Decker raised an eyebrow. "We assumed CUSP took possession of this island because they knew something strange had occurred here."

"If they did, they never left a record of it," Hunt replied. "The island came into our possession way before my time. And don't forget, Celine Rothman vanished in 1912. The organization wasn't even around back then."

"But its predecessor was. The Order of Saint George," Decker said, remembering their entanglement with Jack the Ripper the year before in London, and the organization that had originally dealt with him. Queen Victoria had founded the Order of Saint George to combat threats deemed beyond the scope of the regular police or British Armed Forces. Supernatural threats that would become the responsibility of CUSP when the Allies absorbed The Order into a larger worldwide organization during World War II to combat Hitler's obsession with the occult.

Hunt already knew all this. "That's true. But The Order didn't operate in the United States and by the time our modern organization was formed, Celine Rothman's disappearance was distant history. Even if we had been around back then, it's unlikely CUSP would have become involved, given that most levelheaded people at the time believed she flung herself off the bridal suite's balcony in an act of suicide."

"On her wedding day?" Colum didn't sound convinced.

"Just because she was getting married, doesn't mean she was happy."

"Except we know it wasn't suicide," Decker said. He nodded toward the hotel room. "She's on the other side of that door looking pretty good for a woman knocking on one hundred and thirty-eight years old."

"You're telling me," Colum said. He looked thoughtful. "Hey, maybe this sort of thing happens all the time. After all, lots of people go missing every year and a lot of them are never found."

"Unlikely," Hunt said. "We would have come across more instances of people showing up years after they should have been dead. I would hazard a guess that this is more of a one-off."

"Maybe tied to the location of the island?" Rory said with excitement. "After all, we are in the Bermuda Triangle."

"I think we'd need more proof before we make that leap," Hunt replied.

"Besides, isn't the Bermuda Triangle associated with ships and planes disappearing, not brides?" Colum said.

Rory shrugged. "I'm just throwing out theories."

"Perhaps we should wait to form any conclusions until we can talk to Celine Rothman, herself," Decker said.

"Who knows when that will be," Colum grumbled.

"Maybe not too long," Hunt said, as the bedroom door opened, and Nancy appeared.

She looked at the four men, and then motioned for them to enter. "Come on in. Celine will answer your questions, now."

ELEVEN

CELINE ROTHMAN LOOKED COMPLETELY
different from the drenched and haggard young woman that
staggered through the wedding chapel doors earlier that
afternoon wearing a dirty and wet wedding dress that clung
to her like a shroud. Now she was clean and dry, with hair
that tumbled across her shoulders in a dark and lustrous
cascade. She wore a pair of jeans and a green V-neck that
Decker recognized as belonging to Nancy.

"Some transformation," Rory said as they entered the
room. "She doesn't look like the same person."

"No, she doesn't." If Decker had known otherwise, he
would never have guessed that this woman was a refugee
from the turn of the last century. At least, that was what the
evidence pointed to. He hoped they would have clarification
soon.

"I would really like to know what happened to me,"
Celine said, looking up at the men. She sat perched on the
bed, her hands clasped in her lap. Her eyes were red, as if she
had been crying. "No one has told me anything, so far."

"We were rather hoping *you* could tell us how you got

here," Decker said. He glanced toward the window, and the square of dark and angry sky framed within.

The storm was still in full force. In fact, if anything, it had grown worse since they made their mad dash back to the hotel from the wedding barn. As if to punctuate its observations, a flash of lightning lit up the room, swiftly followed by a deep rumble of thunder. The lights flickered, winked out for a moment, and then came back on.

"I really don't know what happened," Celine said, casting her own nervous glance toward the window. "I was at the wedding reception in the grand ballroom. The band was playing. Irving Berlin. He's one of my favorites. I got caught up with Howard's annoying younger brother. The man wouldn't leave me alone, which is ironic because Howard barely paid any attention to me the entire evening. He was too busy talking to his cronies . . ." Celine's voice trailed off. Tears welled in her eyes again.

"Take your time," Decker said.

Celine nodded and wiped the tears away, then continued with a sniff. "I decided to go upstairs and change into my evening gown. My wedding dress is so cumbersome. But when I got to our suite, the storm was raging. I went to the balcony, opened the French doors. Don't ask me why. I would have stepped out, but the wind and the rain were so bad. This bolt of lightning came out of nowhere and hit the beach right below me. It was really close. I got scared and went to close the doors, but before I could . . ." Celine's voice trailed off again. She looked small and vulnerable sitting on the edge of the bed, more like a terrified child than a grown woman.

"Do you remember what happened next?" Decker asked softly, kneeling next to her.

Everyone else in the room was silent, enraptured by the strange tale.

"I think so." Celine looked perplexed. "I wanted to close

the doors, block out that horrible storm. Change my clothes and go back to the party. But there was another flash of lightning, much closer this time. It felt like the entire sky was tearing itself apart. Ripping open like a piece of thin fabric. Then there was this bright white explosion. I could feel electricity all around me. And I must have passed out."

"That's all you remember?" asked Colum. "There must be more."

"There is," Celine said, her voice trembling. "I don't know how long I was unconscious, but when I awoke everything was different. I found myself lying on the ground out in the woods. I couldn't see the Fairmont, just lots of trees everywhere. The rain was still coming down, so hard. I was soaked through and so cold. I didn't know which way to go or even how I got there. I think I was in shock."

"That's more than likely," Hunt said. "It sounds like you were struck by lightning."

"If I was, then maybe I'm dead." Celine looked around. "Maybe I died, and this is hell."

"You didn't die, and this isn't hell," Colum told her. "Trust me."

"Then what is it?" Celine asked. "Because it surely isn't Singer Cay. Or at least, not the one I remember."

"This is indeed Singer Cay," Hunt said. "And if you're ready to finish your story, perhaps we can figure out what happened to you."

"Okay." Celine nodded. "As I said, I woke up in the forest with no clue how I got there. After a while, I realized that I couldn't stay where I was, so I started walking, looking for the Fairmont. I wandered out there for what seemed like days. It just kept raining so hard, and the thunder . . . I was beginning to despair that I'd never find my way out. Then I came across this place . . ."

"That's when you showed up in the wedding barn," Colum said.

"Yes." Celine blew her nose with a tissue from a box sitting on the bed next to her. She choked back a sob. "You've all been so kind to me, but I don't want to be here. I would very much like to go back to my husband. It's my wedding day . . ."

Nancy and Decker exchanged a look. It was their wedding day, too. Then Decker took Celine's hand in his and spoke in a soft voice. "I'm not sure you *can go home*. I still don't know how you even got here. But I promise I'll do everything in my power to get you back where you belong."

TWELVE

WOULD you mind telling me exactly how you propose getting that poor woman home?" Adam Hunt asked, fixing Decker with a questioning stare.

Decker, Rory, Colum, and Hunt were in a room across the hall from the one that Celine Rothman presently occupied. They had come here to talk in private and discuss their next move. So far, they hadn't gotten very far.

"I don't know *if we can* get her back home," Decker replied. "But I had to say something. She was upset. And it's true, I *will* do everything in my power to get Celine back to where she belongs. She isn't meant to be here."

"Great. Let's hope there's a time machine lying around here somewhere," Colum said. "We'll just fire it up and hop back to 1912 with her. Easy as pie."

"Your flippant attitude isn't helping," Hunt said, glaring at the Irishman.

"Hey, I was just trying to lighten the mood," Colum said. "But one thing's for sure. John's right. She can't stay here."

"She might not have any choice." Now it was Hunt's turn

to pace. "We don't have a clue what brought her here, or why."

"And you found absolutely nothing in the CUSP archives?"

"I already told you, there was no mention of Celine Rothman, or of any unusual events on this island."

"Until now," Colum said.

"That goes without saying." Decker walked to the window and looked out. He couldn't believe how long the storm had been raging. Earlier in the day, the clouds had raced across the sky like they were on a mission, giving him hope the weather would clear before evening so they could hold their reception on the pool deck. But instead, the maelstrom appeared to have come to a halt above the long sliver of land situated sixty miles west of Great Abaco in the Bahamas and showed no sign of wanting to move on. "If we can find out how she got here, we might be able to use the same mechanism to get her back home."

Hunt exhaled a long breath. "We should consider the possibility that she won't ever make it back to her own century. That this happened because it's her destiny. Think about it. We know she disappeared back in 1912. No one ever saw her again."

"Until this afternoon," Decker said.

"Exactly. If we succeed in getting her back to the early twentieth century, how come there's no historical record of her after the disappearance?"

"I don't know," Decker admitted.

"We should consider the possibility that she's trapped here." Hunt didn't look pleased.

"Look, we're dealing with unknowns," Decker said. "The timeline might reset itself once we get her back. Maybe we can't locate any record of her after she disappeared precisely because we haven't found a way to get her back yet. Once we do, time will move forward differently."

"Um . . . I'm not sure time travel works like that." Rory stepped forward. "I know I'm an archaeologist, not a physicist, but I've read up on this stuff. Even if we could return her to 1912, it might create a new timeline from her perspective but leave the original timeline just as we remember it from ours."

"You're talking about alternate realities," Hunt said.

"Yes. Exactly. Nature's way of avoiding a paradox. For example, if I were to invent a time machine and go back to kill my father before he conceived me, that's exactly what my actions would create."

"Because if you killed your father, he wouldn't be around to have a hand in your creation, and therefore you wouldn't be around to go back in time and kill him." Colum looked pleased with himself.

"Right. So that leaves two possibilities. The first is that time travel into the past is impossible and Celine Rothman was destined to arrive here at this moment with no way to get back—"

Colum interrupted. "Which doesn't make sense if time travel into the future is possible, which it clearly is."

"Yes. The second is that the universe has a way of coping with the paradox."

"Your alternate reality theory."

"Some scientists have hypothesized that every potential outcome of a given event creates a new reality where that outcome occurred, thus creating myriad branches that take off along their own timelines. In my example, if I were to go back in time and shoot my father before he conceived me, that act would create an alternate reality where I don't exist because he is dead, but we would both be alive in the original reality. Essentially, it would create a fork in the road of time."

"This is giving me a headache," Colum said. "Do you have proof any of this is real?"

Rory shook his head. "No one's ever traveled backward in time, at least so far as we know."

"But we do know that time travel is possible," Decker said. "Celine Rothman is living proof. And if it happened to her, it could have happened to a lot of other people."

"Which is why the alternate reality theory makes sense," Rory replied. "We might very well succeed in returning her to 1912, but when we do, it will create a new branch of reality that continues independently of our own. Thus, she never reappears on our timeline."

"I'm still not sure I fully understand," Colum said. "But if I'm following you correctly, the only way we'll know is by returning Celine to her own century."

"Yes. But keep in mind, I'm not saying any of this is true or even possible," Rory said. "Only that her absence from our timeline between 1912 and this afternoon isn't necessarily proof she doesn't get home."

"Then how do we proceed?" Colum asked.

"We have to visit the place where Celine Rothman fell forward in time," Decker replied.

"The ruined hotel on the other side of the island."

"The Grand Fairmont," Hunt said.

"Yes. It's the most likely place to find answers." Decker paused before continuing. "And the sooner we do it, the better."

THIRTEEN

THEY RETURNED to the bedroom where Nancy, Taylor, Mina, and Rory's new girlfriend, Cassie, waited with Celine. When they explained their theory, the women didn't look convinced.

Nancy glared at Decker with narrowed eyes. "Absolutely not. It's our wedding day. Send Colum and Hunt to take care of this. They're more than capable. I need you here."

"You know I can't do that," Decker said. "This is my job. Plus, we can't finish getting married until we resolve this situation."

"This isn't safe," Cassie said, clutching Rory's arm. She looked at him. "I don't want you out there in this storm. I agree with Nancy. Let someone else check out that old hotel. Please tell me you won't go."

"John's right. It's my job, too." Rory put an arm around Cassie and pulled her close. He kissed her forehead. "I promise to be careful."

"But why you?" Cassie shook her head. "You're an archaeologist, not a physicist."

"I'm the closest thing to a scientist on this island. They need me."

Adam Hunt stepped up and addressed the group to allay everyone's fears. "I know this situation is not ideal, but we need to investigate the Grand Fairmont Hotel to understand how Celine got here."

"We're just going to check it out." Decker looked at Nancy. "If we see anything out of the ordinary, we'll give it a wide berth."

"I still don't like it, but I understand you need to help this woman," Nancy said, her tone softening. "Promise me you'll be careful."

"I promise. Don't worry. We'll be back before you know it."

Nancy nodded and forced a faint smile, but Decker could tell she still wasn't happy.

"If everyone's ready," Hunt said, "I see no need to delay any further."

"Why don't you stay until the weather clears?" Callie asked.

"I'm not sure we can wait that long," Hunt replied, his gaze shifting to the storm raging outside the window. "Besides, this storm might have something to do with Celine's arrival. She said a bolt of lightning hit right next to her balcony before she ended up here."

"That's true." Celine nodded. She was still sitting on the bed, but now she stood up. "It was so close I thought it would hit me."

"We go now," Hunt said. "That isn't up for debate."

"Sure thing, boss." Now it was Colum's turn to glance at the window. "We should change first, though. Tuxedos aren't exactly good all-weather gear."

"Obviously," Hunt said. "We'll take fifteen minutes to change into more suitable attire and then meet in the lobby."

"Right on." Colum turned to leave.

Decker stepped close to Nancy and took her in his arms. He held her, letting her head rest on his shoulder. "We'll be back before you know it," he whispered into her ear.

"I hope so." She squeezed him tight, then stepped back. "You'd better get going."

"What about me?" Celine asked. "I assume you're taking me."

"I'm coming too," Mina said, a determined look upon her face.

"No to both of you," Decker said. "I'm not putting any unnecessary people at risk."

"That's ridiculous." Anger flashed in Celine's eyes. "I'm the reason you're going over there. If there's an opportunity to send me home, I want to take it."

"I agree with John." Hunt held a hand up. "We don't even know if it's possible to get you home yet. This excursion is exploratory only. We need to understand what we're dealing with and assess the risks before we decide."

Celine took a step toward Hunt. "Now, hold on a minute. You can't just-"

"I can, and I'm going to. You stay here, end of discussion. We'll discuss our findings when we return and plan a strategy from there. Understood?"

Nancy took Celine by the shoulders and steered her back toward the bed. "Let these people do their job. They're good at what they do, and it's your best chance of returning home."

"I just want to see my husband again," Celine said, the tears flowing anew.

"I know you do." Nancy glanced toward Decker and motioned for him to go.

Colum had made it to the door before Celine's outburst. Now he stepped through and disappeared. Hunt and Rory followed behind, with Decker the last to leave. Except he wasn't the last. Mina was following along behind.

They were in the corridor before Decker noticed. "You're not coming," he told her.

"Like hell, I'm not," Mina replied, a determined expression on her face.

Decker had seen this same look in London when he tried to dissuade her from chasing Jack the Ripper. "The last two times you insisted on helping me, you almost got yourself killed."

"But I didn't, did I?" Mina followed Decker, walking fast to keep up as he made his way to the third-floor suite he and Nancy were sharing. "I'm not the same person now. You know that. It's not so easy to kill me anymore."

"We don't know how absorbing Jack the Ripper's life force affected you. Not that it matters. I'm not willing to put you in danger a third time."

"Then I'm in luck. It's not up to you. I'll speak to Adam Hunt."

"He'll give you the same answer."

"We'll see." And with that, Mina hurried past Decker and disappeared down the corridor, leaving him staring at her back.

FOURTEEN

FIFTEEN MINUTES LATER, Decker made his way down to the lobby and found the others already waiting. His tuxedo and dress shirt were gone, replaced by a polo shirt, jeans, and the only coat he had with him. A light rain jacket that now seemed inadequate. He also wore sturdy hiking boots, which he'd brought along to take walks around the island. As he drew close, Decker noticed Mina standing with her arms folded across her chest. She looked pleased with herself.

"I thought I told you to stay here," he said, annoyed.

"You did. And *I told you* I was going to ask Adam Hunt."

"Who agreed with me, no doubt?"

"Actually, I didn't." Hunt looked uncomfortable, which was unusual. "Mina is coming with us."

"That's ridiculous." Decker could hardly believe what he was hearing. "You know what happened in London. She's not equipped for this."

"I read your report. The incident in London was unfortunate, and I agree that it should have been avoided. But this isn't the same situation."

"We don't know what's out there. It's too dangerous."

"Mina can take care of herself." Hunt wasn't budging. "I've made my decision, and I don't want to hear anything else about it."

"This is wrong," Decker said. "You thought Mina was interfering back in Alaska. You were hesitant to involve her in London. Why the sudden about-turn?"

"I don't answer to you." Hunt's voice was even but carried a warning tone. "Mina comes. This conversation is over."

Decker stood in stunned silence. It felt like he'd wandered into one of Rory's alternate realities. Adam Hunt was always cagey, but this was worse than usual. It didn't make sense. There was no reason for Mina to accompany them. But Decker could do nothing to prevent it, so instead, he followed the others when they walked toward the lobby doors.

"We have several vehicles on the island," Hunt said. "I had a Humvee brought from the garage."

"Thank heavens for that," Colum said. "I thought you were going to make us walk through the forest."

"I wouldn't get too excited. We'll take the perimeter road around the island. That will get us most of the way, but the last mile will be on foot. The old access road to the hotel is no longer usable. It would be easier to go by boat and use the Fairmont's old dock, but not in this weather."

"The Humvee it is then," Colum said as they exited the hotel. When he saw the vehicle parked under the portico, he let out a whistle. "Now that's what I call a ride."

The military Humvee was painted dark matte green. It sat on four massive tires with deep treads. Colum took a tour around the vehicle, opening the doors and peeking inside before returning to the rest of the group with a smile.

"It doesn't look very comfortable," Rory said.

"Looks like the perfect vehicle to take for a jaunt around

the island in the middle of a tropical storm, if you ask me," Colum told him. He looked at Hunt. "Naturally, I'm driving."

"Naturally." Hunt smiled. "I know how to get there. I'll sit in the front with you and navigate."

"Hop in, guys." Colum jumped up into the cab. "Last time I drove one of these babies was back when I was an Army Ranger. We were stationed in Afghanistan. This is going to be so much fun."

"I can't imagine this thing has great suspension," Rory complained as he climbed into the rear and sat down, pulling a seatbelt across his lap. "We're going to get tossed all over the place."

"Actually, the suspension is pretty good." Hunt waited for Decker and Mina to climb in, then closed the rear door before taking his place in the front passenger seat next to Colum.

The Irishman fired up the engine and eased the Humvee forward and out from under the protection of the portico, then he followed the winding hotel driveway down toward the coast road that ringed Singer Cay. On the other side of the island the Grand Fairmont waited, and hopefully, Decker thought, the answers they needed.

FIFTEEN

IT WAS ONLY four in the afternoon, so there were still several hours of daylight left, but the sky was so laden with thunderclouds that it might as well already have been the middle of the night. Rain slashed down and thrummed on the Humvee's metal roof, then sluiced over the windshield, making it hard to see. Colum turned on the wipers as fast as they would go and flicked his headlights to full beam as they turned off the hotel driveway onto the dark coast road.

"Weather's getting pretty fierce," he said through gritted teeth, gripping the steering wheel and fighting against a gust of wind that threatened to push them off the road. "I swear, it's grown worse since that bride showed up."

"We'll be fine," Hunt said. "Just watch the road."

"Easy for you to say." Colum snorted. "How far away is this old hotel, anyway?"

"About ten miles if we take the coast road," Hunt replied.

"Ten miles?" Colum looked shocked. "Are you saying that poor woman hoofed it ten miles in a wedding dress?"

"No." Hunt shook his head. "She probably walked

straight across to us. The island is long and thin. They built the hotel on a promontory directly across from La Casa. Going through the middle of the island halves the distance."

"Shame we can't do that," Decker said from the rear. "The less time we're out in this storm, the better."

"Actually, we can. There's an old road that cuts across to the other side."

"Sounds good to me." Colum didn't look like he was having as much fun as his earlier comments back at the hotel would have indicated.

"There's a catch. The road hasn't been used in years and storms blow through this area all the time. If a tree went down, or there was a flash flood, the road could be blocked or even washed out."

"A chance I'm willing to take," Colum said. "Worst-case scenario, we turn back and keep on around the coast. Where is this cut-through?"

"It should be coming up on our right." Hunt leaned forward and peered through the drenched windshield. "There used to be a sign indicating the turn, but who knows if it's still there."

"It is," Colum said, lifting a hand off the wheel and pointing. "I see something up ahead."

Decker leaned forward between the front seats and peered out into the maelstrom. Then he saw it too. A square sheet of metal on a short pole with a reflective arrow pointing inland. "That must be it."

"Taking the shortcut," Colum said, slowing the Humvee and turning. "Keep your fingers crossed."

"Take it slow," Hunt cautioned. "We don't want to wrap ourselves around a tree trunk."

"You forget who you're talking to?" Colum cast a quick glance sideways.

"I know exactly who I'm talking to, which is why I'm telling you to take it easy."

"Relax." Colum shook his head. "I haven't lost a vehicle yet, and I'm not about to start now. I'll get us there in one piece."

"Just make sure you do." Hunt leaned back into his seat.

It was Rory's turn to pipe up. He had been staring out the side window, hands pressed to the glass, cupping his face. Now he turned frontward. "I don't want to worry anyone, but I just saw a sign on the side of the road back there. It said we're entering a restricted area."

"Not anymore. That sign must be decades old," Hunt said, turning to face him. "Back in the early forties, the military used this island for training. They took it from Howard Rothman's heirs."

"When you say took it, you mean . . ."

"Requisitioned it using the War Powers Act, passed by Congress in 1941. The island was deemed vital to the war effort."

"What kind of training did they do here?" Decker asked. "And where?"

"I can't tell you what they were doing. That information has never been released."

"Surely CUSP must know."

Hunt shook his head. "It was different back then. Any records pertaining to that time are either lost to history or still restricted under national security laws that even we can't access."

"To this day?" Decker was incredulous. "They must have been doing some pretty secret stuff here to keep a lid on it for so long."

"Whatever they were up to, looks like they didn't want the general public ever knowing about it," said Colum.

"As I said, it was a different time." Hunt shrugged. "And

bureaucratic red tape has a habit of ensnaring even the most mundane information."

"Where was all this top-secret stuff taking place?" Mina asked, her eyes lighting up. "Sounds fascinating."

"You'll see soon enough," Hunt said. "We have to drive through it to reach the other side of the island."

SIXTEEN

THEY CAME upon the facility Hunt spoke of less than ten minutes later. The trees thinned and gave way to a cleared patch of land several acres in size with ramshackle buildings dotted around that looked like they must once have housed a sizeable contingent of men. There were also two large aircraft hangars alongside a thin ribbon of cracked and weed-ridden asphalt that Decker recognized as a landing strip. The hangar doors were pulled back and open, but the interiors were nothing more than a dim abyss, any contents shrouded by blackness.

The road they were traveling cut across the eastern periphery of the site, giving the Humvee's occupants a fine view.

Colum pulled over near the end of the runway and peered out his side window as lightning flickered overhead lighting up the landscape. "This island is full of surprises."

Decker was curious. "If there's a runway here, why do you bring everyone over to the island by boat?"

"The airfield isn't practical for modern planes, even if we renovated it. Remember, it was built during the Second World

War and constructed in the middle of the island for defense and security reasons."

"It would have been invisible to anyone approaching the island by boat and hard to spot from the air unless you were right on it," Colum said. "Would have been a hair-raising approach for those wartime pilots, with all these trees so close to the landing strip. I've flown a few small planes and can imagine what it would be like. You'd have to drop down in a hurry to avoid clipping them on the way in."

"I see." Decker nodded.

"Plus, the landing strip would be too short for modern jets."

"Couldn't you have extended the runway and cleared the trees to make it safe?" Rory asked.

"Maybe. But there might have been other concerns." Hunt raised his voice over the storm's wrath. "Keep in mind, CUSP has owned this island a long time. Those decisions were made many years before I joined CUSP."

"When was that, exactly?" Decker asked, seeing an unexpected opening to learn more about his tight-lipped boss.

"Nice try." Hunt's face slipped into a slight smile.

"You really don't like people knowing too much about you, huh?" Colum said.

"It's better that way," Hunt replied, without expanding.

"I have a question," Mina said, studying the abandoned facility. "If the military co-opted this place, how did CUSP get their hands on the island?"

"Again, before my time." Hunt shrugged. "But our employer has always had strong government ties. I'm sure someone many decades ago did a backroom deal and took the island off the military in exchange for some kind of service rendered."

"Why did CUSP even need a second island?" Colum asked. "The one in Maine wasn't enough?"

"The island in Maine came afterward." From the tone of Hunt's voice, he was growing tired of the topic. "We're getting off track. There's a job to do and we should get back to it."

"You're right," Colum said, easing the Humvee forward again. "I'd love to research this later, though, if it's all the same with you. Military history is kind of a hobby of mine."

"Be my guest," Hunt replied. "But I doubt you'll find much, at least in the CUSP archives. We're a secret organization for a reason."

"I don't suppose you'd know what that reason is?" Decker asked, unable to resist a playful prod at Hunt.

"Yes, but it's a secret." Hunt gave a small laugh. "If I told you, I'd have to kill you."

"Game, set, and match to Adam," Rory said.

"It would appear so." Decker watched the old military installation slip by as they drove across the overgrown airfield and re-entered the forest.

For the next few minutes, they bumped along on the uneven road surface, and then Colum let slip a surprised exclamation.

"Look at that," he cried. "Up ahead on the right."

Decker craned his neck to see, but all he spied were trees and the torrential rain.

Rory was fairing no better. "I don't see anything."

"You will, once we get a bit closer," Colum said.

For the second time, the Irishman slowed the Humvee, and now Decker saw it. The shattered tail of an airplane sticking out of the undergrowth in the forest near the road. It was almost completely covered with vegetation, which meant the aircraft had been there a very long time. Beyond the broken tail section, he saw part of a wing, patches of aluminum still visible, and the decaying remains of a buckled fuselage.

"Looks like something crashed on landing," Decker said.

"It must be from the Second World War." Colum leaned forward to get a better look. "If I'm not mistaken, it's a Lockheed Electra. I can't tell what model, but it's from the late thirties or early forties, for sure."

"How do you know that?" Decker asked, raising his voice over the wind and rain.

"Look at the double tail with two rounded vertical stabilizers. Pretty distinctive."

"You think the pilots got out okay?" Mina asked, her eyes wide.

"Hard to say. Looks like it hit hard." Decker tapped Hunt on the shoulder. "You know anything about this plane?"

Hunt shook his head. "Nothing. But that's not surprising. A lot of aircraft were lost in the war and not all of them were in hostile territory. Best guess, some poor trainee pilot came up short and clipped the trees."

"Which is a graphic illustration of why putting a landing strip in a forest with no easy approach is a bad idea." Colum snorted. "It also shows why CUSP built their own more accessible runway near the shore."

Hunt was growing impatient. "I think we're done sightseeing if it's all the same with you guys. We have a pressing matter to take care of and I'd rather not be out in the forest after dark, especially in this weather."

"Roger that, boss," Colum said, picking up speed again and driving past the wrecked plane. "Next stop, the Grand Fairmont."

SEVENTEEN

THEY RODE the rest of the way in silence, the combined engine noise and howling storm making it difficult to engage in needless conversation. Soon they reached the coast road again and rejoined it. Then as they approached the turnoff leading to the ruined hotel, Decker unclipped his seatbelt and leaned forward, remembering something Hunt had mentioned earlier. "When we were leaving to come over here, you said we'd have to walk the last mile up to the Grand Fairmont."

"That's right," Hunt replied, raising his voice over the storm's din.

"This Humvee looks like it could scale a mountain," Decker replied. "Surely, the road up to the hotel can't be that bad."

"It's not so much the condition of the road as it is the width," Hunt explained. "No one's taken a vehicle up to the hotel in a very long time. Many decades, I'll wager. The forest has grown back over the access road to the point where anything larger than a compact car would get stuck. Don't forget; it was abandoned over a century ago."

"I hoped you were joking when you said we'd have to walk the last mile," Rory said, sounding glum.

"No such luck, I'm afraid." Hunt turned his attention forward again. A moment later, he slapped the dashboard and pointed as a pair of stone columns with ornate rusting gates still attached came into view further along on their left. "That's it. Bring us to a stop there."

Colum slowed the vehicle and brought it to a stop near the gates. When he cut the engine, the sound in the car diminished by half, leaving only the roar of the storm.

Mina and Rory undid their seatbelts and turned to look out of the Humvee's side window. The entrance gates to the Grand Fairmont Hotel leaned crooked, partially off their hinges. The columns they were attached to were crumbling. Vines had grown up over the masonry, covering it in places. The road beyond was cracked and heaving, with trees pressing in on both sides to form a dark tunnel, the end of which they could not see. Lightning raced across the sky, illuminating the landscape in a staccato burst of white.

Hunt turned to face the backseat. "Ladies and gentlemen, welcome to the Grand Fairmont Hotel. How about we take a little walk?"

EIGHTEEN

THE GRAND FAIRMONT'S iron gates were not just standing askew on their hinges. Someone had wrapped a heavy chain around them and secured it with a padlock. By their rusted condition, the padlock and chain had been there a very long time. Even if the road up to the resort was usable, the Humvee would have been barred from entry. Either way, they were going on foot.

They ducked under the chain and pushed their way through a narrow gap between the gates with their heads bent low against the driving rain. Decker went first, followed by Mina and Hunt. Rory trailed a few feet behind. Colum fell in at their rear, always the good soldier.

It didn't take long for Decker to realize the trek was going to be tough. It might as well have been night under the arching canopy of trees that covered the crumbling road. More trees and bushes had grown up through the asphalt, their roots causing it to heave and crack, creating dangerous ridges that threatened to trip them as they pushed forward toward the ruined hotel. The torrential rain that lashed their faces and soaked through their clothing didn't help.

"Is the weather on Singer Cay always so bad at this time of year?" Colum asked, his voice little more than a low grumble that was swiftly snatched away by the wind.

"We get our share of storms," Hunt replied. "They're more prevalent in the summer months, though. This is unusual."

"I wish it would blow itself out," Rory said. "It's like the damned thing just took up residence above our heads."

"If anything, it's getting worse." Decker squinted up toward the heavens, then dropped his gaze when pelting rain stung his eyes. "I can't believe Celine Rothman made her way all the way across the island in this wearing nothing but a wedding dress."

"No wonder she was in such bad shape when she appeared in the wedding barn," Colum said. "I'm wearing a heavy coat and hiking boots. I've trained in weather like this. Even I'm miserable."

If anyone else chimed in, Decker didn't hear it. At that moment, a clap of thunder rumbled over them. He bent his head and focused on the job at hand. Hunt had said it was about a mile to the ruined hotel and in this weather, it would feel like two. He concentrated on the road ahead. He assumed it would be a straight shot all the way to the Fairmont, but instead the road weaved and meandered as it followed the rocky landscape. Apparently, the builders had taken the path of least resistance rather than blast through jutting boulders that littered the landscape.

He stepped over a thick tree root that had pushed its way up through the crumbling road, then risked a glance backward. Rory looked about as miserable as he had in the Amazon Rainforest months before. The archaeologist found himself in situations such as this on a regular basis, yet he never appeared to get used to them. Mina, however, was taking it in her stride. She moved with a catlike grace that Decker hadn't noticed previously, and if the weather bothered her, she made no show of it. He wondered if this was another of Jack the Ripper's unwanted gifts.

He turned his attention frontward once more. The chatter had died down now. Despite being on a tropical island, the temperature had plummeted since the storm blew in. They were all cold and wet, and no one was in a mood to shout over the rain-laden wind. It whipped through the trees and came at them from all directions, stinging their faces and creeping inside their clothes, finding every small crevice. With grudging determination, they continued on for another twenty minutes, and then the forest thinned, and they came upon the crumbling remains of the Grand Fairmont Hotel.

NINETEEN

THE HOTEL once owned by Celine Rothman's millionaire husband looked nothing like the glitzy pleasure palace he set out to build over a century earlier. Weeds and overgrown bushes clogged the grounds. Terraces and balconies were nothing more than crumbling ruins destroyed by decades exposed to the area's harsh sun and pounding storms. The Grand Fairmont's façade had given in to the ravages of time, its more delicate features and elaborate details crumbling away. The building's windows were cold and dark, and Decker could see several broken panes.

"This place is in a sorry state of repair," Colum said, casting his gaze across the dilapidated landscape. "Hard to believe that it was built as a playground for the wealthy."

"Don't forget, Howard Rothman abandoned the hotel within weeks of its completion," Adam Hunt said, ushering them forward toward the building. "He was grief-stricken at the loss of his wife. There were rumors at the time that he thought the place was cursed."

"If we can figure out how Celine Rothman skipped more than a century and arrived at my wedding, we might be able to send her back and avoid this sorry state of affairs," Decker said.

Rory hurried to keep up as the group crossed the overgrown space in front of the hotel that must once have been lavish lawns. "Don't forget about my theory. We may not be able to return her to the timeline that resulted in the hotel's demise."

"As long as we return her to some form of her own timeline, I'll be happy," Decker said.

"We don't even know how she got here." Colum was making great strides across the open space, less affected by the dire weather than everyone else. "You think we're going to crack that riddle and get her home?"

"That's why we came here."

"I still don't see how any of this is possible," Mina said.

"Before we met up with you in London, would you have believed Jack the Ripper could survive a century's incarceration in a dank basement?" Colum asked.

"I'm still struggling with that," Mina said.

"Guys," Decker said, as they reached the steps leading up to the hotel's grand lobby. "It doesn't matter whether we believe it. Celine Rothman somehow skipped an entire century and ended up stranded in a future she doesn't understand and doesn't belong in. It's our job to get her back, or at least try."

"Well said." Hunt took the steps two at a time.

A veranda ran off to their left and right, the remains of wooden rocking chairs and outdoor tables still recognizable even though they looked as if they would crumble at the slightest touch. Behind these were floor-to-ceiling windows, which were still intact thanks to the veranda's protective overhang. A set of large double doors stood opposite the steps, one of which was standing cracked open on rusted hinges.

Hunt approached the doors and reached out, giving one an exploratory push. When it didn't move, he pressed his face to the gap and peered into the inky blackness beyond.

"I don't see anything."

"I'm not surprised," Colum said. "It's dark enough out here, let alone in there. I bet the place is a death trap."

"We still need to get inside." Hunt put his shoulder to the door and pushed with a grunt.

The door didn't move.

"Let me help." Colum lent his shoulder to the task, and the two men put their backs into it, but to no avail.

"It's useless. Something must be blocking it from the other side." Hunt took a step back and observed the door with folded arms.

"There must be another way in."

"This place is enormous. It could take us hours to find it." Decker glanced around. "We don't have that much time. It will be dark soon, and I don't fancy the walk back down that driveway to the Humvee with no daylight left to guide us."

"I agree." Hunt looked around the group. "Anyone got any suggestions?"

"We could split up." Colum cast a glance along the veranda. "That would make the search go quicker."

"I don't like that idea," Decker said. "Not in this weather."

"I never said it was a perfect plan." Colum slipped the cell phone from his pocket. "If one of us finds a way in they can call the others."

"Um . . ." Rory was looking at his own phone. "That won't work. No service."

"Not possible." Hunt shook his head. "These phones connect to a satellite network in orbit. They always have service."

"Not anymore." Decker checked his own cell phone.

"It's probably the storm," Rory said. "There must be some

sort of electrical buildup in the atmosphere that's blocking the signal."

"That's not good." Colum scratched his chin. "New plan. Let's meet back here in thirty minutes. If one of us finds a way inside, they can lead the others there."

"Thirty minutes? We don't have the time." Hunt grimaced.

"You got a better idea?"

"Oh, for goodness' sake." Mina walked along the veranda to the nearest rocking chair. "There's no need to go traipsing around the outside of the hotel looking for another way in. We'll make our own way in. It's quicker."

"How do you propose to do that?" Hunt watched her with narrowed eyes.

"Like this." Mina picked up the rocking chair, which was sturdier than it appeared at first glance. Then she took a step backward and swung the chair toward one of the floor-to-ceiling windows. At the top of the chair's trajectory, she let go, and it flew into the window with a resounding crack, hitting near the frame.

One of the chair's rockers disintegrated in a hail of rotten wood, but the window held firm.

"Good job," Colum said. "You broke a chair."

"Have a little patience." Mina picked up the remains of the chair and took another swing. This time, instead of impacting the window and bouncing off, the chair sailed on through in a shower of broken glass.

Mina looked pleased with herself. She turned to the others and gestured towards the smashed window. "Anyone want to explore a creepy old hotel with me?"

TWENTY

THE HOTEL'S interior was in much the same sorry state as the outside. After stepping through the broken window, Decker and the rest of the group found themselves in what appeared to be the grand ballroom. Part of the ceiling had collapsed into the center of the cavernous space. A cut-glass chandelier, which would have once been a dazzling sight hanging over the dance floor, now lay in the rubble heap, many of its crystals shattered and missing. The smell of decay was everywhere.

"What now?" Colum asked, glancing around the room.

"We look for anything out of the ordinary." Hunt stepped further into the room. "Something brought Celine Rothman from her own time to the twenty-first century, and I want to find out what."

"Might be easier said than done," Rory said. "This place must have a hundred rooms. I wasn't expecting it to be so big."

Hunt turned back toward the group. "Howard Rothman had a lot of ambition and the money to match. The Grand

Fairmont should have been his crowning achievement. Small wasn't an option."

"You really think he abandoned the hotel right after the wedding because his wife disappeared?" Mina asked.

"Judging by the stuff lying around here, I'd say it's a fair bet." Colum used his foot to nudge a filthy champagne glass that had fallen on its side, somehow still unbroken after more than a century. It rolled sideways and came to rest against the desiccated remnants of a banquet table that had crumbled, leaving silverware strewn across the floor. "Looks like they didn't even bother to clean up the wedding reception."

"Incredible." Decker noticed a pair of tarnished silver salt and pepper shakers sitting upright as if someone had placed them on the floor deliberately. "There must be a fortune in antiques lying around here."

"Maybe. But that's not our concern." Hunt had spotted a sweeping staircase at the far end of the room that led to a mezzanine level. "Celine Rothman said she was in the penthouse suite when the lightning hit. Whatever happened to her did so in that room."

"That's where we need to go," Decker said. "I don't suppose you have a map of this place handy?"

"What do you think?"

"That's what I thought. The penthouse should be at the top of the building."

"That won't be easy to reach." Colum didn't look pleased. "This hotel is a death trap. I'm surprised it hasn't collapsed already. We'll be taking our lives in our hands if we go up there."

"You got a better idea?" Decker knew the Irishman was right, but he also realized they wouldn't find any answers standing around in the remains of the ballroom.

"Wish I did." Colum nodded toward the grand staircase. "Why don't we start over there."

"You think the levels above will hold our weight?" Rory asked.

"Hard to say," Colum replied.

"There's a lot of damage here. The entire building is clearly rotten. One false step and we could end up crashing through the floor. Or worse, trigger a collapse."

"Right." Decker nodded. They risked injury or death if they pressed on and explored the hotel's higher levels in search of the penthouse. But if they confined their exploration to areas deemed safer, like the ballroom and the hotel grounds, they might not find what they were looking for. That meant Celine Rothman would never get home.

"I'll go," Mina said. "I'm lighter than everyone else. The rest of you can stay here."

"Out of the question." Decker shook his head. "It's no safer for you than the rest of us. Besides, you don't know what to look for."

"And you do?"

"She's got you there." Colum chuckled despite the situation.

"The answer is still no."

"That's not your decision to make." Hunt stepped toward Decker. "Mina's right. She's light and agile. It's our best chance of getting answers."

"Now hang on a minute." Decker couldn't believe what he was hearing. "Mina isn't even part of CUSP. You can't ask her to risk her life like this."

"Remember what they used to do in the old West?" Hunt said. "If a town sheriff needed more lawmen, he could deputize folk. I'm the sheriff around here, which means I get to deputize anyone I want. For the time being, Mina is under CUSP's employ."

"You can't be serious." Decker wondered if Hunt had lost his mind. "There are so many reasons this is a bad idea. She's not trained. Our cell phones don't work, which means we can't keep in touch with her. It's wrong. This isn't the way we do—"

"It's the way I'm doing it today. I'm in charge, and I say she goes." Hunt looked at Mina. "If you're still willing."

"Try to stop me."

"It's settled then. Mina will proceed up to the penthouse." Hunt folded his arms and looked at Decker with steely eyes, challenging him to argue further. "The rest of us will retreat out of the building and await her return."

"This is crazy. What if something happens?"

"A risk we have to take."

"She's not going alone," Decker said. "I'll accompany her."

Mina looked alarmed. "That isn't necessary. I can handle this. You know I can."

"I know nothing of the sort. Besides, it's basic safety protocol." Decker expected Hunt to overrule him yet again, but that didn't happen.

"On this point, I grudgingly agree. The increased risk of two people exploring an unsafe building is offset by the safety net an additional body provides."

"You should send me with her instead," Colum said. "I'm more experienced."

"You're also bigger and heavier than the rest of us," Hunt said. "Based purely on body weight, Rory is the next obvious choice, but he's not equipped for such a task. John has the right mix of experience and build."

Decker breathed a sigh of relief. He turned to Mina. "Looks like it's you and me, kid."

TWENTY-ONE

MINA AND DECKER made their way up the grand staircase, moving one behind the other, careful with each footfall. The treads under Decker's feet felt soft and pliable. More than once, he imagined himself falling through the stairs into a dark unknown below. Worse, he could hear water cascading through the building as they climbed toward the mezzanine. Somewhere above them, the rain was getting in. And not a small amount, either. He suspected the collapsed ballroom ceiling had something to do with it.

Moments before, as he and Mina made their way toward the grand staircase, Colum, Rory, and Hunt had stepped back out onto the hotel's veranda. Their departure left Decker feeling uneasy, partly because of Adam Hunt's decision-making when it came to Mina. He shouldn't even have wanted her along on this expedition, yet here she was, climbing into a dangerously unstable building with no hint of concern from their normally levelheaded boss. It didn't feel right, and he wondered if Hunt was thinking straight.

That was something he would have to deal with later,

though. Right now, there were more pressing concerns. Like staying alive.

They reached the top of the stairs and stopped, taking stock of their surroundings. To their right was a row of three elevators. Next to these, a fourth elevator stood apart. Decker guessed this was the Rothman's private elevator and went straight to the penthouse on the top floor. Now, though, it was nothing more than a deadly shaft full of rusty cables. They were not going to reach their destination that way. To their left, Decker saw a grand piano covered in a thick layer of dust. One leg had given way, and the once expensive musical instrument now sat at an angle. Beyond the piano, he saw the remains of sofas and chairs, the fabric long since rotted away to expose their springs. In the Grand Fairmont's brief heyday, Howard Rothman's guests would have lounged in these seats and listened to a pianist while they sipped martinis and smoked cigars. Now the mezzanine level was a rubble-strewn cave, the furthest reaches of which were shrouded in darkness. The sickly odor of decay hung in the air like a shroud.

"I don't like it up here," Mina said with a shudder. "It gives me the creeps."

"Me too." Decker knew there must be a staircase leading up to the floors above. He looked around, wishing they'd brought flashlights with them from La Casa de Playa. But he still had a cell phone, even if it didn't get a signal. He pulled the phone out of his pocket and used its light to push back the gloom. After a few moments, he found an archway, and beyond this, another set of stairs leading higher.

"That looks like our way up," Mina said, starting forward again.

"Take it slow and keep your wits about you," Decker said, hurrying to overtake her so he could go first. "Remember, no one's been this deep into the hotel for many decades. We don't know how stable it is."

Decker tested the first step, then the next. The staircase appeared to be solid enough, and he led Mina upward, sweeping his phone's flashlight from left to right ahead of them. They soon reached a landing with corridors that ran off on both sides of them. Beyond the glare of Decker's phone, there was nothing but inky blackness. No matter. They didn't need to explore here, so they pressed on up the next flight of stairs.

The next landing was the same, and the one after that. Decker was pleased to find the stairs solid under his feet, even as he listened for the telltale splinter of rotten wood. Finally, after climbing up four floors, they came to one last staircase with a sign affixed to the wall next to it that read *Private. Penthouse access only.*

"This is it." There was excitement in Mina's voice as they mounted the last set of stairs and ended up at on a wide landing facing a set of ornate double doors, one of which stood open.

"Looks like they rolled out the welcome mat for us," Decker said, eyeing the door. "Want to see what's in there?"

"Try to stop me." Mina rushed forward, sliding through the gap between the doors and disappearing into the darkness beyond.

"Wait," Decker shouted, too late to stop her.

A moment later, he heard a sharp crack, followed by a terrified scream.

TWENTY-TWO

MINA!" Decker felt his chest tighten. He barreled through the penthouse doors with no concern for his own safety but soon came to a halt. The room appeared to be empty. He couldn't see Mina anywhere.

He swept the phone's flashlight around, fearing the worst. The feeble beam picked out sticks of broken furniture, fallen plaster that had peeled off the walls, and everywhere a thick coating of dust that billowed up with his footfalls, threatening to choke him.

Decker pushed further into the room, hoping that Mina had just tripped on some upturned chair or fallen beam, but he still couldn't find her. Then his gaze alighted on a sinister dark patch in the middle of the floor surrounded by jagged edges. A hole. Had she stepped on weak floorboards and fallen through?

He approached the chasm, his heart pounding against his ribs. Was Mina lying twenty feet below, her body twisted and broken? He feared the worst. Then, before he reached the edge, a voice drifted up.

"Decker, get me out of here."

His heart leaped. She wasn't dead, after all. Decker raced forward and dropped to his knees next to the opening, shining his light down inside.

Mina was a few feet down, clinging to a horizontal support beam. Below her was a yawning pit of darkness.

"Help me," she said, her eyes wide with fear. "I can't hold on for much longer."

"Hang on." Decker placed his phone on the floorboards so that it shone down into the hole, then lay on his stomach and reached toward her. "Take my hand."

"I can't." Mina shook her head. "I'm afraid I'll fall if I let go."

"You won't fall, I promise." Decker extended his arms as much as he could, aware that one false move would send them both tumbling into darkness. "Let go with one hand. Take mine."

"You were right," Mina said, her voice trembling. "I'm a walking disaster. I should have stayed back at the hotel where it was safe."

"Too late for that now." Decker sensed she couldn't last much longer. He could see her arms trembling with the effort to hold on. Her fingers were inching slowly toward the edge of the beam. "Do as I say. Take my hand. I'll pull you up."

"I'm scared."

"I know you are. But you're also the woman who helped take down a Qualapalik in Alaska. You took on Jack the Ripper and won. You can do this."

"That creature in Alaska wasn't a Qualapalik. It was a mutated super-soldier. And Jack the Ripper almost killed me."

"Stop putting off the inevitable and take my hand." Decker leaned further over the edge. His fingers grazed her knuckles, but he couldn't reach low enough to grip her wrist. "I can't do this on my own. You need to help."

"Say you won't drop me."

"That's not going to happen." Decker could feel the jagged edge of the hole pressing painfully against his chest. An image of Mina gripping his hand and dragging both of them down flitted through his mind, so he curled his free arm under the broken planks and fumbled around until he found something solid to hold. If they started to slip, this should stop them. But it meant he only had one arm with which to pull Mina up. He hoped he could do it. But there was no choice. Another few moments and Mina would lose her grip and plummet to her death. "It's now or never."

"Okay." Mina took a long breath. "I'll let go with my left hand. Make sure you grab me quickly."

"On three," Decker said.

Mina nodded. Decker counted. One . . . Two . . . On the third digit, Mina released her grip on the beam and shot her hand upward.

Decker curled his fingers around her wrist. "I've got you."

"Okay. Here goes nothing." Mina let go of the beam with her other hand.

Decker felt his arm muscles protest as he took her entire weight. He strained to heave her upward, but he could sense his strength giving out and he didn't dare let go of the anchor he was holding with his other hand or they would both fall. "I need you to help me. I can't do this on my own."

Mina grunted and lifted her other arm. She curled her fingers around the edge of the hole. "That's the best I can do."

Decker felt the weight on his arm ease a little. It was enough to let him lift Mina higher, and soon she could hook her arm over the lip of the hole and scramble up. They fell back onto the floor, with Mina on top of Decker.

"You saved me," she said, scrambling off him and rolling to one side. "I thought I was going to die."

"We're not sure you can die," Decker said, remembering

Abraham Turner, a.k.a. Jack the Ripper, and how hard it had been to kill him. Mina now possessed at least some of his powers, and that might extend to unnatural longevity. "At least not that easily."

"I'd rather not find out if it's all the same with you." Mina was puffing. She propped herself up on her elbows and looked sideways at Decker. "And anyway, even if I can't die, falling that far would still hurt like hell and possibly leave me maimed."

"Good point." Decker didn't want to move but knew that he must. From somewhere outside there was an ominous rumble of thunder. He could hear the downpour pattering like a thousand drumming fingers on the roof above them.

"This storm is crazy. It's been going for hours now." Mina got to her feet and brushed herself off.

"That might be a good thing," Decker said, standing up. "Celine Rothman disappeared in the middle of the storm and showed up at my wedding during a similar downpour."

"You think her time travel had something to do with the weather?"

"That's exactly what I think," Decker said, moving further into the room, careful to avoid the gaping hole Mina fell through. "If this storm blows itself out, we might lose the ability to find answers."

TWENTY-THREE

CELINE ROTHMAN'S penthouse suite must have been spectacular in its heyday. Decker guessed it was at least three thousand square feet, which was bigger than any of the houses he'd ever lived in. Like the rest of the hotel, the space was filled with decaying furniture, including antique dressers, a chaise lounge, and a large liquor cabinet full of dusty bottles.

Decker ignored all of this and picked his way carefully toward a set of French doors that stood open on the far wall. As he drew closer, Decker saw an expanse of brooding gray ocean beyond. This must have been where Celine Rothman was standing when the lightning struck. He could see black smudges around the doorframe, which looked very much like burn marks. The shattered balcony beyond clung to the side of the hotel, barely hanging on. It certainly wouldn't take their weight. Beyond this, he saw no useful clues regarding Celine Rothman's strange journey across the decades or how to return her home.

"I was expecting something a little more dramatic than this," Mina said, inspecting the burn marks. She kept her face turned away from the open doors to shield it from the stinging rain.

"Me too," Decker said. He wasn't sure what he thought would be here, but this was anticlimactic. He reached out and touched one of the marks. When he withdrew his hand, there was powdery soot on his fingertips. He rubbed it between his fingers. "This feels fresh. Like it only just happened."

"How is that possible?" Mina asked. "The lightning that did this damage struck over a hundred years ago, at least if you believe the strange woman waiting back at La Casa de Playa."

"I don't know." Decker inched closer to the edge and looked down. Beneath them was a crescent-shaped rocky cove at the bottom of a sheer cliff that ran as far as he could see in both directions. Waves crashed against the rocks, frothy and white. The ocean beyond swelled and heaved under nature's wrath all the way to the horizon, which was broken only by the long, slender shape of another island far away. Decker's breath caught in his throat. Howard Rothman had indeed built his hotel upon a promontory, and when it wasn't a howling maelstrom outside, this view must have been spectacular.

"What now?" Mina asked. "Other than a charred doorway, there isn't anything here to back up her story, and certainly nothing that would help us get her home."

"I agree. Maybe we're looking at this the wrong way. Maybe we missed something."

"Or she isn't really Celine Rothman," Mina said. "Maybe she never traveled forward in time at all and she's lying about her identity."

Decker shrugged. "Her story checks out. She looks like the woman in photographs taken at the time."

"She could be descended from Celine Rothman. A family

member would know the stories and might even look like her. It's more logical than time travel."

"Why would an imposter bother?" Decker looked at Mina with raised eyebrows. "What would be their endgame? Come to that, how would they get on the island? The Rothman estate doesn't own it anymore and there are security systems everywhere. We would have noticed an unauthorized craft."

"I'm not saying she isn't Howard Rothman's bride. I'm just saying we need to consider the possibility. Especially since we have found no evidence to support her claim."

"One thing's for sure," Decker said. "We're not going to find anything up here. We might as well return to the others and see if they have any ideas."

"Works for me. This building has already tried to kill me once, and I'd rather not give it a second chance. The sooner we're out of here, the better." Mina backed away from the balcony doors.

Decker cast one more glance out over the churning ocean and turned to follow, just as a finger of lightning raced across the sky, followed by an earsplitting boom.

The hotel shook.

Mina squealed as a large section of the ceiling gave way and came crashing down in a cloud of dust. She jumped back to avoid the falling debris, almost knocking Decker off his feet. He grabbed her and swiveled them around to shield her from the worst of the collapse.

Pieces of roof material clattered all around them.

The hotel made a groaning sound as if its walls were about to fall in.

"We can't stay here," Decker shouted over the howling wind and rain that ripped through the gaping ceiling. Except it was more than that. The room was alive with an electrical hum that crackled and pulsed. The hairs on Decker's arms stood on end. The distinctive smell of ozone assaulted his nostrils, more pungent than Decker had ever experienced before.

There was something else, too.

A blue shimmering glow that hung in the air ahead of them. It looked like a writhing translucent mist with tendrils that snaked out in all directions like feelers.

Mina saw it too. She gave a small gasp and clutched Decker's arm. "What is that?"

"I don't know, but I don't like the look of it." The blue glow was expanding and eating up the air around it like some ravenous beast. Decker pulled Mina backward, looking for an escape route. Then, before either of them could react, the mist collapsed in upon itself, pulsed one more time, and exploded in a flash of brilliant white light that filled the room. Decker felt a moment of searing pain as if the skin were being burned from his body, and then he lost consciousness.

TWENTY-FOUR

DECKER FELT water on his face. Dripping water. No, it was raindrops. He was lying on his back with a hard object pushing into his shoulder blade. For a few seconds, his mind was a blank canvas, but then it all came rushing back. His name. The sodden wedding crasher who showed up right before his and Nancy's vows. Driving across the island to the ruined Grand Fairmont and climbing up into its penthouse suite. He remembered something else, too. A bolt of lightning struck right above them, tearing the roof apart. And an explosion of blinding white light seconds before he lost consciousness. And then . . .

Mina.

Decker opened his eyes and looked around. When the explosion hit them, he and Mina had been in the penthouse suite atop the Grand Fairmont Hotel. But he wasn't there anymore. He saw trees towering above him, and a patch of dull gray sky from which rain fell in sheets. Somewhere in the distance, a rumble of thunder echoed.

Decker groaned and pushed himself up onto his elbows, then staggered to his feet. The sharp pain in his back turned out to be a pointed rock protruding from the earth. He was soaked through and cold despite the tropical heat. He looked around, discovered that he was at the edge of the forest. The Grand Fairmont stood some ways distant, with the jagged edge of the cliffs behind it. There was no sign of Mina. This worried him slightly more than how he'd ended up sprawled on the ground outside when, moments before, they had both been inside the Fairmont's penthouse suite. Did he have a concussion? Had he somehow wandered, dazed and confused, out of the hotel only to collapse here? He didn't have the answer to those questions.

Decker pondered returning to the hotel and searching for her, but it turned out he didn't need to.

"Decker." The voice, instantly recognizable, drifted out of the forest. Seconds later, a familiar figure emerged.

It was Mina.

A rush of relief washed over Decker. He hurried toward her, and they met near the tree line. She looked as wet and miserable as he was.

"Are you okay?" Decker asked, studying her but not seeing any obvious external injuries.

"I'm fine." Mina ran a hand through her hair and squeezed the wetness from it. "Some dry clothes would be nice."

"I'm with you on that one." Decker cast a glance back toward the hotel. "You remember anything? How we got out here?"

"Not so much." Mina shook her head. "One moment we were in the penthouse suite, then the roof caved in and everything went to hell. The next thing, I'm waking up out in the forest soaking wet."

"Pretty much my experience, too."

"How is that possible?"

"Beats me." Decker shrugged. "At first I wondered if the

explosion knocked me into some kind of fugue state and I wandered out here without remembering, but it's unlikely it would affect both of us in the same way."

"Yeah. I don't think that's the answer." Now it was Mina's turn to look toward the hotel. "For a start, the others would have seen us. They were waiting on the veranda."

"Good point."

"Speaking of which, where are Hunt, Rory, and Colum?" A perplexed look passed across her face. "I don't see them anywhere."

"Me either," Decker said, scanning the area around the hotel. "Maybe they all went inside to investigate when they heard the roof come down."

"Maybe." Mina didn't look convinced.

"Yeah. It doesn't sound plausible to me, either." Decker could buy Adam Hunt sending Colum inside to look for them, but it was unlikely he would risk all their lives in an unknown and dangerous situation. Reckless was not in Adam Hunt's nature.

"There's only one way to find out," Mina said. She turned and started back toward the ruined building, taking long, determined strides.

Decker sprinted to catch up with her, but as they drew closer, he noticed something. "Does the hotel look different to you?"

"Huh?" Mina looked confused. "What do you mean, different?"

"Like in better condition. The first time we saw the Grand Fairmont, it was practically falling in. Now it looks . . . I don't know . . . Sturdier."

Mina came to an abrupt halt, staring up at the towering façade. "Holy crap. You're right. It does look better."

"There are fewer broken windows," Decker said. "The paintwork looks brighter, too."

Mina looked down. "You can still see the gravel where the driveway used to be. This is weird."

"Come on." Decker took Mina's hand and guided her forward. "Let's find the others and see what they have to say."

"I don't like this," Mina said as they approached the steps leading up to the main entrance.

"Me either." Decker took steps two at a time and approached the white double doors leading into the hotel lobby. To their left would be the grand ballroom and the window Mina broke to gain access. Except that was different now, too. A chill wormed up his spine, even as Mina vocalized his observation.

"The window. The one I smashed with the rocking chair. It isn't broken."

"I can see that," Decker said, a feeling of dread washing over him.

"That isn't possible."

"I know." Decker felt Mina's hand tighten against his.

Mina looked scared. "What does it mean?"

"Not sure. Come on." Decker approached the hotel's entrance and pushed one of the doors. It opened easily, swinging back with an ominous groan on unoiled hinges. The lobby beyond was full of long shadows, but its condition added more proof to Decker's hunch regarding their predicament. He wasn't ready to admit it yet, though. To himself or to Mina. Instead, he led her into the lobby and left to another set of doors that opened into the ballroom. When he stepped inside, their surroundings cemented his suspicion. "This all looks different. Cleaner. Newer."

"The others aren't here," Mina said, her voice rising in pitch.

"No, they aren't." Decker led her back out of the ballroom and out to the veranda again. He descended the steps and looked up into the sky, toward a break in the clouds. "Look."

"I don't see anything." Mina shook her head. "What am I supposed to be looking for?"

"The sun," Decker replied. "It's in the wrong place. When we came here, it was evening. The sun would have been low on the horizon. Now it's almost overhead."

"You're right." There was a trembling Mina's voice. "Whatever could it mean?"

"You're a smart girl. I think you already know, you just don't want to admit it," Decker told her.

Mina was silent for a moment. She pressed her lips together, looked up at the sky. Then she voiced the Decker's suspicion. "We're not where we should be."

"Right," Decker noted. "We are somewhere else entirely. Some other point in time. And judging by the evidence—the condition of the hotel—we're in the past."

"If that's the case, then . . ." Mina's voice trailed away as if she didn't want to say the obvious out loud.

Decker picked up where she left off. "Then just how far back did we travel?"

TWENTY-FIVE

MINA LOOKED at Decker and bit her bottom lip. "Do you think Adam, Colum, and Rory are around here somewhere, too?"

"Not sure," Decker replied. "I don't see them anywhere, and they were a long way from the lightning strike, so they probably avoided whatever we got caught up in."

"You mean they didn't get thrown back in time."

"Yes."

"That's something, at least," Mina said. "They're safe."

"Doesn't *help us* any," Decker was replaying the events of the past few hours over in his mind, trying to recall any little detail that might provide an answer to their predicament. He drew a blank. "I Sure wish Rory was here. I could use one of his theories right about now. He appeared to have a handle on this time travel stuff."

"We could go back to the penthouse." Mina squinted and looked up at the old hotel. "That's where it happened. Maybe there's a way to get out of here and back home."

"I wouldn't be so sure about that," Decker said. He

glanced up toward the sky again. The rain had stopped now, and the clouds were giving way to a deep blue sky. "Celine Rothman disappeared during a thunderstorm when lightning struck the balcony she was standing on. She reappeared over a hundred years later during a similar storm. We experienced a lightning strike in that same storm and found ourselves here in the middle of a downpour."

"You think the thunderstorms have something to do with what's happening?"

"It is the common denominator." Decker rubbed his chin. "I'm not sure the location matters as much as being near a lightning strike. After all, we were in the penthouse, but then we woke up in the forest."

"Right. The penthouse. The same place Celine Rothman went before she showed up at the wedding barn," Mina pointed out. "That has to mean something."

"Maybe. But don't forget, we went to the penthouse *because* that's where Celine Rothman started out. It could just be a coincidence."

"You believe that?"

"I don't know what to believe," Decker admitted. "But the storms appear to play a part in this, and the weather has cleared up."

"No storm, so no way back to our own time," Mina said.

"I can't be sure of that, but . . ."

"Great." Mina sighed. "So, where does that leave us?"

"I think we need to find out what we're dealing with and what the date is."

"How do you suggest we do that?" Mina asked.

"Well, this island belongs to CUSP, or at least, they own it in the twenty-first century. And according to Adam Hunt, it's been that way for a very long time. First, we should find out if La Casa de Playa is there. If it is, we might be able to get dry clothes and some answers."

"You know what year La Casa was built?"

"No. But it's been there a long time."

"You want to walk across the island." Mina didn't look convinced.

"Unless you have a better idea."

"Is it safe to do that? What about . . . I can't remember what it's called . . ." Mina furrowed her brow as if she were thinking. "The butterfly effect. You know, the theory that if we change some small thing in the past, it will have a huge impact on our future. Like if we accidentally step on a bug and kill it, then we return to our own time and find there are no bees anymore."

"From what Rory said, I'm pretty sure we're safe on that score. He had a theory that time travel creates alternate time-lines to avoid a paradox, so anything we do here will take a separate path from our original timeline."

"Which means when we get back . . . If we get back . . . We won't have caused any problems for ourselves."

"Exactly."

"And we'll return to our original timeline. Safe and sound."

"Yes. If I understood him correctly."

"There's just one problem," Mina said. "All of this is just speculation. Rory has no more clue how time travel works than anyone else. Plus, he's an archaeologist, not a physicist."

"True." Decker nodded. "But he reads an awful lot of books by very smart people, so I'd put my money on him any day."

"What are we waiting for, then?" Mina turned toward the forest with a determined look on her face. "You know how to get to La Casa de Playa?"

"Not entirely. We drove over here, and I'll bet the Humvee won't be waiting for us out on the road."

"Because it's still where we left it in the future."

"Right. We'll have to walk."

"I was afraid you'd say that. How many miles do you think it is?"

"Maybe four or five."

"You think Celine walked that far?"

"She must have. We woke up at the edge of the forest, so I'm guessing that she did too." Decker started towards the tree line. "But she might have found the road running from the old military base. The one we drove along on the way here. That would be easier going."

"We could use it too. Adam Hunt said the base was built in the forties. The road might already be there."

"Maybe. Depending on what year we're in." Decker had already thought of this. But wasn't sure he wanted to telegraph his presence to whoever might be on the island. "I think we should avoid the road until we know more about our situation. A little discretion could serve us well."

"Fine." Mina didn't sound happy. "I guess we're tromping through the woods, then."

"Just until we have more information."

They were now at the tree line near the narrow driveway that ran to the iron gates and the coast road beyond. Decker figured it was safe enough to follow this. The hotel was already abandoned, and there was no one around. After that, they could cut straight across the forest, staying out of sight until they had more information.

As they started down the driveway, Mina tapped Decker on the shoulder.

He turned to her.

"Do you think they know we're gone?" She asked. "Adam and the others."

Decker shrugged. "Don't know."

"What if we never get back?" Mina was chewing her

bottom lip again. "It will be like we disappeared from the face of the earth, just like Celine Rothman on her wedding night."

"Yeah." Decker was trying not to think about that, because then . . .

Mina articulated the thought running through Decker's mind. "Nancy will never know what happened to you."

TWENTY-SIX

THEY REACHED the road quicker than Decker expected and crossed over into the forest beyond. As expected, there was no Humvee parked near the old hotel's gates.

The rain had stopped, and the gray clouds had given way to a gorgeous cerulean blue sky. The sun baked down from high overhead, and the humidity was almost unbearable. Their clothes were still damp, but no longer saturated. Now it was sweat that kept them from being comfortable.

As they walked, Decker thought about Nancy. If he never made it home, she would spend the rest of her life unsure what had happened to him or if he was even still alive.

"If we are in the past, you could probably get a message to her. Write a letter and have it delivered in the future," Mina said, reading Decker's mind.

"And how would I go about doing that?"

Mina shrugged. "I don't know. But there must be a way. At least we're not stuck in the future like Celine Rothman with no way to contact her husband."

"True." Mina's plan had merit, but Decker suspected it

wouldn't work, even if he could send a message up through the decades. "Don't forget Rory's theory about time travel. Any message I send won't reach Nancy in our timeline. It will reach another version of her in an alternate reality created when we arrived here."

"Maybe time doesn't always work that way," Mina said hopefully. "Think about this. It could be your destiny to travel backward in time, and therefore, anything you do here doesn't create a new reality because it was always meant to happen. It was always part of this timeline, not some other random alternate universe."

"And what about the danger of creating a paradox?" Decker wasn't sure Mina was correct. "Nature must have a way of avoiding such situations. Either our actions affect our own history, or they don't. You can't have it both ways."

"Why not? If your actions here and now help create the future we know, there would be no need for another timeline because there would be no paradox. Maybe nature only creates new realities when a paradox occurs to account for the discrepancy. If our actions don't create a problem, everything occurs in the original timeline even when we are in the past."

"If we get back, you should debate that with Rory. He'd love it."

"If we get back, we'll know the answer because the footprints of our actions here will either remain in our timeline, or they won't."

"And how do you propose we find those footprints?" Decker asked. "Unless we do something monumental that we can trace, our actions will simply merge into the river of time."

"It doesn't have to be anything big. We can leave ourselves a clue." Mina stopped and looked around. She soon spied a large and distinctive boulder sticking out of the leaf litter collected on the forest floor. She hurried over to it and found a smaller rock. "We can leave ourselves a message here. This rock is remote enough that it will still be here when we get back to the twenty-first century. We can come and find it. If some trace of these markings survive, it will be proof."

"Not a bad idea." Decker watched as Mina scratched their names into the boulder's surface, using the smaller rock.

She pressed hard, going over each stroke many times, before discarding the small rock and turning back to Decker. "It's not perfect, but these markings should last long enough to provide an answer."

"You sure about that?" Decker asked. "It rains a lot here during certain times of the year. They might get washed away."

"I doubt it. There are rock carvings worldwide made by primitive peoples that have survived many thousands of years exposed to the elements. This only needs to survive a fraction of that."

"Assuming we can find it again."

"It's the best I can do." Mina rubbed her hands on her jeans. "We should keep moving."

Decker nodded, and they started walking again. As they left the boulder behind, he made a mental note of the topography to better locate it if they returned.

They walked for a while in silence, lost in their own thoughts. The going was becoming tougher the further into the forest they walked. The trees were closer together. Tangled and dense understory frequently blocked their path, forcing them to find ways around it.

Eventually, Mina spoke up. "This is getting hard to navigate. You sure we shouldn't just find the road across the island?"

"I'd like to stay out of sight until we know more about our predicament," Decker replied. "Just as a precaution."

"What do you think is going to happen?"

"I don't know, which is why I don't want to reveal ourselves unnecessarily."

"I suppose." Mina cursed as a thorny branch snagged on her coat. She pulled free and inspected the tear left behind by the bush. "We're going to get scratched to hell if we keep walking through this."

"Can't be helped." Decker pushed another bush aside to let Mina pass through, then he stiffened and came to a stop, looking around.

"What is it?" Mina halted mid-step and turned to look at him. "Is something wrong?"

"I'm not sure." Decker scanned their surroundings. "Thought I heard movement to our rear."

"We are in the forest," Mina said. "There must be all sorts of animals out here."

"I'm sure there are. I read that there are rock iguanas, parrots, and even pigs. But I don't think it was any of those things. I've been hearing it for a while. Like we're being followed." Decker took a long breath. "Or stalked."

"If you're trying to scare me, it's working." Mina looked around nervously. "Do pigs stalk people?"

"Not so far as I know." Decker shook his head.

"Then what do you think is following us?"

"Believe me; you're better off not knowing," a gruff male voice said, off to their left.

Decker swiveled, saw a man in green fatigues. He stood fifteen feet away with a rifle leveled at them.

Mina let out a surprised yelp. "Who are you?"

"Never mind who I am." The man waved his rifle. "The pair of you need to come with me right now."

"Not until you tell us who you are." Decker stepped forward and positioned himself between the newcomer and Mina.

"You're not in any position to argue. I'm the one holding the gun." The man waved his rifle a second time. "Now move. We can't stay here. It's not safe."

TWENTY-SEVEN

THE STRANGER in army fatigues hurried them through the woods at a clip. As they went, he glanced to his left and right, studying the underbrush, while keeping Decker and Mina ahead of him where he could see them.

"You look a little nervous there," Decker said, noting the man's unease. "What are you expecting to see out here?"

The man poked Decker in the back with the muzzle of his rifle. "Never you mind. Just keep walking."

"Back when we first crossed paths," Decker said, unphased. "You said we didn't want to know what was following us. Why would you say that? Is there someone else out there that you're afraid of?"

"I'm not afraid of anyone."

"Then *what* are you scared of?"

"Quiet. Save the chatter for when we get back to base."

"Do you mean the airstrip in the middle of the island?" Mina asked. "The one built in World War Two?"

"Built in . . ." The soldier looked confused. "Lady, I don't know who you or your companion work for, but we don't tolerate spies around here."

"Spies?" Mina exclaimed. "That isn't what we are."

"Why would you be worried about spies on an island in the Bahamas?" Decker glanced back toward the soldier.

The rifle's muzzle found Decker's back again. "That's none of your business."

"My name's John," Decker said, taking a different tack. "John Decker. My friend here is Mina. What's your name, soldier?"

"Jim Tarrant. Now for the love of God, stop talking."

Decker spied the insignia attached to the man's arm. Two upward-pointing yellow chevrons. He didn't see any other identifying badges or tabs. "You're a corporal. What branch and unit are you in?"

"That's not your concern."

"Are you even in the military? I've never seen a member of the Armed Forces wear an anonymous uniform."

"Does he always talk this much?" the corporal asked Mina.

"Pretty much," she replied. "Sometimes more."

"Well, he needs to stop, or he'll get us all killed. I need to concentrate."

"There you go again," Decker said. "Acting like we're behind enemy lines instead of an island sixty miles off the coast of Florida. There shouldn't be anything more dangerous than an iguana around here, so what has gotten you so spooked?"

"I won't tell you again," the soldier warned. "Be quiet."

"Maybe if you told us—"

The corporal waved a hand. He came to a stop and cocked his ear. "Hush. I mean it."

Decker exchanged a glance with Mina. The soldier was acting jumpy enough that he was starting to think they might all be in real danger.

From somewhere out in the woods, a twig snapped, the sound disturbing the silence like a firecracker.

The corporal jumped and swung his gun around, pointing it in the direction of the noise.

Mina took a step toward Decker. She leaned close and whispered in his ear. "I don't suppose that was a pig?"

"A big one, maybe," Decker replied in a low voice, but his gut told him it was no hog.

"Would you two pipe down." The corporal cast an angry glance over his shoulder toward them. "It's close by."

Decker wanted to ask what he was referring to, but something told him not to say anything else. The atmosphere in the forest changed. Before, they could hear insects in the understory. The occasional cry of a parrot high in the canopy. Now it was silent as a grave. Even the air had turned oppressive and heavy.

The soldier kept his gun leveled at the surrounding woods and turned slowly, looking for any sign of movement. After a minute, when there was no further noise, he turned to Decker and Mina, motioning them forward. "Let's get out of here while we still can."

They started walking again, picking their way through the forest faster now. Decker could sense their captor's fear. It washed off him in waves, an almost tangible force. He wondered what would terrify a man carrying a large gun in such a benign locale. After all, the chain of over seven hundred islands and cays that made up the Bahamas was a playground for tourists from around the world seeking sun, sand, and cheap booze. Others came to enjoy the diverse ecosystem, including the dry broadleaf forests known as coppices. Decker, Mina, and the corporal were in the middle of one such forest at that moment and on a private island with no significant resident population. It made no sense.

Up ahead, Decker saw the silver twinkle of a stream

meandering between the trees. The water gushed and gurgled, swollen by the recent rainstorm. The corporal led them to a point where a series of flat-topped rocks spanned the watery ribbon like a row of steppingstones. He cast a wary glance over his shoulder, then motioned for Decker and Mina to cross.

Decker went first, picking his way from rock to rock until he reached the other side. When Mina started across, he held out his hand to guide her. She hopped from the last flat boulder just as the corporal turned to make his way across.

He never got that far.

There was a sudden snapping of twigs and rustle of leaves from somewhere in the woods. The corporal turned toward the sound, raising his rifle in self-defense a moment before a sleek dark shape rocketed out of the understory with an earsplitting, animalistic screech.

Mina screamed and stumbled backward until Decker caught her. Momentarily distracted, he dropped his gaze from the helpless man. When he looked back, the creature had vanished into the forest again, and the soldier was nowhere to be seen. All that remained to prove he was ever there, was the rifle lying on the ground, and a slick trail of blood leading off into the underbrush.

Mina clutched Decker's arm. She looked around wildly, eyes wide. He could hear her breath coming in short, ragged gasps.

Then, rising out of the forest, came a scream of terror, quickly silenced.

TWENTY-EIGHT

WHERE DID HE GO?" Mina's voice cracked when she spoke. "You said there were no dangerous animals out here."

"I did," Decker said, eyeing the discarded gun. "And there shouldn't be anything big enough to carry a man off like that."

"Did you see what it was?"

"No. All I saw was a blur of motion. I looked away to stop you from falling over, and when I looked back, we were alone. What did you see?"

"Pretty much the same. Whatever that thing was, it was fast."

"And powerful, too." Decker knew they needed to move before whatever had attacked the corporal came back for them. But the gun lying on the other side of the stream would make him feel safer and might save their lives. "I'm going over there to get that rifle. Stay here. Don't move an inch. And whatever you do, keep quiet."

"No." Mina's eyes flew wide with fear. She gripped his arm, her fingers pressing into his flesh. "Leave the gun. It's not worth it. I don't want anything to happen to you."

"I'll be fine." Decker extricated himself from Mina's grasp and approached the stream. He paused at the water's edge, his gaze sweeping the trees and the underbrush, looking for any threats. He listened, trying to detect any aberrant noise, but the woods sounded normal again now. Parrots chattered in the branches above his head, and cicadas buzzed. It was like nothing had happened. Except for the bloody trail leading off into the bushes. He took a deep breath, steadied his nerves, and stepped on the first rock.

"Be careful." Mina hissed the words in a low voice.

"That was kind of my plan," Decker replied, stepping onto the second rock, then the third. When he placed his foot on the fourth rock, he felt the stone shift, and he lost his balance.

Mina let out a strangled groan.

Decker teetered for a moment, putting his arms out to steady himself as the rock settled back into position, and then he was able to hop across onto the far bank and scooped up the discarded weapon.

He recoiled. The gun's stock was slick with a viscous liquid that he realized was the corporal's blood.

"What are you doing?" Mina stood on the other side of the stream, shifting from one foot to the other. "You have the gun. Get back here."

"Hang on a second." Decker lifted a hand to silence her. He gripped the rifle with the other hand and looked around, hoping to see some sign of the corporal. The blood trail ran about fifteen feet into a cluster of thick bushes. He looked down at the gun. It was an old model he only recognized because his father had collected antique weapons. Decker had grown up being schooled in firearms of all shapes and sizes even though he didn't have a passion for them like his old man. The gun he now held was an M1 Garand, an Army infantry rifle that came into service in the decade before the second world war and hadn't been in use since the late 1950s. Unlike many rifles of the era that still used a bolt action, the Garand was semi-automatic. This provided some comfort. The higher rate of fire would prove useful against what was clearly a swift and deadly enemy, although he hoped they wouldn't have to use it.

"Please . . ." Mina was getting desperate on the other side of the stream. "Come back."

"I can't leave that man behind," Decker said. He took a step forward, following the blood trail until he reached the bushes. When he got there, he found a path of broken branches and crushed limbs that led deep into the understory. He took a tentative step forward, pushing the foliage aside with the gun's muzzle until he came upon a flattened area that held a shocking sight.

Spreadeagled on the ground, his chest flayed down to the bone and stomach ripped open, was the owner of the gun Decker now held. Clearly dead, the corporal looked skyward with cloudy eyes, an expression of rictus horror imprinted upon his face.

Decker felt a pang of sorrow. He didn't know anything about this man or where his allegiances lay, but some unnatural force had stolen his life, and he didn't deserve that.

With no reason to continue exploring further, Decker turned to beat a path back through the bushes to Mina. He didn't want to leave her alone any longer than necessary, especially since the creature that killed the corporal named Jim was still out there.

Then he hesitated and turned back, his eyes alighting on the man's uniform. The corporal's shirt was ruined. It was ripped and stained with blood, but his trousers were still mostly clean. There was a handgun too, tucked into a holster on the man's belt. It was a Colt 1911—a reliable pistol that was so well made it been in service for over a century. During his time as sheriff in Wolf Haven, Decker had encountered several 1911s and even owned one that he kept locked in his gun cabinet at home.

He hated to do it, but if he and Mina were going to survive here, they needed to blend in. The soldier was about Decker's height and build. What was left of his uniform might come in useful. Not to mention the Colt. Moving quickly, Decker kneeled down, removed the gun, and stripped the pants off the dead man. He changed into them, abandoning his own dirty and damp pants, then slipped the belt and gun holster around his waist. He checked the gun's breach then returned it to the holster before retracing his steps to the stream. He was happy to see Mina still standing on the other side, and she looked relieved to see him.

"Hurry up," she said, glancing around. "I swear I heard something moving in the bushes."

Decker lifted the rifle and scanned the surrounding forest but saw nothing. Not that it made him feel any safer. Whatever killed the corporal was so fast the man didn't even have a chance to get off a shot. He navigated the stream, careful not to slip on the slick rocks, and joined her on the opposite bank.

"Here." He pulled the Colt from his belt and offered it to her. "You know how to use one of these?"

"What do you think?" Mina took the gun and inspected it. "I'd rather have that rifle."

"Not going to happen."

"Since you're giving me this pistol, I assume you found the original owner and he has no more use for it?"

"You assume correctly."

"Which is why you're also wearing his pants." Mina shuddered. "That's gross."

"It was also necessary. We need to blend in."

"What about me?"

"We'll figure that out later." Decker glanced around, overcome by a sudden sense of urgency. "We have to leave. Right now."

TWENTY-NINE

DECKER AND MINA hurried through the forest, leaving the torn and mutilated body of the soldier far behind. At first, they moved in silence, afraid that any conversation would draw the attention of whatever creature had been stalking them before they ran into the corporal. After a while, though, Mina spoke up.

"What's our plan now?" She asked, glancing sideways at Decker without slowing down.

"To find the military base," Decker replied.

"That corporal wasn't exactly friendly. You sure that's a good idea?"

"I don't intend to stroll on in there like a chump. At least, not until I know more about who we're dealing with. That soldier wasn't wearing any identifying insignia, and he refused to tell us which branch of the military or unit he was in."

"Maybe he wasn't in the military. He could have been a civilian wearing camo."

"Not likely. Not on this island." Decker shook his head. "He was a real soldier. I'm sure of it."

"Then why are we heading for that base?" Mina asked. "Wouldn't it be better to keep going toward the coast and La Casa de Playa?"

"I have a feeling that would be pointless."

"Why? I'd feel safer there."

"Because it won't have been built yet." Decker tapped the rifle. "This gun hasn't been made since the fifties, yet it looks almost new. That soldier was wearing an old-fashioned uniform, and he had no modern tech. I believe we're in a decade sometime around the second world war."

"That far back?" Mina looked shocked. "I was hoping CUSP would be on the other side of the island and might know how to get us home."

"No such luck, I'm afraid."

"That's bad, right?"

"It's not good. But even if La Casa de Playa was there and we could make someone from CUSP believe our story, it's unlikely they would know what to do."

"They would know more than a bunch of soldiers from World War Two."

"Maybe." Decker shrugged. "But we have other problems."

"The creature that was stalking us. The one that killed the corporal."

"Precisely. There shouldn't be anything on this island big enough to kill a man that quickly and drag him off." Decker scanned the forest as they walked, eager to avoid the same fate. He kept the M1 Garand at the ready, finger pressed against the frame above the trigger so he could drop it down and get off a quick shot if necessary. He hoped he wouldn't need to. "This whole day is just getting weirder by the minute. A few hours ago, I was getting married. Now I've somehow ended up in another era, being stalked through the forest by an unknown predator. Maybe Colum was right. Trouble does find me."

"That's what makes you such a good monster hunter," Mina said. "I can't think of anyone I'd rather be in a jam with than you."

"I'd rather not be in a jam in the first place."

"Bit late for that now."

"Tell me about it." Decker could see the trees thinning up ahead, and beyond that, a thin strip of asphalt running through the forest. They had found the road. He looked at Mina, mouthed for her to keep quiet. They couldn't be far from the military base, given how long they had been in the forest and the direction they were walking.

He was soon proved correct.

As they drew closer to the road, they came to a high chain-link fence crowned with razor wire. It ran away from them in both directions at the tree line. A set of tall gates blocked the road. Two armed guards kept watch from behind the gates, guns at the ready.

Decker cautiously approached the fence, careful not to let the distant guards spot him, and peered through at the base beyond. When they had passed through here in the Humvee earlier that day, the airfield and buildings were in a dilapidated state, but now everything looked new and well-maintained. Three aircraft hangars flanked the airstrip. The doors of two hangars were closed, but one aircraft hangar stood open, and Decker saw several airplanes parked inside. There were more planes parked next to the runway. Five of them. Old single-propeller aircraft with the Navy's distinctive roundel of a white star in a blue circle over a red horizontal bar. Uniformed men hurried back and forth, moving in and out of the hangars and buildings. As they watched, a military truck with several large crates in the bed rolled down the road and arrived at the gates. One of the soldiers took a moment to check the driver's credentials and then pulled the gates back to allow him access. The truck rumbled forward and headed straight for one of the aircraft hangars. The doors opened, and the truck disappeared inside. A moment later, the doors closed behind it.

Decker sensed Mina beside him and turned to her, motioning them further along the fence, away from the gates and the guard booth. She nodded, and they followed the fence through the woods, keeping out of sight until they were far from the landing strip and its associated activity.

Now Mina deemed it safe to talk, albeit in a whisper. "This is more built-up than I remember when we drove through earlier today. I'm sure there were fewer buildings and no fence."

"I'm sure they removed the fence to allow easier passage across the island. The buildings probably collapsed due to neglect. CUSP didn't have a use for this facility. They built their own."

"What's your plan, now?" Mina glanced around, nervous. "I don't want to stay in these woods with whatever killed that soldier."

"Me either, but I'm not going to walk in there and surrender to these people. We don't know who they are or what their agenda is." They were coming to the other end of the base now. Decker could see a second set of gates blocking the road, manned by two more guards.

"Then what *are* we going to do?"

"A little reconnaissance." Decker stopped and crouched down next to the fence. He peered through toward the hangars and buildings. "I want to see exactly what they're doing in there and who they are."

"How do you propose we do that?" Mina asked.

"By sneaking into the back of one of those trucks and letting it carry us in," Decker said, pointing toward the other side of the base where another truck loaded with crates was entering through the first set of gates they saw when they arrived at the fence. "That's the second one in the last twenty minutes. I bet if we wait a while, another will come along."

"You can't be serious," Mina said, looking unsure.

"Would you rather stay out here with whatever killed the corporal?"

"Since you put it that way . . ." Mina watched the truck until it disappeared inside the hangar, following the same route as the previous one. "But how are we going to get up into a truck without being spotted?"

"With a lot of stealth and a little luck," Decker said. He tapped Mina on the shoulder and motioned her to follow him back along the fence toward the first gate. "Come on. I'd rather not stay out here any longer than necessary."

THIRTY

DECKER RETRACED his steps along the fence line, with Mina right behind. He made sure they were far enough into the forest to avoid easy detection. Soon they reached the road, and the original gate they had seen upon their arrival. The two guards were still there, rifles clutched to their chests. They looked warily down the road from behind the gates, as if they expected something more dangerous than a truck to appear. Decker wondered if they knew about the creature in the forest that had killed the corporal named Jim.

"What should we do now?" Mina whispered as they came to a stop near the edge of the road and crouched down behind a large thorny bush.

"We wait for another truck," Decker said, taking out his cell and holding an expectant hand toward Mina. "Give me your cell phone."

"Why?" Mina's hand dropped to her pocket where she held it defensively. "I only just bought this."

"Never mind that. I'm guessing the people in that base have never seen a cell phone, and you won't get a signal for decades. We need to hide them. Give me the phone."

"I hate you." Mina withdrew the phone and handed it to Decker.

"No, you don't." Decker took the phone and dug a small hole under the bush. He dropped both phones in before covering them and pushing leaves over the disturbed earth.

"You're right." Mina shook her head. "But you owe me a new phone when we get back. Even if we come back for these, they'll be ruined."

"Deal. I'll even buy you a shiny new case to go along with it." Decker glanced down the empty road as far as he could see until it took a turn to the left and disappeared among the trees. "The last two trucks were full of crates, and they were coming from the coast. Probably unloading a ship. If we're lucky, another will be along soon."

"What do you think they have in those crates?" Mina asked.

Decker shrugged. "Spare parts for their planes. Munitions. Hell, it could even be a bunch of baked bean cans. Impossible to know without taking a peek inside."

"Which I'm guessing you intend to do."

"Given half a chance."

Mina turned and looked down the road, her attention drawn by a low rumble that grew louder as another military truck with crates strapped to the bed appeared. "You might get that chance sooner rather than later."

Decker nodded. He watched the truck approach the gates, noting the two men in the cab. One driving, the other riding shotgun with a rifle visible in his hands. Even inside their cab, these guys were paranoid about something.

"How do you want to do this?" Mina asked as the truck grew closer.

"We wait for them to stop at the gates, then hop in the back behind the crates and conceal ourselves. If we're lucky, they'll take us all the way into that hangar where the other trucks went."

"Got it." Mina nodded.

"When the time comes, follow my lead and don't lag." Decker watched as the truck came to come to a stop in front of the gates. The guards swung them open, and one man approached the cab while the other disappeared on the far side of the vehicle.

"This looks like a good time to go." Mina started to stand up, but Decker gripped her shoulder and eased her back down.

"Not yet. On my mark."

"Why? The truck is right there."

"Just give it a minute."

Mina let out a frustrated huff, but Decker was soon proved right when the second soldier reappeared at the back of the truck. He raised his foot onto the back bumper, then gripped the truck's tailgate and hauled himself up, peering into the bed with his gun leveled as if he expected to find something there. When he didn't, the soldier dropped back down and completed his tour of the truck, checking the wheel arches before making his way back inside the gates and out of view.

The other soldier was still at the front, talking to the driver through the open window. He was paying no attention to anything else.

"We go now," Decker said, taking Mina's arm. He took a deep breath. They had to cross an open area of about fifteen feet to reach the back of the truck if their plan was to succeed. All it would take was the soldier standing by the cab to glance sideways, or the other soldier to reappear, and the jig would be up. They might even get themselves shot for their troubles.

They needed to go quickly and quietly.

Decker glanced toward the gates one last time to make sure no one was looking in their direction, and then he broke cover with Mina at his side. They raced toward the truck, keeping low and moving with all the stealth they could muster. The open ground seemed to stretch ahead of them. Decker felt like it took forever to reach the back of the truck, but in reality, it was probably only five seconds. He listened for a shout to go up or the crack of a gunshot, but luck was on their side. They fell against the back of the truck and caught their breath. But there was no time to delay. The truck could move at any moment. Decker tapped Mina on the shoulder and motioned for her to climb into the rear. He helped her up and over the tailgate, then followed, hoisting himself into the back and collapsing on the truck bed just as the vehicle shuddered and started to trundle forward on its enormous tires.

"We did it," Mina whispered. Breathless, she wedged herself between the crates and the side of the truck bed.

"We're not in the clear yet," Decker replied. They still must lie low until the truck reached its destination, then sneak back out of the bed without being seen. No small feat.

"These look even bigger up close." Mina reached out and touched one of the crates. Then she withdrew her hand, a look of shock on her face. "I swear something moved inside that crate."

"Are you sure?" Decker placed his palm against the crate but didn't sense any movement. He pressed his ear to it but heard nothing over the roar of the truck's engine and rattle of its frame. "Maybe it was just a vibration."

"I don't think so." Mina shook her head. "It was like something hit the side of the crate. As if it was trying to get out. I think there's an animal in there."

"Animal or not, we have to move soon," Decker said, because the hangar doors were opening for the truck to pass through. The same hangar they had watched the other trucks enter.

Decker pressed himself flat against the truck bed as they passed through the doors into the cavernous and gloomy space beyond. He could hear men shouting instructions to each other from somewhere inside the building. A truck door slammed. Or maybe a tailgate on one of the other vehicles. He stared up toward a ceiling crisscrossed with metal girders. Lights shone down at intervals, casting pools of illumination. Then the truck came to a juddering halt with a belch of diesel fumes.

Someone banged a hard fist on the side of the truck.

The voices grew closer. Mina drew in a sharp breath and inched back closer to the truck's cab.

The voices were right on top of them now.

Decker held his breath. His gaze slid toward the tailgate, waiting for it to open. He looked around, frantic to find a gap between the crates in which to hide, if only for a little while. But there was none. The boxes were packed tight, leaving the slim space between the cargo and the truck's side wall as their only cover. And it would be no cover at all if someone opened the tailgate before they had a chance to sneak out of the truck bed. They would be caught in a heartbeat. And considering the attitude of the soldier they encountered in the forest, Decker hated to think about what would be in store for them then.

THIRTY-ONE

DECKER AND MINA exchanged worried glances. The men unloading the trucks were right next to them. Decker wondered if his plan to sneak into the base was a miscalculation. Worse, he had brought Mina along with him and now they both risked being discovered. But then, just when he thought all was lost, the voices grew fainter again and he heard footsteps moving away.

Decker breathed a sigh of relief. He counted to ten in his head, giving the personnel in the hangar time to distance themselves from the truck. Then he risked a peek out, peering around the back of the cab.

The driver and his companion with the rifle were no longer in the truck. He saw them standing some distance away, talking to a group of other men clad in similar uniforms. He turned back to Mina and pointed to the rear of the truck bed, indicating that they should disembark before their luck ran out.

Mina nodded and scooted toward the back, then clambered silently over the tailgate and dropped to the floor. Decker followed, but not before he reached out and touched one of the crates again, wondering if he would feel movement now that the truck was parked in the engine turned off. But whatever Mina had sensed inside the wooden box was still. If there was an animal inside, it wasn't moving anymore.

Decker withdrew his hand. He climbed over the tailgate and clambered down next to Mina. Then he peeked around the back of the vehicle to make sure they were still undetected. Across the hangar, on the far wall, was a wide door into which two men were wheeling a crate from one of the other vehicles, using a heavy-duty dolly. Decker was burning with curiosity to see what lay beyond those doors and, since they couldn't stay where they were, he decided that was a good place to head for.

"Come on," he whispered, nudging Mina. "Let's see what we can find out."

Mina looked unsure, but when Decker started off along the side of the truck, keeping the vehicle between them and the group of talking men, she followed.

Now came the hard part. Another wide expanse of open space between themselves and the next truck. Beyond that, even more open space to the doors.

Decker wondered how they were going to pull this off. In his haste to escape the forest and see what was going on inside the military base, he hadn't considered all the angles. There were simply too many soldiers around. He mouthed a silent command to Mina, instructing her to stop, and then pulled himself up so that he could see into the truck's cab. There, lying on the passenger seat, was a dark green camouflage jacket. It just might be what he needed.

Jumping back down, he eased the passenger door open and reached inside, snatching the jacket from the seat. Between that and the pants he'd taken from the dead soldier in the forest, he might just blend in if nobody looks too closely. It was Decker's experience that people saw what they expected to see, and he looked enough like a soldier to escape detection so long as no one studied him too closely. Mina, on the other hand, stuck out like a sore thumb. Not only was she wearing civilian clothing, but she was female. Decker had seen no other women on the base.

"What is it?" Mina asked, picking up on Decker's hesitation.

"If anyone sees us, they'll know you don't belong here right away." Decker hitched the rifle over his shoulder. "Give me the pistol."

"No way." Mina shook her head. "You already have a gun. I'm keeping it."

"That's not a good idea. You don't look like you belong here. If someone sees you with that gun, they might shoot first and ask questions later."

"Fine. Have it your way." Mina handed the pistol to Decker. "Just for the record, I felt safer when I had the gun."

"Duly noted." Decker took the gun and slipped it back into the holster on his belt. He peeked around the truck cab. The driver and his buddy with the rifle had finished talking and were making their way to a truck that was already unloaded. They climbed into the cab and started it up, then swung the vehicle around and headed for the hangar doors. A moment later, they were gone, probably to pick up another load. That just left the men tasked with unloading crates and wheeling them away, and their focus was on a fully laden truck parked across the hangar. It should keep them busy for a while, which meant he and Mina might make it across the hangar without being seen. He waited for them to turn away and start lifting a crate from the truck bed, then he nudged Mina. "Let's go. Stay on my right side so that I'm blocking you from the view of those men."

"What if they see me, anyway?"

"Let's worry about that if it happens. Right now, their

attention is on that truck." He nodded toward the door, where they'd seen a crate being wheeled. "Move quickly, but don't run. We need to look like we belong here if anyone glances our way."

"You look fine in that uniform, but I'm wearing jeans and a leather jacket. No one will think I belong here."

"Which is why I want you on the far side of me. Come on." After another quick glance to confirm the men unloading the other truck were still busy, Decker took Mina's hand, and they broke cover.

A moment later they reached the truck parked ahead of the one they arrived in and skirted around the side of it. Decker was glad for the momentary cover, but they were soon exposed again as they navigated the last stretch. But luck was on their side. They reached the door without drawing attention and hurried through, finding themselves in a windowless chamber with a metal cage sitting in the middle surrounding a large freight elevator. The elevator's gate was open, the cab waiting for its next load of crates.

"That's weird," Decker said, approaching the elevator. "Not what you expect to find in an aircraft hangar."

"Where do you think it goes?" Mina asked.

"This building doesn't have a second floor, so I'm guessing it goes down."

"To what?" Mina walked to the elevator and peered inside.

"Let's find out." Decker stepped inside and waited for Mina to join him, then pulled the gate closed. There were only two buttons on the control panel, which meant there was only one level beneath the hangar. Decker was curious to see what it contained. He reached out and pressed the lower of the two buttons, and with a mechanical clank and a shudder, the elevator started downward.

THIRTY-TWO

THE ELEVATOR CREAKED and groaned as it descended through the shaft. There was no illumination in the cab, and for a few seconds, while the elevator was between floors, they were plunged into inky blackness. But then the lower level came into view and weak light spilled through the elevator cage. A moment later, the cab came to a stop with a slight bump.

Decker peered through the cage before opening the door to make sure they were not stepping out into certain capture, but all he saw through the grate was a long murky corridor hewn from the island's bedrock with bare bulbs strung along it at intervals.

"What is this place?" Mina asked, looking over his shoulder.

"Not a regular military base, that's for sure," Decker answered. "It must have taken a lot of effort to dig an underground tunnel like this. They must be hiding something pretty important."

"The contents of those crates," Mina said. "I wish we

could've opened one to see what was inside. I'd love to know what they were transporting."

"Maybe the answer will be at the end of this tunnel." Decker slid the grill back and stepped out of the elevator. Mina followed behind, then turned to close the grill again but Decker stopped her. "Leave it. The elevator can't go back up if the cab is open. I'd rather not have those men in the hangar appearing unannounced."

"Me either." A look of concern flashed across Mina's face. "But how are we going to get back up? If we take the elevator, we won't know if anyone is waiting for us at the top."

"I haven't figured that out yet." Decker started down the tunnel. "It will come to me."

"I hope so." Mina glanced back toward the elevator. "I'd rather not be stuck down here. It's freaking creepy."

"I think it might be about to get creepier," Decker said as they approached a split in the tunnel. A metal sign affixed to the wall on their left with the word menagerie stenciled on it pointed along one branch, while a sign on the other wall with the word reliquary pointed down the other tunnel. Decker turned to Mina. "Got a preference?"

"What's a menagerie?"

"A place where they keep live specimens of animals," Decker replied. "A reliquary is just as it sounds. A place to store relics of some kind."

"I knew it." Mina looked pleased with herself. "I told you there was an animal inside one of those crates. I felt it move."

"Then we take the left-hand tunnel and maybe we'll find out what those trucks were transporting." Decker started off again, leading Mina along the tunnel until they reached a set of steel doors blocking their path. There was another sign here, stenciled directly on the door.

THIRTY-THREE

**Level III Personnel Only Beyond This Point.
Use Extreme Caution.**

"THAT CAN'T BE GOOD," Mina said, suppressing a shudder. "It kind of reminds me of the secret labs we found under the North Tower back in Shackleton."

"I'm hoping there's nothing that sinister on the other side of this door," Decker said. The labs Mina was referring to had been used for genetic experiments. A couple of hapless robbers who didn't understand what they were mixed up in had tried to steal technology from abandoned military labs under a dilapidated tower block in an Alaskan outpost only to end up as victims of the tech they wanted to steal. It hadn't turned out well for the robbers, but it had led to Decker meeting Mina for the first time, and also his current employment at CUSP.

"Either way, we're going to open it, right?"

"That is what we came here for." Decker tried the handle. Incredibly, the doors opened. He glanced sideways at Mina. "I guess they trust their employees to obey the sign."

"Or the soldiers with big guns aren't particularly keen to visit whatever might be in there so they don't need a lock." Mina's gaze shifted back in the direction from which they came. "Maybe we should rethink this and visit the reliquary first."

"Where's the fun in that?" Decker said, pushing the doors wide.

An odor wafted out, cloying and sickly.

Mina gagged and turned away. "Oh, hell. That's bad."

"On that point, we agree," Decker said. It smelled like a mix of feces and rotten food.

Decker poked his head inside. The tunnel continued on for a short distance before opening up into a wider chamber. He could see doors set into the chamber walls. Metal doors with square grates set into them. He moved forward cautiously, wondering if there would be anyone inside the chamber. A guard or some other custodian. But there was not. When they reached the tunnel's end, they found themselves in a large round space empty except for a desk sitting in the middle with nothing but an old-fashioned red telephone on it. Except the doors that lined the walls. Forty of them at least, spread at intervals of about fifteen feet from one end of the chamber all the way to the other. And from beyond these doors came animalistic sounds. Grunts and snorts. The occasional rumbling bark, although the creature that made it didn't sound like any dog Decker had ever encountered.

Decker crossed to the desk and looked at the phone. He saw that there was no dialer. This line only went to one place. "I wonder who's on the other end of this?"

"Not sure I want to find out," Mina said, looking around with wide eyes. "This is awful. It's like some kind of prison."

"Not a prison. I don't think there are any humans behind those doors," Decker said. He picked up the phone, held the receiver to his ear.

Without ringing, a curt voice answered. "State your location and emergency."

Decker hesitated. He didn't want to reply and alert whoever controlled the base to their presence.

"State your location and emergency," the voice said again, this time with a tinge of irritation.

Decker replaced the handset. "That wasn't very helpful."

"What did they say?" Mina asked.

"They just asked what my emergency was." Decker turned his attention to the doors lining the walls of the circular chamber. He approached the closest and put his face close to the grill.

All he could see beyond the door was darkness. He waited for his vision to adjust, and when it did, he saw another set of eyes staring back at him out of the shadows. Inhuman eyes that burned a sulfurous yellow. Then, before he could react, the occupant of the room beyond the door lunged forward.

THIRTY-FOUR

WHATEVER WAS inside the room slammed into the metal door with a thump. Decker stumbled backwards with a strangled shout. He lifted his arms to defend himself against whatever might escape and come hurtling toward him, but the door held firm.

"Decker." Mina rushed toward him. "Are you okay?"

"It's okay. I'm fine." Decker's heart was racing. He took a calming breath.

"What did you see?" Mina cast a fearful glance toward the door. "What is in there?"

"I didn't see much of anything. Just a pair of eyes before it rushed the door."

"What do you think this place is?"

"Upon reflection, I think you were dead on when you said it was a prison. Although what they are keeping prisoner, I couldn't begin to guess, and I have no intention of looking in any of the other rooms."

"Where does that leave us?"

"With no more answers than we had before." Decker looked at the doors surrounding them, then the table with the red telephone sitting on it. "If anything, it raises new questions. Not to mention that we still don't know exactly what decade we are in."

"Or how to get back home," Mina added. She folded her arms across her chest. "I don't like it in here. We should leave. Maybe the reliquary will have some answers."

"Maybe. And it's not like we have anything better to do." Decker led her out of the circular room and closed the door behind them. He was glad to be away from that chamber and the horrors he suspected it contained. He wondered about the red telephone and the voice on the other end of the line. Was it connected to somewhere else in the base, or was the voice much further away, like on the mainland? This was just another question to which he didn't have a satisfactory answer.

They retraced their steps back along the tunnel until they reached the fork, then headed toward the reliquary. At the end of that tunnel was another set of doors, much like the ones they had just left behind, except this one didn't have a dire warning printed on it. Decker felt like that was progress. Just like the other doors, these were also unlocked. Beyond them was another large room, only there was no telephone this time. Instead, heavy duty metal racks lined the walls. More racks occupied the middle of the room, forming rows. A small table and a single chair stood at the end of each rack. The overhead lights bathed everything in a dull yellow glow. They flickered occasionally, as if the power source feeding them was not constant. Decker guessed it was a generator somewhere on the base.

Decker ushered Mina into the room and followed her, then turned and closed the doors behind them. He looked around. Each rack had six shelves, upon which sat archival boxes gathering dust. He approached the closest rack and studied one of them. There was a number written on the front in neat block lettering, but nothing else. Decker surmised it must be a reference number of some sort, probably linked to a ledger that would tell them what the box contained. But there was an easier way to see what was inside.

Decker lifted the box off the shelf and took it to the desk at the end of the rack, where he placed it down.

"Wait," Mina said, placing her hand atop the box. "Are you sure you want to open this? Remember what happened when you looked in that room just now."

"It's just a box." Decker lifted Mina's hand away. "And there were no warnings printed on the door to this room, so I'm sure that whatever is inside will be safe."

"I wouldn't be too sure about that," a male voice said to their rear.

Decker and Mina spun around to find three uniformed men standing in the doorway, two of which were holding rifles. The closest man's insignia identified him as a captain, but he wore no other identifying badges, just like every other soldier they'd seen.

"It's been a busy couple of weeks for unauthorized visitors," the captain said, stepping closer to them; his hand resting on a holstered colt pistol. "I can't wait to hear what the two of you have to say for yourselves."

"I'm not unauthorized," Decker said, hoping the uniform he had cobbled together would be enough to bluff their way out of trouble. "I was told to bring a specialist down here to—"

"Don't waste your breath." The captain waved a dismissive hand. He moved close to Decker. "I'll take those guns, if you please."

With no other choice, Decker handed over the rifle, then removed the pistol from his belt and offered that up too.

"Very good." The captain took the guns and stepped back,

then motioned his companions. "Take them away and put them with the others."

"There are others?" Decker asked. "You mentioned more unauthorized visitors. Who were you talking about?"

"I'll be the one asking the questions, thank you very much," the captain replied as his men moved forward to apprehend Decker and Mina. "But not yet. I have more urgent matters to attend to."

"What urgent matters?" Decker asked, thinking of the creature that attacked them in the forest. He resisted the urge to shrug off one of the soldiers, who placed a hand in the center of his back and pushed him forward while the other soldier took charge of Mina. "Let us go and maybe we can help you."

"I hardly think so. And you're in no position to bargain."

Wait . . ." Decker protested.

But the captain was having none of it. He looked at his men. "Get them out of here. Quickly now."

With those parting words, he turned and left, while Decker and Mina were hustled back out into the tunnel toward an unknown fate.

THIRTY-FIVE

THE TWO SOLDIERS led Mina and Decker back through the tunnels to the freight elevator and up. As the elevator ascended, Decker tried to engage their captors in conversation.

"I don't suppose you want to tell me what branch of the military you work for?" He asked, not really expecting an answer.

"Quiet," came the not entirely unexpected reply from the burly soldier on the left.

"Does that extend to me, too?" Mina asked in a silky voice that surprised Decker. She looked at the soldier with wide, innocent eyes. "I really don't know what's going on, or how I got caught up in all of this. Can you at least tell us what the date is?"

"You don't know what date this is?" The two soldiers exchanged glances.

"No." Mina shook her head. Her voice trembled and a tear rolled down her cheek. "I really don't. I'm sure you're not supposed to engage in conversation, but it can't hurt to tell us the date, surely?"

"Just like the other ones," the taller, thinner soldier on the right said to his companion. "I swear, this place gets weirder every week."

Decker burned with curiosity. This was the third time someone had alluded to more unauthorized people on the base. He wanted to quiz the two soldiers, but Mina was doing a good job of tugging at their heartstrings, and he didn't want to interrupt that.

As if she sensed Decker's approval, Mina ramped up the drama. She wiped the tear from her cheek and stared at the soldiers. "I just want to know where I am. I'm so scared. Please, tell me the date if nothing else?"

The burly soldier on their left hesitated, then shrugged. "It's June twentieth."

"I know this will sound crazy, but what's the year?"

"Sister, you don't know the half of it." The soldier chuckled. "Believe me, you're one of the less crazy things I've seen around this place recently."

"Like what?" Mina asked.

"Just tell her the damn year," his companion said. "Nothing else unless you want to get sent to the front."

"Fine. 1942." the burly soldier shook his head. The elevator clanked to a halt. He pulled the door open and nudged Mina with his gun. "Now move. And keep your trap shut from here on out."

"Alright, already." Mina glared at the man; all pretense of innocence now dropped. "You don't need to poke me with that thing."

"Let's just do as they say." Decker took Mina's arm and stepped out of the elevator. Then he leaned close and whispered in her ear. "Good job."

The merest hint of a smile touched Mina's lips before it vanished as she stepped from the elevator.

They passed through the hangar and out into onto the

grounds of the base, where they were roughly escorted to a block building on the far side near the fence. A sign hanging above the door told them it was Barrack C. Barracks A and B stood alongside it. Decker guessed this was where the base personnel lived. But not building C. This was going to be their prison, apparently. The soldiers marched them inside and into a corridor with three sturdy doors on each side, two of which were secured with chains and a padlock. Two guards stood in the hallway, guns at the ready.

"Got some more for you," the lanky soldier said. "Caught them mooching around the reliquary."

"The reliquary?" The closest guard raised an eyebrow. "How did they get in there?"

"Beats me." Lanky shrugged. "Captain Hawkins was not happy, I can tell you."

"I bet. He has to answer to the colonel. Rather him than me." The guard visibly shuddered.

"Yeah. I agree with that." Lanky nodded. "Where do you want them?"

"They can go in with the other three civies." The guard took a set of keys out and unlocked the nearest door on the left while his companion covered them with his gun.

"In you go," Lanky said, giving Decker a hard shove in the back.

He stumbled forward through the opening, then turned and caught Mina as the door slammed shut behind them.

She straightened, then let out a startled gasp. Decker turned, afraid of what he would see, but instead, a familiar figure stepped from the shadows. The last man he expected to find locked in a barrack room eighty years in the past . . .

THIRTY-SIX

DECKER. MINA." Colum raced to them and embraced Decker in a tight bearhug before doing the same to Mina. "You're a sight for sore eyes."

"We thought you were dead," Rory said, approaching them with Adam Hunt a step behind.

"That's for sure," Hunt said. "We didn't think anyone could survive that lightning strike that hit the hotel."

"Well, we did. Although I'm not sure our current situation is much better." Decker looked around. The room was long and narrow, with cots placed along the walls. It looked exactly like Decker's impression of a World War Two barracks. "I hoped you guys had avoided our fate."

"Yet here we are," Colum said. "That lightning strike was a helluva thing. Hit the roof and then sent what looked like ribbons of energy down to ground level. Damned near fried us alive."

"It was almost like the lightning was searching for us. Like it knew we were there." Hunt rubbed his neck. "There was no time to evade it. One moment we were on the veranda waiting for the pair of you, the next we were waking up in the forest."

"That was two days ago," Rory said. "We'd all but given up on ever seeing you again. Figured that since the lightning nearly killed us, you two must be goners."

"Two days?" Decker exchanged a look with Mina. "We've been here less than six hours."

"Interesting." Rory paced back and forth. "Whatever process brought us here is not very accurate. It dumped us days apart."

"Maybe because we weren't all in the same location?" Colum asked.

"Possible." Rory shrugged. "Or maybe that's just how it works. You get sent to some approximate place in time with no guarantee that anyone else will arrive at the same point."

"Hardly encouraging for getting back to our own time," Hunt said.

Decker went to the door, tried the handle. As he expected, it was locked. "If we can't get out of this room, we'll never find out."

"Not to mention that we need another storm to roll in," Rory said. "I have a hypothesis about our predicament."

"That the disappearances in the Bermuda triangle are linked to those storms?" Decker asked. "I came to the same conclusion."

"Yes." Rory nodded. "A lot of eyewitness accounts of strange happenings in the triangle talk about electrical storms and strange cloud formations. The sky turning odd, shimmering colors. There's a famous account of a pilot in a Beechcraft single-engine plane flying from the Bahamas to Florida with a couple of passengers back in the seventies. He flew into an area of black clouds which he couldn't avoid. There were flashes of bright light similar to lightning, and he ended up in a dark tunnel inside the clouds that appeared to be closing around him. His equipment started going wrong and he couldn't get his bearings. Even so, he managed to escape right before the tunnel swallowed him up and found himself in clear blue skies once again. The weirdest thing of all was that his entire trip took less than forty-five minutes. A flight that should've taken an hour and a half at top speed."

"Time travel," Mina said.

"That's one theory."

"A theory borne out by our own experience, and the fact that we have a bride from the early twentieth century sitting back at La Casa de Playa." Decker gave up on the door and returned to the rest of the group. "But there's something else going on here, too."

"The creature in the woods," Mina said. "The one that killed the soldier."

"Wait. What creature in the woods?" Hunt looked at Decker with narrowed eyes. "Tell me."

"There's not much to tell." Decker quickly explained what had happened in the forest. He told Hunt about the corporal they came across, and his untimely end. He recounted breaking into the military base, finding the underground chambers.

Hunt listened to all of this with a blank expression, then he nodded. "Very interesting. We haven't had much interaction with the people here, but I thought they were acting jumpy. Nervous. That might explain why."

"Have they questioned you?" Decker asked. "Tried to find out who you are and where you came from?"

"Not so much," Hunt replied. "I was expecting an interrogation within hours of our capture, but so far, they've just kept us in here. As prisons go, it's not too bad. They bring us a meal in the morning and another in the evening. The beds are bearable, and they even gave us a pack of playing cards to pass the time. I've tried to get information out of the guards, but they're tight-lipped. We're not even sure what decade we are in, although given the military hardware around here, I'm guessing the forties or fifties."

"Try 1942." Decker jerked his thumb toward Mina. "She played one of our captors pretty good. Got him to open up, at least a little."

"Forty-two." Hunt nodded. "Makes sense. This place was built during the early years of the war. According to our records, it was a training base, but that secret underground facility you described doesn't sound much like a training base to me."

"Me either," Decker said. "They were actively transporting something down there. Mina thought one of the crates in the truck we hid in contained a live animal."

"Maybe related to whatever killed that soldier in the forest?" Colum asked.

"It's possible." Decker thought for a moment. Something had been bothering him. None of the men they encountered were particularly surprised to see them, even though Mina clearly didn't know what year it was. He looked at Hunt. "Do you find it odd that a bunch of unusually dressed strangers showing up on a secret military base in the middle of the war doesn't seem to have phased these people? As you said, they haven't even bothered to interrogate you. It's like they already know what our deal is."

"Or at least they suspect," Colum said. "Maybe that's because we're not the first unannounced guests to show up here."

"What do you mean?" Decker asked.

"Did you see the torpedo bombers out there on the airstrip?" Hunt asked. "Five of them. TBM Avengers."

"Sure. I also saw what looked like a Lockheed Electra inside one of the hangars. Hardly unusual for an airbase."

"Except we've already established this isn't a normal airbase."

"I still don't see the relevance of those planes."

Colum stepped forward. "I'm not sure the TBM's are meant to be here anymore than we are."

"And why would you think that?" Decker asked. "There were plenty of TBM Avengers that flew throughout the Second World War, completing thousands of missions. And not just for the U.S. Navy. The British and Canadians flew them too."

Colum folded his arms and met Decker's gaze. "Because if the planes are yours, you don't lock up the men who were flying them. Crazy as it sounds, I think we might have solved the mystery of Flight 19."

THIRTY-SEVEN

YOU THINK those planes out there are Flight 19?" Decker looked at Colum, incredulous.

"Flight 19?" Mina said, her gaze shifting between the two men. "No way. I read a book on them a few years ago. They were a squadron of TBM Avenger torpedo bombers that took off from the Naval Air Station in Fort Lauderdale, Florida, a few months after World War Two ended. They were flying a training exercise east toward the Bahamas before flying north and then turning back toward home. After a couple of garbled radio communications, they were never heard from again. The Navy attributed their loss to the Bermuda triangle."

"That's right," Colum said.

"They must have encountered a storm just like us and Celine Rothman." Rory was talking fast. "I bet they traveled backwards in time and ended up landing here years before they took off."

"You think the people that run this base know those airmen are from the future?"

"I guarantee it," Colum said. "Those men would have

been mightily confused when they landed. From their point of view, the war is over, but to everyone else here it's still going on."

"Not to mention that earlier versions of them would still be wandering around out there somewhere," Rory said. "It wouldn't take much digging to figure out there were two versions of the same men occupying the same point in time."

"Exactly."

"None of this helps us," Decker said. "We're still trapped here with no way to get home, and I can't imagine our captors have cracked the secret of time travel even if they are willing to help us."

"Are you saying we're trapped here forever?" Mina asked.

"No." Decker shook his head. "I don't believe in impossible situations. There's always a solution. We're just not going to find it locked in this room."

"What do you propose we do?" Colum asked. "I know you have a plan, by the look on your face."

"Not really a plan so much as a course of action. I'm still playing this by ear. Get us out of here first, then deal with the next problem." Decker walked to the door. He bunched his fists and hammered on it, then shouted as loud as he could. "If there's anyone out there, I need to talk with the base commander. I have information that can help him."

"What are you doing?" Rory asked, hurrying toward Decker. "Drawing attention to us like this might only make things worse."

"The men out there have barely spoken to us in two days," Hunt said. "I think John has the right idea."

"Me, too." Colum crossed the room and clenched his own fists, then joined Decker pounding on the door. "You need to listen to this man. He can help you."

A gruff voice drifted from the other side of the door.

"Keep it down in there. If Colonel Spear wants to talk to you, he'll tell us."

"You need to take a message to him," Decker shouted back. "Tell him we know what's going on here. We know all about those airmen you're holding in the opposite barrack room. We know about Flight 19."

"I won't say this again, be quiet." The guard in the hallway was having none of it.

"Tell him we saw the creature in the forest." Decker played his last card.

"You know about the creature?" The guard asked. "You saw it?"

"We did more than see it," Decker replied. "We survived it. I'm guessing you have a real problem on your hands."

"Nothing we can't handle," came the reply.

"Really? I'm going to dispute that assessment."

"And why would you do that?" The guard sounded unsure of himself now.

"Because we know what happened to his corporal, too." Mina joined in. "A man named Jim Tarrant."

Decker flashed a thumbs up to Mina. "If you haven't discovered that he's missing, you soon will."

There was a brief period of silence from the other side of the door before the guard spoke again. "I'll send someone to relay your message to the commander."

Decker grinned. His plan had worked. It wouldn't set them all free, but at least someone was paying attention now. That was a start.

"Thank you," Mina shouted. She held her hand up for Decker to give a high-five.

"You'd better not be lying to me." The guard didn't sound happy. "Now shut up. I don't want to hear another peep out of you until I get an answer back."

"Works for me." Decker stepped away from the door and turned to the others.

"What do you hope to achieve by talking with the base commander?" Rory asked. "You think he'll let us all go?"

"Not sure. But we'll never get out of here if we don't open a line of dialogue. Besides, I have a feeling they need our help."

"The creature in the forest," Hunt said. "You don't think it should be there."

"I know it. There should not be anything on this island big enough to drag a man off and kill him. Whatever that thing is, it was huge. And it was stalking us."

"It could have been me or Decker killed instead of that soldier," Mina said. "We were lucky to escape."

"Other people are going to die," Decker said. "I'm sure of it."

"What makes you think they'll accept your help?" Colum asked.

Mina grinned. "Because he's John Decker, monster hunter. That's what he does. And this time he has reinforcements . . . us."

"Except they don't know any of that," Colum said. "Those men out there are from eighty years in the past. They've never heard of CUSP."

"Maybe it's time they did," said Decker. He paced back and forth, hoping the guard would hear from his commander soon. He was eager to do something other than stand around.

As it happened, the reply came quickly. Less than ten minutes after Decker spoke to the guard, they heard a commotion on the other side of the door, and it swung open.

Four mean looking soldiers stood there, including the two guards. One of them glared at Decker with narrowed eyes. "You. Come with us."

"Looks like we got the answer we wanted," Decker said, stepping forward.

"Hang on a moment." Colum followed him. "Where he goes, we all go."

"Just the mouthy one," the guard said. He reached out and grabbed Decker's jacket, then pulled him through the open door while the other soldiers held Colum and the rest at bay with their guns. "The rest of you stay here and keep a lid on it."

Then he slammed the door and locked it as the soldiers led Decker away at gunpoint to see their base commander.

THIRTY-EIGHT

BASE COMMANDER COLONEL GERALD P. Spear had a face that looked like it might have been chiseled from granite. The deep wrinkles on his forehead looked more like fault lines, making him appear older than his true age, which couldn't be more than fifty-five given his lean yet muscular frame, and hair tinged with gray but not yet entirely silver. He sat in his office behind a large desk and observed Decker with tented fingers while the pair of soldiers who delivered him hovered nervously in the background. On the desk, three CUSP-issued cell phones that Decker knew belonged to Hunt, Colum, and Rory were sitting in plain view.

"You may leave now," Spear said, addressing his men. "Wait outside. I'll shout if I need you."

"Very good." The soldiers snapped to attention, then filed out, closing the door behind them.

Decker was now alone with the imposing base commander, which was precisely what he hoped would happen. He waited for the man to speak, but instead, the commander studied Decker as if he were an insect caught in a sample jar.

"What's your name?" Spear asked.

"John Decker."

Spear nodded. "I hope you're not lying to me."

"I'm not." Decker cleared his throat. He glanced at the phones, noting Spear's disinterest in the devices. "I assume you know where we came from, or at least, you suspect."

"The future." Spear spoke the words in such a matter-of-fact manner that Decker found it hard not to be impressed. Here was a military man running what was purported to be a training base who spoke with no hint of doubt when faced with a claim of the impossible and technology that appeared to be from the future. Either he was a believer, or Decker did not wish to sit opposite him in a game of poker.

Spear extricated his fingers from the tent they formed and tapped the cell phones with a bony finger. "The only question is, how far in the future?"

"I'm not sure I should answer that question." Decker was unwilling to provide any details regarding events yet to come. He didn't know if Rory's hypothesis of alternate timelines was true, but either way, he did not wish to influence events that had not yet occurred.

"Not an entirely unexpected answer," Spear replied. "You appear less alarmed by your predicament than the first group of men who showed up here."

Decker suspected he wasn't talking about Hunt, Colum, and Rory. "The airmen in the TBM Avengers."

Spear nodded. "They claim to be from 1945. They are also under the impression the war is over, which I sincerely hope is true."

"I can't comment on that."

"Naturally." Spear eyed Decker's clothes. "Perhaps you could tell me where you got that uniform. I know it doesn't belong to you. It's too ill-fitting. Not to mention that none of your companions are similarly dressed."

"I took the pants from one of your soldiers. A corporal named Jim Tarrant. I found the jacket in the cab of a truck."

"And you thought you could pass yourself off as one of us?"

"I thought it was worth a try." Decker felt like he was playing a game of cat and mouse with the base commander. Unfortunately, he was the mouse.

"And Corporal Tarrant?"

"Dead. But I didn't kill him."

"I never said that you did. This brings me to my next question. What do you know about the creature in the forest?"

"Not much. My friend and I had only just arrived here when we encountered it. I can tell you it's not indigenous to this island and that it's a deadly predator much more dangerous than anything that should be here."

"So, you didn't see it?"

"Not clearly." Decker shook his head. "But it was tracking us when we encountered your corporal. It took him so quickly we barely saw it. Just a blur. Dragged him off into the forest. I found his body later. It was ripped open. A savage attack. If it's any consolation, he wouldn't have suffered for long."

"It is. My men might as well be family. I take it personally when I lose even one of them." Spear sighed. "What else can you tell me?"

"Not much. As I said, we barely saw the creature. After the attack, we made our way to this base. It was the only safe place to go. The creature would have found us again, eventually."

"You're probably right. But I'm curious why you broke in rather than seek our help?"

"I didn't know who you guys were. Still don't. Your soldier wore no identification other than his rank, and as you already pointed out, we're in the middle of a war. Spies must be a concern. A couple of unannounced visitors waltzing up to the gates of a secret base on an island controlled by the military . . ." Decker smiled wryly. "Well, let's just say I didn't expect to be welcomed with open arms."

"For what it's worth, I don't believe any of you are spies." Spear folded his arms. "And in your situation, I would probably have done the same thing."

Decker nodded.

"But that doesn't excuse you breaking into a secure facility," Spear said. "Be that as it may, we need to focus on the future, and what to do with you all."

"I was rather hoping to help with your problem in the forest, and in return, you might help us find a way back to our own time."

"Is that so?"

"It's a win-win situation. I'm sure you don't want us here, any more than we wish to be here. By my reckoning, you are racking up quite a collection of time travelers. There's the five of us, not to mention the three-man crews of five Navy Avengers. That puts the total headcount at twenty. You certainly can't release any of us. The TBM crews are only a few years displaced from their own time. That means there will be two versions of them occupying the same point in time. Not an easy situation to explain to your superiors. Not to mention the obvious fact that we all have knowledge of future events. Depending on your ideology, that information could be weaponized, and not just to win the war. It could alter world history if the wrong men were privy to it."

"Or even the right ones," Spear said. "The temptation to open a Pandora's box of knowledge under the guise of the greater good is tempting. A little too tempting. Thankfully, yourselves and those pilots appeared in the one location that can protect the world from that misguided ideology."

"The Bermuda Triangle."

"I have no idea what you're talking about. We're nowhere near Bermuda," Spear said. "I was referring to myself and the other men on this island. We have a higher purpose. One that transcends the petty rivalries of our time."

"Your little menagerie buried under that hangar." Decker was forming an opinion regarding their captors. One that he found unlikely yet fit the facts as he knew them. "I'm curious. Why don't your uniforms show the branch of the military or unit you all belong to?"

"There's a good reason for that," Spear said. He looked thoughtful for a moment. "I appreciate your offer of help with our little problem in the forest, but I'm not inclined to take you up on it just yet. I need time to think. To make sure my decision is the correct one. For the moment, I'm going to return you to the barracks."

Decker sensed he was about to call the guards back in. "Would you at least tell me who you are, what military unit you represent?"

Again, Spear looked thoughtful. Then he nodded. "I don't see how it can hurt. We're a new unit, formed as an alliance between the British and other Allied countries. The reimagining of a much older organization."

"What's the name of that unit?"

Spear settled back in his chair and fixed Decker with a somber gaze. "Classified Universal Special Projects."

THIRTY-NINE

COLONEL SPEAR SETTLED back in his chair and watched his guards lead the man, who said his name was John Decker, out of the room. One of them reached back and closed the door, leaving Spear alone with his thoughts. There was a lot he still didn't understand about his uninvited visitors. And not just the five men who showed up over the last few days during an unusually violent and long-lived tropical storm. A few weeks before that, a squadron of Navy planes dropped out of the sky during another thunderstorm and landed one by one as the wind buffeted them and lightning cracked around.

It hadn't taken long to figure out there was an issue with the five TBM Avengers. The torpedo bomber crews believed it was December 1945, more than three years distant. Worse, he had checked on several of the men and discovered they were not even old enough to join the military yet—unlike their *future* versions who were sitting across the base in barrack three. The commander of the training squadron was another matter. He was old enough to serve but shouldn't have been anywhere near the Bahamas. The Navy had him assigned to a scouting squadron in the Pacific and discreet inquiries proved that to be exactly where he was. Which made the man who landed a TBM avenger on Singer Cay either an imposter or a time traveler just like his story made him out to be. There were other discrepancies, too. Three of the aircraft carried Bureau Numbers that were reserved for future use. Those aircraft were not even built yet.

To any other base commander, these things would seem impossible, but not to a man like Colonel Gerald P. Spear. He had been hand-selected as head of Classified Universal Special Projects because of his ability to take the paranormal and the unusual in stride. And with good cause. The Nazis had developed a keen interest in the occult and the Allies wanted a weapon to bring to the front lines of that strange fight. The British Order of St. George was the logical choice, having battled the paranormal since Victorian times. But the organization needed to be global. It must answer to Allied Command rather than one single country. This was why the name had been changed and the structure reorganized.

Spear stood and walked to the window. He looked out over the base just as another truck made its way through the south gate laden with more crates. If he had known all the problems this island would bring when they were selecting a location for their headquarters, he would have picked some-where less troublesome. First those airmen showed up out of thin air. Then the liberty ship SS Winston Box ran aground on the south tip of the island during the same foul storm that brought Decker and his group here. Worse, it was laden with cargo from England. And not just any cargo. The Order of St. George had accumulated quite a collection during fifty-odd years, and none of it was safe in a London bombarded by Axis bombs on an almost daily basis. Which was why the SS Winston Box was heading for Singer Cay, its hold full of precious cargo. No one could have foreseen the ferocity of that storm, or the speed with which it descended upon the island. Now, thanks to that wrecked ship, a man under his command was dead. At least if the newcomer John Decker was to be believed, and there was no reason not to believe him. Colonel Spear gave a long sigh. He was starting to think Singer Cay was cursed.

He turned away from the window and went to the door. The least he could do was make sure no one else died today.

His secretary Burt Calder, a wiry young man with a crop of curly brown hair and a pair of thick, black-rimmed glasses perched at the end of his nose, looked up when Spear opened the door and poked his head out.

"Can I help you, sir?" Calder asked.

"It will be dark soon. Tell Captain Myers to bring the men in from the forest and secure the perimeter. We'll start our search again in the morning."

"Very good, sir." Calder nodded and reached for the telephone sitting on his desk.

Spear watched for a moment as his underling lifted the receiver and started to dial the guard room. Then he turned and retreated into his office, closing the door behind him. It was going to be a long night, but at least his men would be safe.

FORTY

WELL, WHAT HAPPENED?" Colum said as soon as the guards thrust Decker back into the barrack room. "Are they going to let us out of here?"

"Not so much." Decker heard the door lock behind him. "The base commander was suspicious of me. He knows we're from the future and doesn't appear terribly distressed by it. He's pretty calm and collected, actually. You were right about Flight 19, too. Those airmen are from 1945. I'm sure he's keeping them locked up for the same reason he's keeping us in here. He doesn't know what to do with them, and he's afraid of the repercussions if he leaves them to their own devices."

"I don't like this." Colum pulled a face. "That base commander should be confused as hell. Why is he so open to the possibility of time travel?"

"Maybe because he's not a normal base commander," Decker replied.

"What do you mean?" Hunt asked.

"Really? You haven't guessed the truth yet?" Decker looked at Hunt and raised an eyebrow.

"Just spit it out, man."

"This base belongs to us. Or at least, what we were eighty years ago." Decker looked around the group, waiting for it to sink in. "That's Classified Universal Special Projects out there. The reason CUSP owns this island in the twenty-first century is because they selected it as their headquarters during the Second World War after being created and absorbing the Order of St. George."

"No way." Mina's jaw dropped.

"I'm afraid it's true. This is no ordinary training base. The military didn't build it for the Navy or Air Force. They took it from Howard Rothman's heirs so the newly formed CUSP would have somewhere private to go about their business."

"So that underground chamber with all the creatures locked inside is some sort of . . ." Mina's voice trailed off.

"Holding area for the supernatural and pseudo-mythical creatures CUSP deals with."

"In other words, the Zoo," Colum said.

"The Zoo?" Mina asked, looking between the men. "What's that?"

Hunt looked uncomfortable. "It's where we keep the more . . . dangerous creatures we encounter."

"You still maintain a facility like that horrendous place under the hangar?"

Now Hunt looked like he wished the ground would swallow him up. "We do. Yes. At our island facility in Maine."

"That's horrible." Mina shuddered. "It's barbaric."

"I can assure you; we take excellent care of the residents of our Zoo," Hunt said. "The accommodations are more than adequate."

"I don't care if you provide a suite of rooms with a view and king-sized beds." Mina glared at Hunt. "It's still wrong."

"On that point, we shall have to disagree."

"Adam's right," Decker said. "Sometimes, we have no option. The Zoo is for creatures that present a clear and present threat. It's a last resort when there's no other option."

Mina edged close to Decker, turned her back on the others, and spoke under her breath so only he could hear. "I'm a monster now. Did you think about putting me in that place?"

"You're not a monster," Decker replied, his voice low. "And no, that was never an option."

"Good to know." Mina turned and walked away.

"What's up with her?" Colum asked, watching her go.

"She's fine," Decker said. "Just stressed, that's all. Seeing that menagerie really freaked her out."

"I get that." Colum snorted. "I can't believe these people built a Zoo on this island. Of all the places to keep your collection of dangerous monsters. The freaking Bermuda Triangle. Idiots."

"I'm not sure anyone out there knows what the Bermuda Triangle is," Decker said. "The base commander looked blank when I mentioned it."

"Not surprising," Rory said. "The concept of the Bermuda Triangle and the mysterious disappearances associated with it originated with a Miami Herald article in 1950. That article won't be written for another eight years. Even then, the term Bermuda Triangle hadn't been coined. That wouldn't happen until 1964."

"Which means when CUSP selected this island for their headquarters, they didn't know it was within the boundary of an area prone to paranormal events."

"Correct. There have been strange occurrences in the area for centuries, but no one put them together into a coherent narrative." Rory was in his element now. "For example, the disappearance of the USS Cyclops in 1918. There are also less well-known disappearances like the USS Wasp and the USS

Pickering that both vanished in the early nineteenth century. Even Christopher Columbus got in on the act when he claimed to see strange lights from the deck of the Santa Maria a day before they landed on the Bahamian island of Guanahani, now known as San Salvador Island. There are many more—"

"I think we've heard enough to prove your point," Hunt said, interrupting the archaeologist. "The question is, what are we going to do next?"

"We sit tight and wait for the base commander to make his mind up," Decker said. "I don't see that we have much choice, at least in the short term."

"The crates being transported in those trucks," Mina said. "They must contain creatures for the menagerie."

"That would be my guess," Decker said. "And possibly artifacts for the reliquary, too."

"Which leads to an obvious question." A shadow passed across Mina's face. "If they are keeping the monsters locked up, then what attacked us and killed the corporal out in the forest?"

"I don't know," Decker admitted. "But I think the base commander does, and I have a feeling he's not doing a good job dealing with it. I offered to help, and for a moment, I thought he would take me up on it. But then cautiousness got the better of him."

"Which means we're back at square one," Colum said, looking disappointed.

"Not necessarily." Decker shook his head. "He didn't give me a firm no. He said he wanted to think about it. I guess all we can do now is wait and hope he comes to the right decision."

"Did you tell him who we are?" Hunt asked. "Is he aware we also work for CUSP?"

"No." Decker shook his head again. "I had my suspicions,

but I didn't know for sure that we were dealing with an earlier version of Classified Universal Special Projects until the end of our conversation. By that time, his guards were hustling me out the door. Still, it gives us some leverage for a future conversation."

"Great. We sit around here with nothing to do until that base commander has an epiphany." Rory pushed his hands into his pockets. "Yippee."

"Have you got a better idea?" asked Decker.

"No. But I was rather hoping to start work on a way to get us home so you can finish marrying Nancy. Not to mention getting back to Cassie. It figures that I finally meet an amazing woman who actually likes me too, and now she won't even be born for another fifty years. Just my luck."

"Don't remind me," Decker said. He felt a tug of longing. Did she even know he was missing yet? He hoped not. He forced the thoughts from his mind and walked further into the room, studying the cots lining the walls and stopping in front of an undisturbed one. "Is this bed free?"

"Sure. There are ten beds in here and five of us," Colum said. "Take your pick."

"Perfect." Decker sat down and kicked his shoes off, then removed his socks, which were still damp. He discarded the jacket he'd found in the truck cab and lay back with a sigh, closing his eyes as his head sank into the pillow. "It's been a long day. I'm exhausted. Wake me up when something interesting happens."

FORTY-ONE

CAPTAIN EDDIE MYERS was enjoying a few minutes of peace with a mug of steaming coffee and a three-day-old edition of the Daily Globe—because it took that long for a copy to reach Singer Cay—when the guard room phone rang and made him jump.

He muttered a curse under his breath and laid the paper down. He hadn't even gotten to the baseball scores yet, which was the bit of the newspaper he most looked forward to. The Sox were trailing the Yankees in the American League and coming off a trio of wins over the Detroit Tigers. Next up were two games against the Browns and if they won both, it might just tighten the race to the finish line with the despised Yankees. But the first of those scores, and the associated good fortunes it might bring, would have to wait.

"Myers here," he said, snatching up the handset and lifting it to his ear.

A second later, the voice of Burt Calder, Commander Spear's secretary, crackled over the speaker. He listened to his orders from on high, relayed his understanding of those same orders, and replaced the handset wondering why the message couldn't have been relayed straight to the north and south gates where the guards stood ready with flare pistols-the easiest way of signaling the thirty men spread throughout the forest. Giving the newspaper one last, longing glance, Captain Myers put down his coffee and hurried from the guardroom.

On the way out, he encountered a staff sergeant strolling the other way. He couldn't remember the man's name but thought it was Timmy, or maybe Larry. Either way, it didn't matter. He barked an order for the staff sergeant to proceed to the north gate and tell the men there to send up signal flares, then watched the man turn and hurry back across the airstrip in the same direction from which he just came. Satisfied that his orders were being obeyed, Myers headed in the other direction, toward the south gate.

As he approached, the men there snapped to attention.

"Send up the red flares," Myers said, as soon as he was within earshot. "Let's get our boys in for the night."

"Sir." The closer of the two men saluted and turned toward the guard box. He reached inside and brought out a standard issue Type AN-M8 flare pistol. The stubby wide barreled aluminum gun looked more like a toy pistol than a real weapon, but it would send a searing bolt of blazing light arching high into the sky, which would be visible even on a sunny day. Now, with the sun already behind the horizon and darkness creeping across the island, it would be even more obvious. The only downside to the flares was the forest canopy, which obstructed a clear view of the sky. That was why they would fire several flares at different trajectories from both gates to alert any men that hadn't already started back with the approaching darkness, that it was time to retreat behind the safety of an eight-foot chain-link fence topped with razor wire.

Myers waited while the guard loaded the pistol and raised

it above his head, pointing the barrel skyward. With a pop, the first flare barreled skyward. Myers watched it arch over the treetops and descend, flickering red. By the third flare, the first men, those closest to base, appeared out of the forest and trudging toward the south gate. They looked tired and scared. And with good cause. The creature they were searching for was more deadly than any natural predator these woods ever held. It was a fast, sleek killing machine and Myers was glad he wasn't part of the search detail. He watched a moment longer, then relayed one more order to the guards.

"Coordinate with the north gate. Conduct a headcount as the men return. When you think you have everyone that's coming back, lock us up tight. I want nothing getting in that shouldn't be here."

"Yes, sir." The guard nodded.

"And keep your guns at the ready. Anything comes out of the darkness, shoot it."

The guards exchanged a nervous look, then nodded.

Myers cast one last glance toward the forest, then turned to make his way back across the airfield. His newspaper was waiting, and with it a chance to defeat the Yankees.

He heard a rumble to his rear and turned, stepping out of the way as the evening's last truck laden with crates from the beached and stricken SS Winston Box grumbled along toward hangar four. The soldier riding shotgun had the barrel of his rifle leaning on the doorframe through the open passenger window. He raised his free hand in a silent greeting as the truck passed Myers. Then the vehicle slowed as it reached the hangar and maneuvered through the doors, which soon closed behind it, blocking Myers's view.

It was almost dark now. Lamps on poles around the airfield flickered on one by one, bathing the space in pale yellow light that pushed the darkness back, banished it to the spaces between the hangars and other buildings.

Myers was almost back to the guardroom now. He wondered if his coffee would still be warm, hoped no one had taken the newspaper for themselves.

He passed close by hangar four, but as he approached hangar five, a movement caught his eye. It was slight. Nothing more than a shifting of the gloom that settled between the two hangars. But it was enough to draw his attention.

He stopped, then turned and studied the narrow space.

Everything was quiet. Peaceful. He wondered if it was nothing more than his eyes playing tricks. He started off again, but hadn't gone more than three steps when another movement flickered at the edge of his vision.

This time, he knew he hadn't imagined it.

He swiveled, changed direction, and headed for the narrow alley between the hangars. Only that afternoon, he'd come across two interlopers in the reliquary. That on top of the ones his men had apprehended two days before out in the forest. Maybe there were yet others.

His hand fell to his service weapon, wishing he had a rifle, deciding there was no time to fetch one. He looked around, hoping to flag down a passing soldier, but there was no one coming his way. The closest men were too far to hail, and he had no intention of letting an intruder escape.

He stepped into the alley, made his way along under the shadow of the hangars. He slipped his pistol from its holster, continued on. A prickle of fear wormed its way up his spine. He was alone here in the darkness between the buildings, and he still had a ways to go before he reached the back of the hangars. Myers took a faltering step, almost turned back around, but then admonished himself. He was no coward.

Myers paused and glanced down at his gun, checked to make sure there was a round in the chamber.

When he looked up again, the darkness seemed thicker, more intense. For a moment he wasn't sure why, but then he realized, too late. There was a shape blocking the alley ahead of him, silhouetted in the meager glow of the lights positioned around the perimeter fence. It crouched low, heckles raised, reminding him of how the pet cat he'd had when he was a child hunkered down when it saw a frog. Except a frog was much smaller, and his cat couldn't rise up onto its hind legs like this beast was now doing, front limbs stretching to reveal muscular arms that ended in wicked-looking curved claws. And there was something else, too. A pair of eerie blue eyes that seemed to glow from within. Eyes that watched him with cold, compassionless hunger.

Myers's breath caught in his throat. He lifted the pistol, hand shaking as he fumbled to find the trigger and failed.

Then it was too late. The dark shape lunged forward with a guttural grunt, too fast for Myers to aim his service weapon, let alone fire a shot. He lifted his arms in self-defense. A scream bubbled up in his throat, soon silenced as sharp teeth found his windpipe. And then, as the blood pumped from his body and oblivion closed in around him, a last unhinged thought flickered through Captain Eddie Myers's mind. A thought of the newspaper lying unread back in the guardroom, and how he would never know if the Sox defeated the Browns.

FORTY-TWO

DECKER LAY on his cot and listened to Mina's rhythmic breathing as she slept in the next bed. Beyond this, somewhere in the darkness, Colum was snoring softly. He didn't know what the time was, but knew it was after midnight, the early hours of the morning.

Several hours ago, their captors had provided a meager meal of bread and soup, which he'd eaten with gusto despite the food's lackluster taste. He had eaten nothing since before the wedding got started, which felt like an interminably long time ago. The irony that it also hadn't happened yet and would not for another eighty years was not lost on him. After the guards collected the empty bowls, they announced it was lights out. He had laid there ever since, unable to fall asleep despite his weariness. He couldn't help thinking of all that had occurred. Of how he'd been ripped away from his bride on their wedding day and tossed back three quarters of a century in time with no clue if there was any way to return.

"Decker?" A small voice drifted out of the darkness. It was Mina. She wasn't sleeping, after all.

"Yes?" He glanced her way but only saw a vague shape

silhouetted by a shaft of moonlight that lanced in through a narrow clerestory window near the ceiling. A window he'd studied earlier in the evening but soon discarded as a means of escape when he noticed the vertical bars on the window's exterior casing.

"Can't sleep?"

"No."

"Me, either." Mina sighed softly. "I can't help feeling we're not going to get out of this situation."

"You mustn't think like that." Decker kept his voice low so he wouldn't disturb the others. "I won't stop until I figure this out."

"I know." Mina's voice trembled.

"Our current situation aside, how are you doing?" Decker asked.

"You mean how am I coping with the unwelcome gift I received from Abraham Turner?"

"Yes."

"About the same as ever. Coming to terms with the fact that I may be immortal, or near as dammit." There was a moment's silence. "And that my brain will always be a jumble of discordant memories inherited from the thousands of people he killed."

"You have their memories, too?" Decker felt a shudder of horror. "I thought it was only Abraham Turner's life that you remembered."

"It is, mostly. They live inside me like a gentle tide lapping the beach. Sometimes it's easy to block them out, while other times . . ."

"It's harder."

"Yes. And then there are snatches of other lives that bubble to the surface, too. Just bits and pieces, nothing coherent. They are like flotsam riding the tide of Turner's own memories. Maybe he could remember more details of his victim's lives, and if so, I pity him."

"He had the choice to stop killing."

"Are you sure about that?" Mina drew in a long breath. "Does a cat have any choice but to chase the mouse?"

"Mina, I don't know what to say, I don't-"

"There's no need for you to say anything." Mina cut him off. "This is my burden. My cross to bear. Besides, you have your own problems."

"I suppose that I do," Decker admitted. His thoughts turned once again to Nancy, waiting for him across the chasm of time. When his mind was otherwise occupied, he could push those thoughts to the side, but at times like this, when all was quiet and he had no other way to occupy himself, they filled his head and left no room for anything else.

"She'll understand, you know."

"Understand what?"

"That you did what you had to do. And even if she never sees you again, your sacrifice, and hers, were for a greater good."

"You really believe that?"

"Don't you?" Mina asked. "Think of all the people you've helped. All the lives you've saved."

"I wasn't much help to you."

"Anything that happened to me was because of my own headstrong nature. I would've gotten myself into a whole heap more trouble if it wasn't for you. But we're not talking about me. We're talking about everyone else. I don't know what Adam Hunt has had you doing since London, but it must've been important."

"It was."

"Look what you accomplished back in Shackleton before you ever even joined Classified Universal Special Projects. What about all the stuff that happened prior to that? Taylor told me how you saved her life in Wolf Haven. Helping people is what you do, and Nancy understands that."

"Okay, you've made your point." None of this made Decker feel any better about the prospect of losing Nancy for good. "Let's not think about the possibility that we'll never return home. Not just yet, anyway. I haven't given up on finding a way back."

"You really think we can?"

"I think if we could travel backward in time, there must be a way to travel forward. After all, Celine Rothman did it."

"If only we had access to that same storm that snatched her out of 1912 and dropped her in our laps."

"We have no guarantee that we'd end up in the same place she did," Decker said. "We were all hit by the same storm while we were exploring the Grand Fairmont, and the others arrived here days before us. It could just as easily have been months, or even longer. They might've ended up on Singer Cay years before us. Or vice versa."

"You don't know that to be true."

"I don't know that it's not true. None of us have any idea how this time travel stuff works. Not that it matters. Celine Rothman has been gone for thirty years at this point in time and won't reappear for another eighty. We can't use her to find our way home even if we wanted to."

"I know," Mina said. "And I'm sorry. I don't mean to be so glum, but I don't mind admitting, I'm scared."

"We all are," Decker said.

"You know what the worst thing is?"

"No, what?"

"If we get stuck here in the past for good, I'm going to have to wait half a century for my next Starbucks."

Decker snorted despite himself. "All the more reason to find a way back."

"Guys?" Another voice drifted out of the darkness. It was

Adam Hunt. "I know you can't sleep, but for the rest of our sakes, could you just pretend?"

"Sorry." Mina sounded sheepish.

"We'll stop talking," Decker said. He whispered a quick good night to Mina, then closed his eyes and pushed the maudlin thoughts of Nancy and their predicament from his mind. Instead, he focused on happier events, like the first time he'd stepped into Cassidy's Diner after returning from New York to take the reins as Wolf Haven's Sheriff. He could still remember how his heart leaped for joy when he saw her behind the counter and how he hoped against hope there was still a chance for them after so many years. Then, with those happy thoughts, Decker finally drifted off to sleep.

FORTY-THREE

THE SOUND of the barrack room door banging open shook Decker from his slumber. It took him a moment to regain his senses. It was still early. Weak dawn sunlight spilled from the narrow barred window above the beds, casting a slanted oblong of brightness into the otherwise shadowy room. He sat up and wiped the sleep from his eyes, his exhausted body protesting the movement, and looked toward the door where a quartet of soldiers now stood with stern expressions on their faces.

The rest of the group was awake now, too. Colum was half out of bed. Mina scooted back against her cot's utilitarian metal headboard and pulled her knees up tight to her chest, wrapping her arms around them defensively.

"I have a feeling you're not bringing us breakfast," said Colum, studying the new arrivals with a mixture of wariness and defiance.

"You." The closest soldier ignored Colum's comment and pointed at Decker. "On your feet."

"Why?" Decker asked, even as he swung his legs off the

bed and stood. He sensed it would be unwise to argue with this gruff posse of men.

"Colonel Spear has requested your presence."

"Just me?" Decker wondered if the Colonel had reconsidered his offer to help, and what had happened overnight to facilitate such a decision so early in the morning. There was a sense of urgency about his summons. The soldiers looked uneasy. No, scratch that. They looked scared, even though they were doing a good job of hiding it.

"Just you, for now." The soldier stepped further into the room while the others guarded the door. He motioned for Decker to join him. "Hurry up. You don't want to keep the colonel waiting."

"All right. I'm coming." After donning his boots, he joined the soldiers and let them lead him out of the barrack room, casting a reassuring glance back toward Mina as he went.

The soldiers secured the door and hustled him out of the barracks. He expected to be taken to the base commander's office in a block building on the west side of the compound, as he had the day before, but instead they led him in the other direction toward the row of hangars sitting next to the airstrip.

There was a cluster of men here, standing in the narrow space between two of the large buildings. As he approached, accompanied by his guards, the group parted down the middle and Decker saw a dour faced Colonel Spear standing to one side, hands on hips.

Decker wasn't sure what the commotion was about, but then he noticed a ragged form sprawled on the ground between the hangars. At first he thought it might be an animal, but as he drew closer, he recognized the remains of a uniform, and the unmistakable form of a man. There was blood, too. Lots of it spreading around the figure like a grotesque halo.

Colonel Spear glanced sideways at Decker's approach. "Does this look familiar to you?"

"If you're asking if I had something to do with killing this soldier, I didn't." Decker was careful not to step in the blood as he drew level with Spear. "Your men had me locked up in the barrack room all-"

"Settle down. I'm well aware you weren't responsible for the death of this man. You witnessed that creature in the forest attack Corporal Tarrant and kill him. You also saw his body. I'm asking if these wounds look similar."

Decker studied the corpse, forcing himself to take in every detail despite its gory condition. He'd seen plenty of dead bodies before, from homicide victims in New York City to those who had tangled with the likes of Grendel in Ireland and the Cyclops deep in the Amazon rainforest. Which was why he wasn't turning away in horror despite his profound sadness at this violent death. He kneeled to get a closer look, noting the lacerations to the man's chest, as if he'd been flayed with knives. But unlike the corporal in the forest, there were additional wounds to this body. Notably, a single powerful bite had opened up his neck. Decker stood and turned his attention back to the base commander. "This attack is more ferocious than the one I witnessed in the forest, possibly because this man was on his own and the creature could complete its kill undisturbed, but the wounds look similar."

"I was afraid you would say that." Colonel Spear nodded, his gaze shifting briefly downward to the mangled corpse before lifting again to meet Decker's. "Do you have any observations you would like to share?"

"I thought you were on the fence about accepting my help, and that of my companions," Decker said.

"I am. Consider this an audition."

"Very well." Decker glanced back along the narrow alley

between the aircraft hangars, then in the other direction to where the boundary fence ran beyond the buildings. The razor wire glinted in the sunlight. "You and your men have trampled the earth leading up to and around the body, making it impossible to isolate any boot prints that might belong to the deceased which would confirm the direction from which he came to arrive at this spot. That said, it seems most likely that he approached from the direction of the airstrip, given the position of the body lying on its back with the head pointing away from the fence. The mortal wounds to the chest and the neck around his windpipe support this theory. This was not a stealthy ambush but a full-frontal assault."

"He saw his killer."

"Undoubtedly. Is there any logical reason for this man to be where he is?"

"You mean here, between the hangars?"

"Yes."

"I can't think of one. I sent orders for him to recall the men from the forest last night which he did. He sent a man to the north gate with instructions to fire flares, while he proceeded to the south gate. That was the last time anyone spoke to him. He would have returned to the guardroom after that."

"Except he didn't, because someone would have crossed paths with him if he'd returned there."

"Probably."

"Which means he was returning from the gates when this happened. If he didn't have a valid reason to be between the hangars, my guess is that something unusual drew him here. Maybe he saw movement and went to investigate." Decker noticed the service weapon lying next to the dead man's right hand. He glanced around at the assembled soldiers. "Does anyone have a handkerchief?"

"Here." A soldier dug into his pocket, then handed him a white square of fabric.

"Thank you." Decker took the handkerchief and carefully plucked the gun from its resting place. He examined it before speaking again. "The victim was holding this weapon but didn't fire it. Whatever happened was fast. Too quick for him to defend himself."

"I don't like where this is heading," Colonel Spear said. "You think something got in here last night and did this?"

"Unless one of your men is a depraved killer, the answer is yes." Decker stepped around the body and moved toward the back fence.

"What are you doing?" Colonel Spear followed behind.

"Looking for proof that something deadly breached the base perimeter overnight."

"That's impossible. Both gates are under twenty-four-hour armed guard and the fence is eight feet tall and topped with razor wire."

"Nevertheless, you had an uninvited visitor." Decker pointed to a section of fence behind the hangars that had been ripped vertically open with the wire peeled back to make a hole large enough for Decker to easily fit through. "You might want to make up your mind about my companions and myself, because it looks like you can use all the help you can get."

FORTY-FOUR

FIRST THINGS FIRST, why don't you tell me who you people are and why you think you're qualified to help us?" Colonel Spear navigated the wide desk that sat in the center of his office and settled into his chair.

Less than five minutes before, Decker had discovered the broken fence and surmised that the creature he and Mina witnessed in the forest-the same one that killed Corporal Tarrant-had used it to gain access to the base and kill again. Unwilling to have a sensitive conversation in front of his men, Spear had ordered Decker to accompany him back inside to continue their discussion.

Decker closed the office door and took a seat on the other side of the desk before he answered Colonel Spear's question. "We're just like you."

"I'm listening. Elaborate."

"With the exception of the girl, Mina, we work for a future version of Classified Universal Special Projects." Decker waited for this to sink in, studying the Colonel's face for some show of surprise. When it didn't come, he continued. "I sense you already suspected that just as I had a hunch regarding your own identities."

The Colonel nodded. "We have a lab on site. I had our science wonks take a look at the devices we confiscated from your friends. I got the report back this morning before Captain Myers's body was discovered. It made for some interesting reading. There appeared to be some sort of passcode required to unlock the devices, and your colleagues were unwilling to help us, but my scientists were able to make some deductions, anyway. The devices are some sort of miniaturized television screen based wireless telephone. But not only a phone. They have a host of other features. A camera that doesn't require film. A recording device. Even a flashlight. Who knows what other functionality we cannot access. It's the sort of thing a technologically advanced spy might carry."

"I can see how it would look that way from your perspective," Decker said.

"Precisely. Interesting thing was, when activated, the screens of all three devices displayed the same symbol. A modified version of the shield used by the Order of Saint George. A snake coiled around a pyramid maze with the Latin motto Verum Conquisitor within."

"And the name of our organization, too," Decker added.

"Yes, that too. Although a sophisticated spy network seeking to infiltrate the organization might engage in such tactics to win our trust."

"Except the only spy network with a reason to do that would be the Axis powers, and I know for a fact they couldn't come close to replicating the technology you see on our phones."

"Precisely what my scientists tell me. Which leads to the only other rational conclusion. That you are exactly who you say you are. Members of my own organization from the future that either came here using some technology we don't yet have or ended up here accidentally. The squadron of torpedo bombers and their crews who claim to be from 1945 would appear to back up this hypothesis."

"Does that mean you trust us?"

"It means I'm keeping an open mind but will also be keeping a close eye on you." Colonel Spear leaned back in his chair and studied Decker. "I'm also inclined to accept your offer of help. If you really are members of CUSP from some future decade, then you will have knowledge that might prove useful."

"I can't tell you anything about future events or technology," Decker said. "Just so we're clear."

"Understood." Spear nodded. "But truth be told, we're all in over our heads. This command post came out of the blue and I'm still finding my feet. Likewise, with most of my men. That creature out there in the forest is the first we've dealt with in such a crisis."

"Well, it's not *my first time*," Decker said. He was curious why there would be so little experience in the fledgling CUSP. "What about the Order of Saint George? Surely they have knowledgeable operatives. After all, they've been around since the late nineteenth century."

"That is true. Or rather, it was. But when war broke out, most of those men got sent to the front lines. Sadly, we lost many of them before the Allies realized they needed a specialized organization to fight on the supernatural front. Just like everyone else, we scrambled to adapt and have not yet found our feet. I don't know what Classified Universal Special Projects are like in your time, but here and now, it's not the effective unit we hoped it would be. At least, not yet."

"Well, hang on in there. It gets better."

"I'm pleased to hear that."

"It's also not controlled by the military in my time," Decker said.

"The necessity of war, unfortunately. We need to operate in a cohesive manner alongside more conventional forces."

"I understand." Decker felt the time was right to press his position. "If you want our help, I'll need you to release the rest of my people."

"Anything else?"

"I also need the phones you confiscated. I cannot allow future technology to remain in the past. The danger is too great."

"I'll take that under advisement. Will there be anything else?"

"Yes. One of my group is a physicist," Decker said, fudging the truth. He was thinking of Rory, who was an archaeologist, not a scientist, but nobody in 1942 knew that, and he was the only one who had any chance of figuring out a solution to their dilemma. "I'd like you to extend the full range of your facilities to him in order to research a way for us to get home."

"That's a tall order."

"But one that will also benefit you. There are five TBM avenger crews sitting in the barrack room opposite our own. They present as much a dilemma to you as we do, maybe more. You can't release them, but I'll wager you don't want the responsibility of locking them up for the rest of their lives." Decker paused to let this sink in.

"Go on." He had the commander's undivided attention.

"If we can find a way to get back to our own time, we might be able to return the airman to their time, too. There will be no need to lock anyone up."

"You make a compelling argument." Colonel Spear leaned forward and rested his elbows on the desk. "But unfettered access to our base and technology is a tremendous risk should you turn out to be enemy spies with cleverly constructed identities tailored to prey on our particular weaknesses instead of genuine CUSP operatives stranded in the past."

"Which is why you'll have to make a judgment call." For a moment Decker thought he'd lost the base commander, that he'd overplayed his hand.

But soon Spear relaxed and stood up. "How about a compromise? I'll give your man the access he needs to do his work, but with an escort. If he steps out of line, proves my instincts were wrong, I'll throw all of you into the menagerie with the monsters instead of a comfortable barrack room."

"Sounds fair to me," Decker said. He only hoped Rory could live up to the scientist persona without a misstep that would get them all incarcerated alongside the denizens of their worst nightmares.

"Excellent." Colonel Spear clapped his hands together. "I'll make arrangements for your people to be released in short order. And then, there's something I need to show you."

FORTY-FIVE

THEY'RE LETTING us go free, for real?" Rory asked, when Decker relayed his conversation with Colonel Spear.

He was back at the barracks now, returned there by two soldiers who were visibly more relaxed than his previous escorts. Decker guessed it was because they no longer felt threatened by the group, who Spear had decided to trust, albeit on a short leash. Decker had also arranged for fresh clothing for himself and the others, which had arrived at the barracks in short order. He was pleased to be given the opportunity to change out of the dirty and ill-fitting dead man's pants into clothes provided by the base quartermaster. This turned out to be another uniform, but at least it was clean.

"Are you sure we can trust the colonel?" Hunt asked, ever wary.

"I am," Decker replied. "He's even agreed to let Rory work with his scientists here at the base to find us a way home."

"What makes you think I know any more about getting us home than anyone else?" Rory asked. "I'm an archaeologist, not a quantum physicist. And even if I were a physicist, I'm not sure I'd know where to start."

"You're the best we've got," Decker replied. "It was you that came up the time travel theory in the first place when Celine Rothman showed up at the wedding. So yes, I do think you know more about getting us home than anyone else."

"Since you put it like that . . ." Rory tried to suppress a smug grin and failed.

"But I wouldn't get too cocky if I were you. Colonel Spear is placing his trust in us, up to a point. But he made it clear that if we step out of line, there will be consequences. One false move could scuttle our chances of ever seeing the twenty-first century again."

"Okay, I get it." The grin faded from Rory's face. "No need to pile on the pressure."

"I'm not trying to put you under any pressure," Decker said. "But you might not want to mention your masters in archaeology. I kind of told these people that you actually are a physicist."

"You did what?" Panic flashed across Rory's face. "You want me to work alongside a bunch of wartime scientists and pretend I'm one of them when I probably know ten percent of what they do?"

"Don't worry about it. Like you said, they're wartime scientists. If you get into trouble, just dazzle them with some 21st-century mumbo-jumbo that's too advanced for them. You'll be fine."

"Easy for you to say." Rory stomped off and sat on his cot, wringing his hands.

Hunt picked up the conversation. "I assume you didn't give the base commander any information about the future of CUSP or the world in general?"

"What do you think?"

"Just had to ask." Hunt scratched his chin. "Where do we go from here?"

"Colonel Spear gave us thirty minutes to freshen up and change our clothes and then he wants to show us something."

"Do you know what that might be?"

"Not a clue." Decker shook his head. "But I'll wager it has something to do with the creature that's been killing his men."

"You mean the one they must have let escape from that menagerie of theirs," Hunt said, shaking his head. "Amateurs."

"He all but admitted that they're not on top of it here," Decker replied. "But I'm not sure that whatever is on the loose escaped from the menagerie. I have a feeling there's another explanation."

"Any ideas?"

"No. Not yet. But it probably has something to do with whatever Spear wants to show us."

Mina raised her hand as if she were a schoolgirl trying to draw the teacher's attention. "I don't want to butt in, but you said we had half an hour to freshen up."

"That's what the base commander told me."

"Wonderful. I don't suppose that extends to taking a hot shower? After waking up soaking wet in the forest, then being stalked by a monster, before ending up thrown into a barracks that doesn't have any air-conditioning, I could use one of those."

"Me too," Rory said, looking up with renewed interest. "The rest of us have been here days longer than the pair of you."

"The guard that brought me back here said there are communal showers at the other end of the building. We're free to use them, and they've left the barrack room doors unlocked." Decker looked at Mina. "We could all use a shower, but why don't you go first."

"Perfect." Mina looked happier than she had in days. "But is there time for me to shower alone before everyone else?"

"Probably not, but we'll do the best we can."

"In that case, I'll take the quickest shower in history," Mina said. Then she turned and hurried from the room.

FORTY-SIX

DECKER, Mina, Colum, and Hunt sat facing each other on hard wooden benches in the canvas covered back of a GMC CCKW military truck as it headed south from the base toward the lower tip of Singer Cay. Rory had stayed behind, escorted to CUSP's laboratory to meet his World War Two counterparts, and start working on a way to get them all home.

"Where do you think they are taking us?" Colum asked. He grimaced as the truck bounced over a pothole, jarring the vehicle's occupants.

"We'll find out soon enough," Decker replied. Colonel Spear, who was sitting up front in the cabin next to the truck's driver, had been tightlipped regarding their destination, opting to let them see it for themselves rather than fill them in ahead of time. "We're heading toward the shoreline, so I'm guessing the ship?"

"Back in our time, there's an old wreck down near the south tip," Hunt said. "It's nothing but a rusting heap of metal sitting out on the sandbar. Could be that."

"Do you know anything about the wreck?" Decker asked.

Hunt shook his head. "Only that it's been there a long time, and wrecks aren't that rare in these parts. Ships have been sinking around the Bahamas for hundreds of years, so it might not even be relevant."

"Speaking of knowing things," Colum said. "How come you weren't aware CUSP built this base? You told us it was an old military installation when we passed through it in the Humvee. You said Special Projects took over the island after the war."

"I thought they did." Hunt shrugged. "From what John has found out, CUSP started as a military organization. It would've been top-secret back then."

"It's hardly common knowledge even in the twenty-first century."

"True. But in the Second World War, its existence would have been known only to the highest levels of the Allied military and their respective governments. Mostly us and the Brits. I imagine they sealed the records pertaining to that time for national security reasons, buried them never to see the light of day because releasing such documents would shine a light on the modern organization."

"Except that CUSP doesn't answer to any government on either side of the Atlantic," Decker said. "Unless there's something you're not telling us."

"It isn't so much that we don't answer to any government, it's more that we have a symbiotic relationship. How do you think we're able to access spy satellites and classified intel across the globe? CUSP is autonomous but linked by necessity to sympathetic governments around the world. Think of us a bit like a supernatural United Nations serving the greater good while being free of the influence of any single country."

"Still doesn't explain how our organization doesn't know its own origins." Colum gripped the bench as the truck's front wheel dropped into another pothole.

"Or why they can't do a decent job of paving a road?" Mina said, gritting her teeth.

"Road construction aside, it's possible that the military did not want to give us the records of the early, militaristic organization when it transitioned into a more independent institution. Don't forget, the origins of CUSP lie in the Order of Saint George, which had its own military roots. They drew the first members from Queen Victoria's Grenadier Guards, as we well know from our excursion to London last year."

"Jack the Ripper," Decker said.

"Yes."

"Which brings me to another question," Colum said. "Frederick Abberline and Thomas Finch didn't take Abraham Turner to a menagerie or zoo. They walled him up in the basement of his own house."

"They did. Probably because they were newly formed and didn't yet have any type of facility in which to hold the creatures they went up against. I imagine the fledgling organization quickly realized that such threats needed tighter control."

"Hence the menagerie," Decker said.

"Which eventually became the Zoo."

"Makes sense." Colum huffed as the truck bounced over something in the road, jolting them on the hard benches. "They could've put some cushions back here given the awful suspension on this truck and state of the roads."

"For a man who spent so much time in Special Forces, you sure complain a lot," Decker said with a grin.

"I'm just saying it wouldn't kill them to make it more comfortable back here."

"He's gotten soft since he left the service," Hunt said, unable to resist an easy shot. "Apparently we're not working him hard enough."

"You give me my share of hard work." By the tone of

Colum's voice, he wasn't happy with the ribbing. "And I'm not soft."

Decker chuckled and settled back on the bench. A few minutes later, he sensed the truck slow down and make a turn. Then it came to a stop and the rumbling engine cut out.

"Wherever we're going, it looks like we've arrived," Colum said.

"This should be interesting." Decker glanced toward the rear of the truck as the canvas flaps were pulled back. He squinted against the sudden onslaught of bright sunlight. When his eyes adjusted, he saw Colonel Spear standing tall with his arms folded. Two stern faced soldiers holding rifles flanked him, one on each side.

"Gentlemen, if you wouldn't mind disembarking the truck, we have reached our destination."

"Anything to get off these hard benches," Colum said, standing and jumping down out of the truck.

Decker let Hunt go next, then followed behind before turning and helping Mina down.

He noticed they were on a narrow sandy beach lined with palm trees that arched overhead. Light blue waters lapped the shore in a gentle ebb and flow. The road they had come along was nearby, disappearing back into the forest. It was a tropical paradise, spoiled only by the presence of their truck and three other military vehicles that stood near the shoreline. Not to mention the soldiers that scurried back and forth, and further away, sitting in shallow water and listing heavily to one side, a huge slate gray cargo ship.

FORTY-SEVEN

COLUM WALKED past Spear and his men across the beach toward the shoreline. He peered out over the water. "That's a Liberty Ship." He turned and waited for the others to join him. "I toured one a few years ago in San Francisco. There are only four left, but they built thousands of these things during the war, completing them at an average of one a day. It was an incredible feat given the logistical—"

"Colum." Hunt interrupted the Irishman. "That's enough. We're not supposed to be discussing the future, remember?"

"Sorry, boss." Colum looked sheepish. He glanced back toward the ship. "Man, is that boat huge. It must be at least four-hundred feet long."

"Four hundred and forty, to be exact." Colonel Spear came up behind them. He watched a group of soldiers pull a wooden crate much like those Decker and Mina had seen the day before from a smaller vessel, one of several moving back and forth between the stricken Liberty Ship and the shore. As the men lifted the crate into a waiting truck, Spear spoke again. "The SS Winston Box was heading for the docks on the other side of the island twelve miles from here when it ran aground in foul weather. The same storm that brought all of you here. We hoped to move it off the sandbar, but the damage was too great."

"I can see that," Decker said. There was a large vertical gash in the ship's hull. Worse, the stern section appeared to have twisted away from the bow, further opening the hole in the ship's side. There was no way this vessel would ever float again. If it wasn't for the sandbar, the ship would already be on the bottom. He looked at Spear. "What were you transporting on that ship? What's in those crates?"

"You can't guess?"

"Items belonging to the order of Saint George," Decker said. "And not just items. I saw that menagerie hidden underneath the aircraft hangar. You're transporting creatures, too."

"A necessity, I'm afraid." Spear gazed out over the water toward the cargo ship's immense hull. "The Order has performed their duties well over the last half a century, but London is no longer safe. The Germans have been carrying out a deadly bombing campaign over the last two years that only spared the Order's headquarters by good fortune. There is talk that Hitler may try to invade the British Isles. Allied Command could not let the Order of Saint George fall into enemy hands. They took control, built a new and safer headquarters here in the Bahamas where it would go unnoticed, and began the mammoth task of relocating everything of value."

"And so rose Classified Universal Special Projects from the ashes of the Blitz," said Hunt. He looked to Colonel Spear. "How many creatures did you have on that ship?"

"Upwards of fifty. A few didn't survive the storm. There was significant damage to the hold when the ship ran aground."

"And the rest?" Decker asked. "Are they all accounted for?"

"Therein lies the problem." Spear looked uncomfortable. "When the ship foundered, several of the pens holding the creatures smashed open."

"How many did you lose?"

"We're not sure. When we surveyed the damage, there were six empty pens."

"Six?" Colum glanced back toward the forest with narrowed eyes. "Are you telling me there could be half a dozen dangerous creatures roaming around this island?"

Spear shook his head. "I doubt it. I imagine most of them were killed during the grounding and subsequently washed out to sea when the hull split open. We have some evidence to support this. The body of an ogre washed ashore a mile down the beach yesterday morning."

"Just great," Mina said. "Ogres are real. You'll be telling us you let a fire-breathing dragon escape, next."

"No dragons," Spear replied. "The last one of those was dispatched almost nineteen hundred years ago by the man whose name the Order took."

"Saint George," Colum said. "You don't really think any of that was real?"

"Heavens, no. Just because someone created a myth doesn't mean it must always be true. Besides, the Order had no documentation of real dragons."

"Good to know," Decker said, happy to know that at least dragons really were mythical. "I guess we can strike one creature off our suspect list. I don't suppose you have a cargo log detailing exactly what live specimens *you did have* aboard that ship?"

"Lost when the ship ran aground."

"Naturally," Colum said. "Why is nothing easy?"

"Where did the ship originate?" Decker asked. "Which port?"

"Liverpool," Spear replied. "We transported everything

overland from the capital and steamed out from there, avoiding the major trans-Atlantic routes. It was too risky to use the Port of London or anywhere on the English Channel. Too many U-boats."

"Would they have a manifest?"

"Even if they did, it would take weeks to get here."

"That's unfortunate." In the twenty-first century, they could send such documents in the blink of an eye, but in 1942, information still moved at a snail's pace.

"How are we going to stop a monster if we don't even know what is?" Mina asked.

"A good question." Decker rubbed his neck. The narrow cot back in the barracks was even less comfortable than it looked, and the solitary pillow was hard. He missed his comfortable suite at La Casa de Playa. "To which I don't have an answer. At least, not yet."

"Should we look inside that ship?" Colum asked. "Maybe we'll find a clue there."

Colonel Spear shrugged. "Be my guest, but my men have been going back and forth between the ship and shore for two days, rescuing everything possible from the hold. If there were any clues regarding the creature that escaped, we would have found them already."

"I agree with the Colonel," Decker said. "Searching the ship would be a waste of time. The creature isn't aboard anymore, and I doubt it's returned here since being released. The only thing that would tell us more about it is the cargo manifest, which we already know is missing and presumed lost. We'll need to come up with another plan if we are to identify and trap this creature."

"In that case, there's nothing more we can do here," said Colonel Spear. "We should return to base and figure out-"

"Sir?" A panicked voice cut the base commander off mid-sentence.

As one, the group turned to see a young man in combat fatigues racing down the beach toward them. He came to a halt and leaned over with his hands on his knees to catch his breath.

"Well? What is it, man?" Spear snapped his fingers at the soldier. "And stand up straight when you're addressing the superior."

"Yes, sir." The soldier, a lance corporal, straightened his back and saluted. "You need to come quickly. There's been another incident."

"What kind of incident?" Decker asked, overcome by a sense of foreboding. He hoped he was wrong about what the new arrival was about to say. But he wasn't.

"A soldier on the search team in the forest. Private Harry Benson. Something attacked him. It must be the creature we're looking for."

"And?" Spear was clearly growing impatient. "Speak up. Quickly now."

"And it killed him, sir. Private Benson is dead."

FORTY-EIGHT

THE BODY WAS deep in the woods on the west side of the base. It took them almost half an hour to reach it, first by road, and then over a mile on foot through dense forest.

As they walked, Decker kept a wary eye on the surrounding foliage. He'd already tangled with this beast once, and he knew how quickly it could strike. This time, he didn't have the luxury of a weapon with which to defend himself and would have to rely on the reflexes of the two scared looking soldiers Colonel Spear enlisted to accompany them to the scene. Mina stayed close to Decker's side, and even though she did her best to hide it, he could tell she was just as scared.

The corpse of Private Harry Benson lay in a small clearing created by a fallen log, surrounded by wild tamarind, red cedar, and pigeon plum trees. The private had ended up sprawled on his back near the downed tree in a pose much like that of the other two victims, with his chest cavity splayed open. But when Decker looked more closely, he saw vicious claw marks extending around the torso and realized his assailant had attacked from the rear. The man must have rolled onto his back to defend himself. The position of his arms, raised as if to fend off blows, or maybe even a mouthful of sharp teeth, further supported the hypothesis. And if Decker needed any more confirmation, there was a witness to the attack.

He stood with two other men under a thick trunked mahogany tree. He held his rifle across his chest, finger close to the trigger. His eyes darted from left to right, as if he expected Private Benson's attacker to return for him at any moment.

Decker took another look over the corpse, then straightened and approached him. "Were you here when this man was attacked or did you come across the body afterward?" Decker asked.

"Yes. I was here when the attack happened, sir." The man's voice shook. "It was horrible. Damned thing came out of nowhere."

"It's okay, you're safe now. Calm down, son." Decker could see the terror in the man's eyes. "What's your name?"

"Slattery, sir. Private First Class Richie Slattery."

"A pleasure to meet you, Private Slattery." Decker glanced back toward the body. Someone had placed a jacket over the man's face, although he wasn't sure if it was out of respect or to cover the look of rictus horror frozen there. "Can you tell me what happened?"

"Sure. I mean, I'll try." The private drew in a deep breath to steady his nerves. "We were searching for the creature in pairs today. Captain Bartholomew thought that would be safer after what happened yesterday. I guess it wasn't."

"Okay. You were out here in pairs, combing the woods," Decker said. "What then?"

"We hadn't been out very long. Only an hour. Benson thought something was behind us, that we were being tracked. I wanted to signal the rest of the searchers. Each group carries a flare gun loaded with a green flare. We use green because red flares are fired to summon us back to base. If one goes up, everyone is supposed to head toward it and close a circle around the creature. But Benson didn't want to do that, and he was the one with the flare gun. He said we should keep moving, act like we hadn't seen it. Try and lead it closer to the base, where there would be more men around, before we sent up a flare. Then maybe we could capture it easier . . . or kill it."

"That was a mistake," Decker said.

"I know that now."

"Although I doubt you would have fared any better even if you sent a flare up right away when you realized you were being followed. The creature would most likely have attacked before anyone else could reach you."

"I suppose you're right. I guess we'll never know. Maybe the flare would have scared it away. As it was, the creature was upon us almost right away. I was in the lead. It hit Benson from behind. I heard him go down. When I turned, he was on the ground with the creature on his back. Somehow he managed to roll over and fight back. He tried to push it away, but it was no use. The beast just kept tearing at him. He was screaming so much. It was awful. Like something out of a nightmare. I mean, look what it did to him."

"You saw the creature?" Decker felt a surge of hope. If this man could describe Private Benson's attacker, they might narrow down what it was. And if they could do that, there might be a way to defeat it.

"I wish I hadn't seen the damn thing. After it killed Benson, it looked up like I was next. Looked right into my eyes, even as Benson's blood was dripping from its mouth. Then it gave this weird bellow, and I thought it was about to leap at me, so I fired my rifle and kept on firing. I didn't dare turn and run. I knew what would happen if I did."

"Did you hit it?" Decker asked. "Did you wound the creature?"

"I couldn't say. I'm sure I must have. But as soon as I started shooting it disappeared into the trees again. I could hear it moving around in the underbrush like it was trying to circle behind me. But my shots attracted the attention of another search team. They must've scared it off when they arrived. And thank God they did."

"You're a lucky man," Decker said.

"I know." Slattery didn't look like a man who felt particularly lucky. He looked like one who wanted to find a deep, dark hole and crawl into it.

"Can you tell us what the creature looked like?" Decker asked.

"Kind of looked like a wolf, but not quite. It was hairy, and really muscular. And those teeth." Slattery shuddered. "They were so big. Like steak knives."

Decker felt a shiver run down his spine. An image of the Loup Garou weaved its way into his head. Please God, he thought, don't let it be one of those. He forced himself to focus. "Anything else."

"The eyes. They were this real intense shade of blue."

"Blue?"

Slattery nodded.

Hunt stepped forward. "Could you identify the beast if you saw it again?"

"It's kinda hard to forget a thing like that." Slattery glanced from Hunt to Decker, then back again. "So yeah, I figure I could."

"Good man," Hunt said. He turned to Decker. "We must get PFC Slattery back to base, quick as we can."

"Why?" Decker asked, bewildered.

"Because I might have a way of identifying the creature, but we don't have much time. It may already be too late."

FORTY-NINE

I NEED MY PHONE," Hunt said as soon as they arrived back at the base.

"You mean the one you wouldn't give us access to." Colonel Spear didn't look inclined to go along with Hunt's request. "How do I know you can be trusted?"

"We've already gone through this," Decker said. "Either you trust us and want our help, or you don't. Right now, you have three dead men and come morning, there could be more. Your choice."

Spear hesitated a moment, then nodded. "Okay. I'll give you access to the device, but only under supervision. I can't take any chances."

"Whatever makes you comfortable." The tone of Hunt's voice indicated that he was growing impatient. "Where's the phone?"

"It's in the lab," Colonel Spear replied. "I'll take you there."

"You can take us all there," Decker said. "I want a status update from Rory, anyway."

"Fine. This way." Colonel Spear started off across the

airstrip without looking back. Behind him, a pair of soldiers escorted PFC Slattery.

Decker looked at Hunt. "I hope you know what you're doing."

"You're not the only one," Hunt said, then turned and followed the others.

———

A few minutes later, they arrived at the lab. It occupied a large block construction building on the other side of the hangars. When they entered, Rory was deep in conversation with a gray-haired man wearing a white lab coat. A name tag on his coat identified him as Colin Blanchard.

Rory looked around and smiled when he saw Decker, but before he could say anything, Colonel Spear took charge.

He approached the man in the lab coat with Adam Hunt a step behind. "Bring the devices we confiscated from these people and give them back to this man."

"Sir?" Blanchard hesitated. "I thought we were-"

"Don't argue with me, Mr. Blanchard. You may be a civilian, but you're still under my command."

"Yes, sir. Of course." Blanchard scuttled away, disappearing through a door at the far end of the lab. A few moments later, he returned carrying the three cell phones that belonged to Colum, Rory, and Hunt. He offered them up with a look of extreme disappointment. "I don't suppose you'd consider showing me how these work?"

"Not a chance," Hunt said, snatching the phones from the crestfallen scientist. He glanced back toward Slattery, who was standing at the edge of the group with a shellshocked expression on his face. "Find this man a chair and sit him down."

Decker exchanged a puzzled glance with Mina, then

focused his attention back on Hunt. "What are you planning to do with those phones?"

"Not all the phones. Just one of them. Mine." Hunt placed the other two phones on the table but kept his own. "I have an app that connects to CUSP's secure cloud server. All the knowledge in our database is accessible to me from anywhere in the world. That database contains a catalog of every creature CUSP has dealt with, many of them with photographs."

"How far back does this database go?" Decker wondered why Hunt hadn't mentioned this before, or why his own phone didn't contain such information.

"Since at least the early sixties. At first everything was on paper, but we've since digitized the entire archive."

"What's a cloud server?" Blanchard asked, suddenly perking up. "Or a database, for that matter?"

"Give it about eighty years and you might find out," Hunt said. "Or at least, your grandchildren will."

"I hate to burst your bubble," Decker said to Hunt. "But that's about how long you're going to have to wait if you want to connect to that cloud server. Did you forget where we are?"

"I did not. I keep a locally encrypted copy of the important stuff directly on the phone. The problem isn't connecting to the cloud, the problem is whether the battery has run out of juice since we arrived here." Hunt was examining his handset. He pressed the side button and was rewarded with an electronic chime seconds before the screen lit up. He let out a satisfied grunt. "It would appear someone in this lab turned the phone off, either by accident or design."

"That would be me," Blanchard said. "I deduced the device must need to be replenished from an external power source. Since we don't have one of those available, I tinkered around until I found a way to shut it off. I wanted to preserve the device's power for as long as possible to afford myself more opportunity to study it."

"Thank goodness you did," Hunt said. "You may just have inadvertently helped us identify a monster."

"Excellent." Blanchard beamed with pride. "Does that earn me a little peek at the contents?"

"Nice try. The answer's still no." Hunt approached Slattery, who was sitting in a chair provided by one of the soldiers. He typed his code into the lock screen. "I have a gallery here containing photographs of different creatures. You can flip through it using your index finger on the screen like this." Hunt showed him how the touchscreen worked, swiping first one way and then the other through the images. Then he handed the phone to the bemused private.

"I just touch my finger here and slide?" Slattery asked, dragging a digit across the screen. His eyes lit up when one photograph disappeared, to be replaced by another.

"That's the way," Hunt said. "You're getting the hang of it."

"How many creatures have you got on that phone?" Decker asked.

"Hard to say. Hundreds."

"There are that many monsters roaming around?" Colum looked aghast. "It's no wonder we never get a moment's peace."

"It's not as bad as it sounds," Hunt said. "We might have encountered the same species of creature on more than one occasion, in which case each individual will have their own record."

"That's still a lot," Colum said. "With that many creatures running around, it's a miracle people don't come across them more often."

"They mostly like to stick to the dark places." Hunt turned his attention back to Slattery. "Just keep looking through those photographs. If you see anything that looks familiar, shout."

"Nothing yet," Slattery said, sliding another photograph. He looked up at Hunt with wide eyes. "Are all these different monsters really out there?"

"Just keep looking," Hunt said, directing the man's attention back to the screen.

"This might take a while," Colum said. "Are we just supposed to stand around here and wait?"

"That's exactly what we are going to do." Hunt looked down at the phone in Slattery's hands, then toward Blanchard, who was hovering a few feet away. "I'm not letting this out of my sight while it's still unlocked."

"In that case, I'm going to get a status update from Rory," Decker said. But before he could take a step, Slattery let out a triumphant cry.

"I found it," the private said, looking up at the group gathered around him. He held the phone out for everyone to see. "I found the monster. This is what attacked us in the forest."

FIFTY

AS ONE THE group moved closer, tightening into a circle around PFC Slattery. Even Rory made his way over and inserted himself between Mina and Decker. The creature on the phone screen was unlike anything Decker had seen before. It was captured in a black-and-white photograph of undetermined location. A hulking catlike beast with powerful haunches, thick neck, and dappled fur. It looked almost like an oversized house cat, except for the two curved daggers protruding from its upper jaw. Teeth that would make quick work of anything unlucky enough to cross its path.

"What in blazes is that thing?" Colum asked. "It looks like someone bred a leopard with a wolf. It's just wrong."

Hunt lifted the phone out of Slattery's hand. "That, gentlemen, is a saber-toothed cat."

"A real-life Smilodon." Rory pushed closer to get a better look. "This is unbelievable."

"Aren't those things supposed to be extinct?" Colum asked.

"The last ones died out around ten thousand years ago," Rory said. "Or at least, they were supposed to."

"Apparently some of them survived," Decker said.

Hunt enlarged the image on the screen. "This one was caught in Cornwall, England, in the fifties, a member of what we surmised to be a small breeding population that fueled the legend of the Beast of Bodmin Moor. There are other big cat legends in the British Isles, too. Lots of them, probably related to sightings of similar animals."

"Like the Beast of Exmoor," Colum said. "The sightings were so credible they sent a team of Royal Marines to hunt that one down. Didn't find it, though."

"But the Order of Saint George must have fared better and caught at least one Smilodon. Big cat sightings go back many centuries in Britain. It must've been among the cargo on that liberty ship and escaped when the vessel ran aground."

"Then this isn't some supernatural creature," Mina said. "It's just an unruly big house pet."

"It's more than that," Rory said. "Smilodon were ruthless killers with razor-sharp, extended canine teeth that could rip your throat out in a second. They could take down prey as large as a bison. Not a creature you'd want to come across during an evening stroll in the woods."

"That explains its cunning and speed," Decker said. "It was able to track us, then kill Corporal Tarrant so quickly we barely saw it."

"Where has a thing like that been hiding all these years in a place like England?" Mina asked. "It's not a big country."

"It might not have the wide-open spaces of locations like the American Midwest or the African savanna," Colum replied. "But there are a lot of sparsely populated regions in the British Isles. A big population could easily live on the moors or up in the Highlands of Scotland and go unnoticed. Even in countries where big cats are more prevalent, they're rarely seen by humans, which will make a small population even harder to detect."

"And is going to make catching this one difficult," Rory said.

Decker exhaled. "Except it has a taste for human blood and knows where to find us."

"What are you suggesting?" Colum looked at Decker. "We just let it stroll back in here and then ask it to get into a cage?"

"Something like that." Decker turned to Colonel Spear. "Do you still have personnel in the forest?"

"No. We recalled everyone after the attack. All my men are safely back behind the fence."

"Hardly safe," Rory said. "A big cat like that could easily climb the fence. Might even be able to jump over the barbed wire at a push."

"It doesn't need to," Decker said. "It made its own way in. Tore a hole through the chain link."

"Which we should patch up immediately," Colum said.

Decker shook his head. "There's no point. If it could rip through the fence once, it can do so again. And closing off a means of entry the creature is already familiar with will just send it somewhere else to break through in a place we can't predict. Leaving that hole open gives us an advantage if we want to capture it."

"I still don't see how we're going to do that," Colum said. "It would be better to set a trap and just shoot it."

"That's not what CUSP does," Hunt said. "At least not in our time."

"And not in this time, either," Colonel Spear said. "Shooting the beast is our last option. First, we attempt to capture it alive and send it to the menagerie."

Decker felt Mina's eyes upon him. He knew how she felt about the menagerie. But she kept quiet.

"In that case, I hope someone has a better plan than just hanging around that hole in the fence and seeing if it shows up," Colum said.

"I do," Decker said before turning to Spear. "Do you have sedatives on hand? Something that could put down a large animal long enough to move it safely?"

"That would be a question for the team who look after the menagerie."

"Where would I find those people?"

"You wouldn't."

"Still don't trust us, huh?"

Colonel Spear gave Decker a wan smile. "I think some compartmentalization would be prudent. Let's leave it at that."

"A man after my own heart," Hunt said.

Spear turned to a soldier standing at his left flank. "Go see Doctor Padian in menagerie intake and ask what sedatives he has that will work on a large predator."

"Yes, sir." The soldier snapped off a quick salute, turned on his heel, and hurried from the lab.

Spear focused his attention back on Decker. "I trust you actually have a plan to rid us of this Smilodon?"

"I do," Decker said. "Or at least, the start of one. Much will depend on the availability of that sedative and a tranquilizer gun with which to administer it."

"I'm not sure I know what one of those is," Spear said. "The only guns we have around here shoot bullets."

Decker looked at Rory. "Let me guess, tranquilizer guns haven't been invented yet."

"Don't ask me. I know nothing about guns," Rory replied. "Tranquilizer or otherwise."

"I'm sure if there was such a thing as a tranquilizer gun in the 1940s, they would have one here," Colum chipped in. "Considering the number of dangerous creatures they deal with in that menagerie."

"That could be a problem." Decker's plan was slipping

away from him. He shifted his gaze to Rory again. "Any ideas?"

"We could try putting the sedative into a chunk of raw meat and hope it prefers steak to a fresh victim."

"That won't work," Colum said. "Normally a sedative has to be injected into the bloodstream."

"How would you know that?" Rory asked.

"My father used to have horses on his land back in Ireland. He thought he was going to breed the next thoroughbred Derby winner."

"Did he?" Decker asked, curious.

"Not so much. But he did rack up a hefty pile of bills that would have earned him a divorce anywhere but Ireland." Colum pushed his hands into his pockets. "Since tranquilizer guns apparently aren't invented yet, what's your backup plan?"

"I don't have one," Decker admitted. "Which is going to make it much harder to catch that creature before it kills again."

FIFTY-ONE

WE NEED TO TALK," Rory said to Decker as Spear's men led PFC Slattery away to get checked out by the base medical team. "It's about how we got here, and how to get back home."

"Very well," Decker said. There were still several soldiers loitering around the lab, so Decker tapped Hunt on the shoulder to gather the others, then took Rory's arm and led him to a quiet corner. "What have you got?"

Rory didn't reply. His gaze shifted from Decker, toward the rest of the group, and one person in particular. Colonel Spear, who had noticed the five of them retreating from earshot and tagged along.

When he realized all eyes were upon him, Spear puffed out his chest and raised himself to his full height. "If you think I'm going to let you talk among yourselves unsupervised, you're wrong. If your man has information, I want to hear it, too."

Decker knew it was pointless to argue. He nodded to Rory. "It's fine. Go ahead."

Rory hesitated, drew a breath, before continuing. "Ok. Well, I've been doing some digging into what brought us here, with Professor Blanchard's help."

"What did you find out?"

"Not much, at first. To be honest, it's hard work with the primitive equipment in this lab. I'd give a month's pay for ten minutes' access to the Internet right now."

"I guess it would be too much for someone to tell me what the Internet is?" Spear asked.

"You guessed right." Decker motioned for Rory to continue. "Have you found anything or not?"

"Like I said, it was slow going at first, but I think I'm getting a handle on it. As you know, I theorized that the intense storms in this region must have something to do with the time displacement we experienced. But it's more than that. The island itself plays a part, too."

"Singer Cay does fall within the Bermuda Triangle," Colum said.

"It does," Rory agreed. "And if you believe the stories, the triangle can produce electromagnetic fields more intense than other places on the planet. That got me thinking. Maybe this island is a hotspot for those electromagnetic fields."

"And is it?" Decker asked, hopefully.

"I believe so, yes. We ran a bunch of tests and discovered unusual levels of electromagnetism. More than should be here. There may be other spots in the triangle with similarly high levels. But the fields aren't constant. The electromagnetism fluctuates. I believe that's why pilots and mariners sometimes report their compasses spinning or acting strangely, and other times, everything is fine."

"Where do the storms fit into this?" Decker asked.

"That's the kicker. Thunderstorms can also produce electromagnetism. Lightning creates waves known as Schumann

Resonances that get trapped in the Earth's atmosphere and bounce around there repeating in a predictable pattern. These are low-frequency and harmless, and also difficult to detect. But it's possible much more powerful high-frequency localized electromagnetic radiation might be produced when lightning strikes the ground."

"And in a place already susceptible to spikes of electromagnetic energy, the effect would be amplified," Decker said, realizing where Rory was going.

"That's exactly right. And get this. Albert Einstein postulated that powerful electromagnetic fields could create curvatures in space-time."

"Which is why people disappear during storms around this island," Decker said. "And the Bermuda Triangle in general."

"That's my belief. They get caught in some sort of space-time distortion. The stronger the storm, the larger the curvature. But only if the storm coincides with a period of unusually high electromagnetic activity in the Triangle. They feed off each other, creating an effect greater than the sum of their parts."

"In other words, we need a mighty powerful thunderstorm to come along at the just right time if we are to get home," Colum said.

"How do we know it would take us home?" Mina asked. "We could end up somewhere else entirely, like the Middle Ages, or even in the future, like Celine."

"We don't know. Not for sure, anyway." Rory rubbed his chin. "But it's possible we contain a kind of temporal homing beacon. A code buried deep in our DNA linked to the time and place of our origin."

"Do you have any proof of this?" asked Decker.

"No. It's purely speculative. But it makes sense. Time

travel upsets the flow of the universe. It creates paradoxes that must be resolved and unbalances the natural order of things. It's much more likely that a time traveler would be thrown back to their own time than taken to some other random point. Think about it like this. It's easier to move with the current in a fast-moving river than against it. Going back in time might be like swimming against the current. It can be done, but the minute you stop swimming, you will be swept back in the other direction."

"If your theory is true, then we can get home," Decker said.

"Yes. And we can also return those airmen in their TBM Avengers and get Celine Rothman back where she belongs."

"There's one thing I don't understand," Colum said. "If nature doesn't want people to travel in time and always tries to return them to the point of their origin, how did we end up back here in 1942? For that matter, how did the TBM Avengers get here, or Celine Rothman show up at John's wedding?"

"Because the combined energy created by the extremely high natural electromagnetism in this region, and the power of the thunderstorm, overcame that natural tendency to anchor people where they should be. It punched a literal hole in the fabric of time and dropped us through it."

"Sheer brute force."

"Precisely."

"Fantastic." Colum clapped his hands together. "To get back home, all we need to do is wait for another thunderstorm. Problem solved."

"Not exactly." Rory paused, as if he didn't want to say what came next. He gave a deep sigh. "It's not that simple."

"Why not?"

"Because conditions have to be pinpoint perfect. We need

a thunderstorm of sufficient magnitude to generate a lot of electromagnetic energy. We also need this island to be doing the same thing. Remember the electromagnetism in this area ebbs and flows. The storm that brought us here might have been a one in a thousand confluence."

"Which is why there aren't more disappearances," Decker said. "Because the conditions are only right once in a great while."

"You got it. But there's another problem, too. We need to be near a powerful lightning strike. Like right next to it. Remember, it's the lightning that creates the energy. If we're not close enough, it won't work even if everything else lines up. Celine Rothman was standing real close to the lightning strike that displaced her. As were we. Those TBM Avengers were flying through the heart of a raging storm. Their metal fuselages would have attracted lightning."

"Wait," Colum said, shaking his head. "First you say we can get home if the conditions are correct, and then you say that everything coming together in the right way is an almost impossible long shot."

"I wouldn't say it's impossible," Rory said. "But the odds are against us."

"What about all that talk of swimming upstream and going with the current?"

"It's all valid, in theory. The trouble is, if we aren't near a lightning strike when the conditions are perfect, there is no stream."

"And therefore, no current to go with," said Decker.

Rory looked down at the ground. "That's about the size of it. And if we're too near a lightning strike that doesn't have the power to tear a hole in space-time, we'll just end up fried instead."

"By fried, you mean dead," Mina said in a small voice.

Rory nodded. "As door nails."

"Perfect. Just great." Colum clenched his jaw. "So, what you're saying is we're stuck here in 1942 for good."

"Yes," Rory said. "Without an incredible stroke of luck, I guess I am."

FIFTY-TWO

DECKER LAY on his cot and stared up at the ceiling. They were back in the barrack room, having returned there when it became clear that an answer would not be quickly forthcoming to Decker's request for a sedative with which to immobilize the Smilodon. This time they were not locked in, and Spear had even allowed Hunt to keep his cell phone, as he had Rory and Colum. There was still a guard outside their door, though. Colonel Spear trusted them, but only to a degree.

"If we're going to be stuck here in 1942, we're going to need new identities," Colum said from his own cot.

"Why?" Rory asked. "None of us will be born for decades. I can't imagine it's going to matter so long as we don't try to hang out with our grandparents."

"First thing I'm going to do is open a stock market account," Colum said. "With our knowledge of the future, we'll end up millionaires."

"That's not terribly honest," Decker said.

"It's also insider-trading," Hunt added.

Colum snorted. "Unless the Securities and Exchange

Commission have time machines, which I'm betting they don't, they're going to have a hell of a time proving it." He sat up and propped himself against the wall with a pillow behind his head. "Anyway, it's a victimless crime. Someone's going to buy those shares. Might as well be me. If I have to live in this backwards age with no Internet or streaming TV or cell phones, then I intend to do it in style. Heck, maybe I'll invent the Internet myself."

"Do you even know how it works?" Rory asked.

"No, but I bet you do."

"I do and I'm not inventing it just so you can look at porn."

Colum feigned shock. "I have never used the Internet for such a thing."

"Yeah, right." Rory snickered.

"Don't you think we're getting ahead of ourselves?" Hunt said. "You're assuming Colonel Spear will ever allow us to be free any more than he intends to let those airmen in the barrack room across the way leave this place."

"Why wouldn't he let us leave?" Mina asked. "We're no threat to him."

"If I were in his place, I wouldn't ever let you leave." Hunt let the statement hang in the air for a moment before continuing. "It's not about whether we are a threat. It's about making sure the public doesn't learn about things they should not know."

"I believe you would keep us here," Decker said. "After all, you have experience with this kind of scenario, and that's exactly how you handled it."

"I assume you're referring to the submariners on that U-boat."

"What's this about a U-boat?" Rory asked, looking at Hunt from across the room. "Have you already had dealings with time travelers?"

"In a manner of speaking," Hunt replied. "And I can assure you, I handled the matter with compassion and dignity."

"But you didn't let them go home, did you?" Decker wondered why he was even prolonging this conversation. It wouldn't help their situation. He wondered if it was because he wanted to find a justification for the possibility that the very organization they worked for in the future may hold them as prisoners for the rest of their lives.

"No. I did not, because it would raise too many uncomfortable questions and possibly reveal our organization to the world. But neither are they locked up. I can assure you of that. In fact, they are living very comfortable lives."

"Under the never-ending supervision of CUSP."

"Yes." Hunt cleared his throat. "Much like the fate that awaits us, I fear."

"Well, at least you're honest about it." Decker folded his arms and watched a small green lizard run across the ceiling and down the wall, where it disappeared into a crack between two bricks. "Maybe Spear will go easy on us if we help with his saber-toothed cat problem."

"Or maybe he'll use us as bait to lure it out and kill two birds with one stone." There was no mirth in Colum's tone.

"Let's hope he doesn't decide on that course of action." Decker was finding the waiting intolerable. He swung his legs off the bed and stood, then paced back and forth between the cots. "What's keeping these people so long? Either they have a sedative, or they don't. You'd think they would know."

"Maybe that doctor of theirs is busy and hasn't gotten around to looking for it yet," Colum said.

"Or maybe it's his day off," Mina added.

"Does it matter?" Hunt asked. "Even if we can get our hands on a drug that will send that monster to the land of nod, we have no way to deliver it. No one around here knows what a tranquilizer gun is, and I can't imagine we'll find many volunteers to sneak up behind a beast like that and give it a jab in the rear."

"I was rather hoping Rory would have an idea about that," Decker said. "Come up with a way to modify a regular rifle to fire a dose."

"Why me?" Rory was sitting on his cot. Now he stood up. "You've already told these people I'm a physicist. Now you want me to be a ballistics engineer, too?"

"If you don't want me to enlist your help with such things, maybe you shouldn't share your knowledge on so many subjects."

"It's actually a compliment when you think about it," Colum said.

"In that case, I wish he wouldn't compliment me so often." Rory looked up at Decker. "It doesn't matter, anyway. They aren't exactly hurrying to let us know about that sedative."

Decker was about to answer, but at that moment the barrack room door opened, and Colonel Spear walked in accompanied by a pole-thin older gentleman dressed in black trousers and a white shirt with a couple of pens jammed into the breast pocket. The man had a hawkish face, with a hook nose and narrow-set eyes that darted around the room from behind wireframe spectacles.

"Gentlemen," Spear began, then adjusted the statement when he saw Mina look up. "And young lady, of course. This is Doctor Emile Padian. He's the keeper of our reliquary, and an expert on all it contains."

"Pleased to meet you all." Padian raised a timid hand in greeting. "I believe you are looking for a strong sedative. One that will stop the creature Private Slattery identified as a Saber-toothed cat."

"We are," Decker said, approaching the doctor. "Do you have it?"

"As a matter of fact, yes. I have a concoction that might work. But only if you have a means of administering it. Do you?"

Decker glanced back at Rory. He could feel all the eyes in the room upon him. He shook his head slowly. "Not exactly."

FIFTY-THREE

AN HOUR LATER, they were back in the lab with an M1 Garand semi-automatic rifle on the table in front of them next to a small bottle of clear, colorless liquid with a label Decker couldn't read. The sedative they hoped would bring the Smilodon down.

Rory stood with the scientist, Colin Blanchard, on one side and Doctor Padian on the other, with Colonel Spear standing behind them, arms folded. Mina, Hunt, and Colum lingered in the background while Decker stood across the table, leaning on it with flat palms.

"The goal here is to build a projectile for that gun that can deliver a dose of sedative without injuring the target," Decker said, pointing to the M1.

"I've told you once already, I'm not an engineer," Rory said. Then he added, "I also hate guns, in case you hadn't noticed."

"That had not escaped my attention." Decker turned his attention to Blanchard. "Do you have any ideas?"

"Wish I did." The scientist eyed the gun with a wary stare,

then turned his attention to the bottle. "How much of this sedative do you need to deliver?"

Decker looked at the doctor. "That sounds like a question for you."

"But not one I can answer effectively," Padian said. "It depends on the animal's weight, its central nervous system, and how susceptible the creature is to the drug. There are a lot of unknowns."

"I can answer at least one of those points," Rory said. "I worked on a dig with a paleontologist back in my university days. A hiker in California found bones that turned out to be the fossilized remains of a saber-toothed cat. The skeleton was mostly complete, with only a few bones missing. We estimated the animal's weight when it was alive to be around five hundred pounds."

"That big?" Mina's eyes flew wide.

"These were powerful, muscular animals," Rory said. "A modern-day comparison would be a Siberian tiger."

"And we're supposed to catch that with nothing but an old gun and a bottle that looks like it has water in it?" Mina didn't look convinced.

"This isn't water, I can assure you." Padian glanced toward her. "And the drug in this vial is more than capable of incapacitating large mammals. I know because it's the only way we can get close to many of the creatures in the reliquary."

"How do you administer the drug to those animals?" Colum asked. "Couldn't we just do it the same way?"

"We use a special apparatus with a needle built into the end, which we can pass through a grill in each animal's enclosure without having to step inside with them."

"In other words, a hypodermic syringe strapped to a stick," Colum said.

"A crude analogy, but somewhat accurate."

"Why can't we do the same with this creature?" Mina asked. "Seems easier than trying to invent the tranquilizer gun."

"Are you going to stand there with a long stick and try to jab an angry prehistoric cat that wants to eat you?" Decker asked.

"Point taken." Mina fell silent.

"Which brings us back to the problem at hand." Decker tapped the rifle. "Making a delivery system that will work with this gun."

"We'll need some time," Rory said. "And I can't guarantee we will be successful."

Decker glanced at the clock hanging on the wall. "It's almost four in the afternoon. Come nightfall, that creature might try to enter the base again, looking for prey. When it does, we need to be ready and in place."

"Does that mean you have a plan beyond jury-rigging a rifle?" Colum asked.

"I have the start of one." Decker nodded. "But everything hinges on our ability to sedate it."

"We could just do the old-fashioned thing and shoot the beast," Colum said.

"We've been through this already. I don't want to kill the beast unless it's absolutely necessary. Even if we can administer the sedative, I will still have marksmen ready in case things go south. But shooting the beast is a last resort."

"I agree," Padian said. "I would love to get that creature into the reliquary where I can study it. A real living saber-tooth. Just think about what we could learn."

"It would be a boon to science," Rory said. "Just the thought of that creature is terrifying, and even I want to study it."

"Figure out a way to make that rifle work in the next couple of hours, and you may get your chance," Decker said.

Because we may be stuck here a long time, he thought to himself.

"In that case, I need to concentrate." Rory pointed toward the door. "Anyone who isn't vital to this task should scoot right now."

"That sounds like our cue to leave," Colum said, turning toward the door with the others at his heel.

Decker looked at Rory. "I'll be back in two hours. Don't let me down."

"I'll do my best," Rory said.

Decker nodded. His gaze wandered briefly toward the rifle and the vial of sedative, then he followed the rest of the group out of the room.

FIFTY-FOUR

DECKER WALKED across the airfield with Hunt, Mina, and Colum by his side. Colonel Spear had taken his leave, retreating to his office with express instructions to be kept informed of their progress. In his place, he left a pair of armed guards who followed behind them.

"You've got Rory working on the projectile, which is great if he can pull it off, but you haven't told us how you intend to trap the beast," Colum said, as they approached the wide ribbon of asphalt that made up the runway.

"I'm working on that," Decker said. "But right now, there's something else I want to check out."

"You want to let us in on it?" Hunt asked.

"Not yet." They were approaching the line of TBM Avenger torpedo bombers parked in a row next to the airstrip.

As they drew level with the closest plane, Colum broke away from the group and headed straight toward it. "This thing is incredible." He squinted against the bright late afternoon sunlight, looking up at the aircraft with its wings folded back in their park position. He reached out and touched the propeller. "This type of aircraft fought in every major U.S. Navy air battle of the Second World War. At one time there were thousands of them, but in the twenty-first century there's less than a hundred left and many of those don't even fly anymore. To be standing next to such a famous squadron, Flight 19 . . . It's breathtaking."

"I think he's in love." Hunt grinned. "Do you think we should give them some private time together?"

"Very funny," Colum laughed. "How are you all not in awe of this? Arguably the most famous Bermuda Triangle disappearance, and we're the only people on earth who know the truth."

"Actually, I'm kinda disappointed," said Mina. "I've read every book there is on the Bermuda Triangle, and I was rooting for it to be aliens."

"Sorry to disappoint you," Decker said. What he didn't mention was that aliens were real even if they weren't responsible for the disappearances in the Triangle. He discovered as much when he journeyed to Habitat One the previous year to investigate what the Habitat's crew thought was a haunted U-boat. It turned out to be nothing of the sort, but in the course of his inquiries he discovered advanced tech stolen from a Foo Fighter that led him to the inexorable conclusion mankind was not the only sentient race in the galaxy. Now he focused on their destination, which was the hangar containing the Electra he and Mina spotted when they were checking the base out from beyond the fence. He placed a hand on Colum's shoulder. "You can check these planes out later. We have more important things to do."

"Like what?"

Decker didn't immediately answer. He was aware of the two guards assigned to them by Colonel Spear. They would undoubtedly report back to him with any suspicious activity on their part. He thought for a few seconds, then nodded toward the row of hangars. "The creature entered the base from this direction, so it's likely this is where it will enter tonight. We should split up and familiarize ourselves with the terrain. Find the best spot to bring it down."

"Really?" Hunt looked skeptical. "You want to split up?"

"I'll take Colum," Decker said. "You take Mina. We'll go in opposite directions."

Hunt furrowed his brow. For a moment Decker thought he was going to query the instructions, but when their eyes met, an understanding passed between them.

"Come on." Hunt turned to Mina. "Let's do as the man says."

Mina shot Decker a questioning glance, but then she nodded. "Okay. Let's do it."

Decker breathed a sigh of relief. He already knew the best place to confront the creature, but he didn't want the two guards assigned by Colonel Spear to know that. He wanted to separate them, and the best way was to split up.

They moved off in different directions. Hunt led Mina through the narrow gap between the aircraft hangars toward the back fence and then turned right. Decker and Colum turned in the other direction and went toward the front of the hangars—specifically the one where Decker had seen the Lockheed Electra airplane. This forced their guards to separate, one going with each pair.

"I hope you know what you're doing," Colum said under his breath as they skirted the front of the hangars. "Because if Colonel Spear thinks we're up to no good, he won't hesitate to lock us up again. And next time, you might not talk your way out of it."

"Just follow my lead," Decker said.

They were approaching the first hangar now. The cantilevered doors stood partially open with the Electra's nose visible within. Decker didn't dare lead Colum inside the hangar—that would have given the game away—but he took a circular route around the front.

As they drew level with the doors, he spoke under his breath, making sure the guard at their rear could not hear. "You think you can fly that plane?"

If Colum was surprised, he didn't show it. Instead, he turned his head just enough to see the plane without drawing their guard's attention. Then he broke away from Decker like he'd only just spotted the aircraft inside the hangar and approached the doors. "Is that a Lockheed Electra 10E?"

The guard stepped between him and the hangar. "Sir, I can't let you go in there. Off-limits."

"I only want to look." Colum raised his arms in deference. "I've never seen one up close before."

"Sorry, sir. Orders." The guard ushered Colum back toward Decker.

They continued to the corner and walked along the side of the hangar toward the fence. Their guard relaxed now, no doubt deciding the crisis was over, which meant they could pull ahead out of earshot.

"So, what do you think?" Decker whispered, keeping his gaze firmly frontward.

"Piece of cake," Colum replied under his breath. "I trained on PC-9M turboprops and then moved on to Learjets when I was in Special Forces. Even flew a DC-9 once. An old plane like that should be no problem."

"Glad to hear it," Decker said.

"You mind telling me what you're thinking?" Colum asked, keeping his eye on their armed escort a few steps behind.

"Once we've taken care of the Smilodon, we might need an exit strategy," Decker said. "If we can't get home, I sure as hell don't want to spend the rest of my life under lock and key."

"You intend to steal that plane," Colum said as they rounded the back of the hangar.

"If it comes to that." Decker saw Hunt and Mina walking back toward them near the fence. "You on board?"

"Try to stop me," Colum said. "The food in this place ain't the worst I've ever had, but I bet they can't cook a decent Irish breakfast."

FIFTY-FIVE

A FEW MINUTES after their surreptitious inspection of the hangar, and the Electra contained within, Decker and Colum spotted Mina and Hunt walking toward them along the back fence line. They met near the jagged hole used by the creature to access the base the previous evening.

"Is that where the dang thing got in?" Hunt asked, reaching out and touching the bent and twisted fencing.

"And where it will return this evening if we're lucky," Decker said. He hoped his hunch was right, because if the saber-tooth gained access to the base via some other entry point, the trap he intended to lay would be useless. Not that he even had the means to set a trap yet. Rory was working on that back in the laboratory. If the nerdy archaeologist failed, they would have no way to bring the creature down.

Decker glanced at his watch. An hour had passed already. He'd given Rory two hours to complete his task but hoped he would finish sooner. There was much to do before darkness fell, and Decker was growing impatient.

"You want go to see how Rory is getting on?" Hunt asked, as if he'd read Decker's mind.

"I do." Decker started back between the hangars.

As they reached the airstrip, a faint rumble reached their ears, getting louder.

Decker glanced skyward and saw the outline of a large aircraft in the distance, silhouetted by the sun. He stopped and watched as it drew closer, dropping altitude as it went.

"I think they're coming in for a landing," Colum said, shielding his eyes against the glare as the plane made a lazy half circle to line up with the runway.

"What you think they're doing here?" Mina asked. "Bringing more monsters for that buried menagerie of theirs?"

"The plane is certainly big enough," Colum replied. "That's a C-47 Skytrain. But I doubt it's carrying anything classified, and certainly no monsters. It's painted in U.S. Air Force livery."

"I agree," Hunt said. "CUSP wouldn't use an Air Force plane for that purpose. If they were moving something clandestine, they would do so with their own unmarked aircraft."

"Are you sure?" Decker asked. "This isn't our CUSP. These people are trying to get up to speed in the middle of a war."

Colum snorted. "And not doing a very good job of it, judging by the grounded ship and the monster that's running around eating people."

"I'm sure," Hunt said. "Colonel Spear may be inexperienced in his command position here on Singer Cay, but everything he's done since we arrived points to a shrewd and competent man doing his best to keep the true nature of this place a secret."

"Whatever that plane's doing here, we might be in the way," Decker said, realizing how close they were to the runway.

They retreated to a safe distance and watched as the

aircraft flew low, barely missing the treetops as it dropped toward the runway. It was a large twin prop painted a dull matt green with black and white stripes on the wings and rear fuselage. Across these was a white star on a dark blue background. There was no mistaking the plane as military.

"I sure hope there's a good pilot at the controls," Colum said as the C-47 hit the runway with a squeal of tires. "This airstrip isn't very long. If they're not careful, they'll overrun."

But they didn't. Decker held his breath as the plane came to a lumbering halt mere feet shy of the end of the runway. A moment later, the engines cut out, and the propellers slowed. Someone scurried from a hangar and chocked the wheels to prevent the plane from rolling. Decker was curious to see more, but their guardians had decided enough was enough. The soldiers assigned to them by Colonel Spear had stood quietly up to this point, but now they hustled Decker and the others away from the airstrip and back toward the building where Rory was working on the makeshift tranquilizer gun.

"I guess the show's over," Colum said as they stepped inside the building and walked down the corridor toward the laboratory.

"Looks that way." Decker pushed the lab doors open and stepped inside with the others close behind.

Rory looked up as they entered, a slight smile playing on his lips. "That's good timing. I was about to send someone for you guys."

"Does that mean you figured out how to get the sedative into that Smilodon?" Decker approached the table.

Rory nodded. "It's a crude solution, but I think it will work."

"What have you got?" Decker noticed the rifle lying on the table. "This gun doesn't look any different from when we left."

"Because it isn't, mostly." Rory picked up the gun and

turned it over in his hands. "It's all in the delivery system. Ideally, it would be better to work with an air rifle, but there are none of those on the base, so we had to come up with a solution that uses a .30 caliber cartridge. First, we combined a two-inch length of narrow metal tubing small enough to fit inside the guns bore—which we got from the aircraft machine shop with a needle provided to us by Doctor Padian. We closed off the back end of the pipe and inserted the whole contraption into the live shell casing after removing its bullet."

"Genius," Colum said. "What about the sedative itself?"

"That was the easy bit. We put a spring-loaded plunger in one end of the tube and then pumped the rest of the tube with sedative before capping the needle. The cap keeps the whole thing pressurized until the needle buries itself in an object with enough force to punch through the cap, at which point the pressure is relieved and the sedative administered."

"But does it actually work?" Decker asked. "Have you fired the projectile?"

"Not personally," Rory said. "As you know, guns aren't my thing. But we had one of the soldiers take a prototype outside and test it."

"And?"

"Worked like a charm." Rory looked pleased with himself. "At least the projectile came out of the gun. As for the sedative, unless someone wants to be a guinea pig and let us shoot them, we'll just have to keep our fingers crossed I got it right."

"How much sedative can you get in each dart?" Decker asked.

"We could get about 15 mL in there."

"Is that enough?" Decker looked at Doctor Padian, who had been loitering in the background until now.

He shook his head. "If that animal really weighs five-hundred pounds, a dose that small might make it woozy, but it won't drop it. To be sure of sedating the animal long enough to get close and restrain it, I wouldn't go with anything less than double that amount."

"We have to shoot it twice," Colum said, scowling.

"At least. And even then, it might take a while for the sedative to have an effect. It certainly won't be instant."

Colum sighed. "Just great."

Decker looked at Rory. "How many of these darts did you make?"

"Six, in total. But we wasted two making sure they wouldn't get stuck in the gun's barrel."

"So that leaves four."

Rory nodded. "It's the best I could do in the time I had."

"Then we better make sure we don't miss." Decker looked around the group with a somber expression. "Because if we do, we'll find out what chickens feel like when a fox gets into the henhouse."

FIFTY-SIX

FORTY-FIVE MINUTES LATER, Decker was on his way across the airstrip toward Colonel Spear's office, accompanied by the ubiquitous guards who appeared hell-bent on keeping him in their sights. He entered the building and climbed a set of stairs to the second floor, appearing in front of the Colonel's startled secretary. Less than a minute later, he was allowed into the Colonel's inner sanctum while the guards loitered in the outer office.

"I was just about to send for you," Spear said, looking up from his desk.

"Now you don't have to." Decker didn't wait for an invitation to settle into a chair opposite the Colonel.

"Your man figure out how to build a delivery system for the sedative yet?"

"He did," Decker replied, nodding. Then he added, tactfully, "With Colin Blanchard's help, of course."

"Colin's an asset to the organization, for sure." Spear studied Decker with an unwavering gaze. "You want to put your plan into action, I assume?"

"I do. When night falls, that creature will come back here looking for more prey. I don't want anyone else to die."

"You also want to prove yourself to us, no doubt."

Decker returned the Colonel's stare. "If we are to be stuck here for the rest of our lives, I'd rather not be locked up. Once we can earn your trust, I hope you will find a place for us inside CUSP."

"What about cause and effect?" Spear asked. "How could you avoid using future knowledge to aid us in the present? Even if you tried not to let it influence your actions, there would be no way to avoid such an outcome."

Decker shrugged. "Just doing my best to prevent us from spending the rest of our lives locked away in some remote facility."

"I understand." Spear pursed his lips. "Your man, Rory, believes that storms play an integral part in the time travel phenomenon that brought both yourselves and the TBM crews here."

"That's right." Decker didn't mention that Rory also believed the circumstances under which time travel could occur to be rare, which was why the past wasn't inundated with such travelers.

"In that case, I have some good news for you." Spear drew in a long breath, as if he wanted to create dramatic tension ahead of his next statement. "A supply flight out of NAS Fort Lauderdale landed an hour ago."

"We saw it come in," Decker said. "A C-47 transport plane."

"Yes. The Air Force provides basic logistical services for us, even though they don't know exactly what we do here. We get resupply flights weekly carrying food, toiletries, and any necessary parts or equipment from the mainland."

"So, what's your news?" Decker asked.

"The flight crew reported a powerful storm crossing the

Florida peninsula and heading our way. They estimate it will be here within the next two to three hours. Maybe it will create the conditions necessary for you to get back home."

Decker remained silent for a few seconds, processing this information. Rory's words rang in his head. They must get close enough to a lightning strike during a specific set of conditions that ripped a hole in space-time to even stand a chance of returning to the twenty-first century. But it was a dangerous proposition with dire consequences for failure. If those conditions were not met, they would be killed instead, electrocuted by three-hundred million volts of raw power. His stomach clenched when he thought about that, but at the same time, he felt a surge of hope. Nancy was waiting for him across the decades, and it was his only way back to her. In the end, he shot Spear a wary look. "Why are you sharing this with me now?"

"Because I would like to avoid keeping you locked up for the rest of your lives, just as much as you wish to remain free. Your presence here is more than a little bothersome. I have enough problems without trying to safeguard the future."

"You also have a vicious predator running around the island. One that needs to be stopped before it kills again."

"I'm well aware of that. It will need to be taken care of before I will allow any attempt on your part to return to the future. We made a deal, after all."

"Quid pro quo," Decker said.

"Precisely."

"And flight 19?"

"Ah, yes. The TBM avenger crews. It would be in everyone's best interest if they were to go with you. Hopefully, they will return to their own time, too."

"Very well." Decker nodded. "A deal's a deal."

"It's settled then. You take care of this creature for me, and I'll assist your efforts to get home when that storm arrives."

"I appreciate that," Decker said, even though he wasn't sure what Colonel Spear could do to help, if anything. "And if we fail in our attempt to return home?"

"We'll worry about that if it happens." Spear settled back in his seat. "Why don't you tell me your plan to capture this beast, and what you need from me to make it happen."

"Very well," Decker said, and then he told the base commander what he had in mind.

FIFTY-SEVEN

THE FIRST BANDS of rain arrived with nightfall. Decker had left Spear's office and wasted no time in setting a trap for the beast, which he prayed would work.

As for returning home, a quick conversation with Rory confirmed his worst suspicions. Not only was it ridiculously dangerous to attempt such a thing given the lethal nature of the lightning required to rip a hole through space-time, but the odds of being in the right location at the exact moment a suitable lightning strike occurred were several million to one. As Colum pointed out, they had already done that once, albeit inadvertently, when they were sent back in time, and doing it again was akin to winning the lottery jackpot twice in the same week. Not impossible, but hardly probable.

Decker didn't need to mention the consequences of being within the vicinity of a lightning strike that did not open a portal back to the future, because none of them wanted to entertain thoughts of that deadly outcome. In the end, with no clear plan regarding the storm and their return home, they turned their attention back to defeating the creature.

"You really think this will work?" Hunt asked, as they

stood between the hangars at the location of the previous attack.

"I think it's the best we can do," Decker said, glancing up toward the roof of the hangar to his left. He could see a dark figure crouched there, barely visible against the night sky. This was Colum. In his hands was the M1 rifle with the modified ammunition developed by Rory and his 1940s counterpart, Blanchard. They had four of the homemade tranquilizer darts but only one could be placed into the adapted rifle at a time, which meant their margin for error was small. Once he fired a dart, Colum would need to reload before shooting again. Worse, Doctor Padian thought it would take at least two darts to bring the creature down based on the amount of sedative contained within them. Decker's plan was to lure the beast into the narrow space between the hangars where Colum could fire upon it from above. To do that, they would need bait, and he already knew who that bait was going to be. Him.

As an added precaution, there was a sniper with real ammunition positioned on top of the hangar opposite Colum. If the tranquilizer darts failed to penetrate the beast's hide, or if Colum missed, the sniper was their last defense. Two more men with rifles were positioned on rooftops out in the main compound as insurance should the beast escape the narrow alleyway between the hangars. Decker hoped they wouldn't be necessary.

"We ready to do this?" Hunt asked, lifting his collar against the rain, which was getting harder as the storm drew closer.

"I'm not sure ready is the right word," Decker replied. "But it has to be done."

"I don't like this." Rory was shifting from one foot to the other. "It's too dangerous. What if the creature kills you?"

"I'll be fine," Decker replied. He glanced down the alley

toward the wire fence, and the hole he knew was there, made by the creature on his previous deadly visit the night before. Somewhere out in the darkness, high on their own rooftops, Colonel Spear had placed lookouts to watch the forest beyond the fence for the Smilodon. To this end, each man carried an SCR-536 radio transceiver. These rudimentary walkie-talkie units had a range of only a few hundred feet thanks to the densely forested terrain around the base but would be vital to Decker's plan. They were the only surefire way to alert Colum and the sniper on the opposite roof if and when the saber-toothed cat made its appearance.

Decker, acting as a lure to draw the creature out, did not carry a walkie-talkie and must rely on his wits. But he had a loaded colt pistol in a holster at his hip, although he wasn't sure how effective it would be unless the beast was right on top of him, a scenario he would like to avoid.

"Please don't do this," Mina said, clutching Decker's arm. "Let someone else, anyone else, be the bait."

"I must," Decker replied. "This is my plan. I'm not willing to put another person's life on the line."

"I don't want to lose you."

"You won't. I promise." Decker moved Mina's hand from his arm. He looked back up at Colum, saw the Irishman wave in the darkness, then he turned to Hunt. "It's time."

Hunt sighed. "For the record, I hate this plan. If I was in charge-"

Decker cut him off. There was no time for a long discussion. "But you're not, And I made a deal with Colonel Spear."

"Where is the Colonel, anyway?" Hunt looked around. "You'd think the least he could do is hang around to wish you good luck, considering what you're about to do."

"He's already inside the hangar with Doctor Padian," Decker said. "Which is where the rest of you should be right now."

"I'm staying," Mina said, a determined look on her face.

"Like hell you are." Decker shook his head and pointed toward the hangar doors, which stood open just enough to allow everyone inside. "Go."

"But-"

"I won't tell you again."

"Come on," Hunt said, taking Mina's arm and pulling her gently toward the hangar. "Let the man do his job."

Decker breathed a sigh of relief as Hunt led her away. The last thing they needed was the Smilodon showing up while Mina was distracting him with her stubbornness.

Rory hesitated a moment. He swallowed hard, drawing in a quick breath as if he wanted to say something but wasn't sure what. Then he stepped forward and threw his arms around Decker in a brief hug. "Don't die."

"I'll try."

"Thank you," Rory said, then he turned and hurried after the others, disappearing inside the hangar.

Decker watched the door slide closed.

A flash of lightning momentarily illuminated the landscape. A few seconds later, thunder rumbled across the sky. The rain was coming down harder now, driven at an angle by a gusty wind.

Decker studied his surroundings. He saw no one. Colonel Spear had confined all unnecessary personnel to their quarters. Somewhere up on the rooftops in the darkness, Colum and the sniper watched. Otherwise, Decker was alone. He gathered his thoughts, took a deep breath, and waited for what might come.

FIFTY-EIGHT

DECKER STOOD in the space between the two aircraft hangars, his attention on the small patch of fence beyond the buildings. Further away still, the dense outlines of closely packed trees. Somewhere out there in the forest a deadly killer was roaming. A prehistoric beast of immense power and speed.

The rain was getting worse. It was coming down in sheets now. He pulled his jacket close around his frame and shivered. Despite the subtropical heat, he felt a chill seeping into his bones. Not only was there no sun to warm the air, but the storm brought along with it a fierce wind that whipped through the space between the buildings and worked its way under the folds of his soaked clothing.

He clapped his hands together and paced back and forth, going between the hope that the beast would make a quick appearance and that it would not show up at all. Eventually, after more than an hour of waiting, he began to think it would be the latter.

"You doing okay down there?" Colum asked in a low voice from the roof above him.

Decker barely heard the words before the breeze snatched them away.

"As well as can be expected," he replied. "How about you?"

"The longer this takes, the jumpier I'm getting."

"I hear you." Decker ceased his pacing and glanced toward the hangar where the others were sheltering. The cantilevered doors were still closed, but he could imagine their anxiety, not knowing if the beast was tardy, or if it had come and gone already, leaving a slew of dead bodies in its wake.

Beyond the hangar's low-slung arching form, the airfield was lit by the warm yellow glow of sodium lamps. There was no other lighting. Not even along the airstrip. In a time of war, the last thing you wanted to do was light up your runway at night and announce your location to anyone who cared to come looking for it.

Decker rubbed his hands together, slicked his hair back to stop water running down his face. His stomach was in knots. He felt like a ceremonial lamb put out for the slaughter. *How much longer is this going to take?* He wondered as another flash of lightning lit the sky. Colonel Spear would allow them to find a way home if Decker first took care of the beast. Which meant the clock was ticking. The storm currently bearing down on the island was an opportunity Decker didn't want to squander, even though he didn't know if it provided a doorway back to the twenty-first century, or an agonizing death with millions of volts coursing through them. It might not matter. If Rory was to be believed, they could be stuck here whether or not they captured the creature. Apart from anything else, Decker wasn't sure how to predict where a bolt of lightning would strike, let alone get close enough to jump through any hole in time it created without being killed in the process.

"Decker." A hoarse voice called out from the darkness, breaking his train of thought. It was Colum again. "Look sharp. It's here."

The knot in Decker's stomach tightened.

His hand slipped to the colt pistol in its holster at his hip.

He waited, eyes searching the darkness ahead of him, straining to decipher the gloom beyond the fence.

Nothing. All he saw were branches tugged by the wind, and silvery streaks of rain lit up with each brief flicker of lightning.

The seconds passed like hours.

Where was it?

His gaze drifted up toward Colum. He could see the Irishman's squat, muscular silhouette as a black shape against the lesser darkness of the cloud choked night sky. He wanted to call out, ask if Colum could see the creature, but something told him that making a sound, any sound, would be a bad idea. Instead, he forced his eyes downward again, swept the terrain ahead of him, then turned toward the airstrip, overcome with a sudden conviction that the beast was creeping up from the rear. A silent predator savoring the moment before the kill.

But there was no stealthy prehistoric cat there. Just an empty storm-drenched airstrip.

He turned his gaze frontward again, was starting to think Colum was mistaken, or that the creature had sensed a trap and slunk back into the forest, when the crack of a rifle shot split the air.

The sudden unexpected sound made him jump. Decker's heart slammed against his rib cage.

The shot had come from on high, and at first he wondered if Colum's modified M1 and its ammunition of sedative had found the beast, but the narrow space between the buildings was still empty.

Another sharp crack echoed between the buildings, and this time Decker pinpointed its location, not atop the building to his left where Colum hid, but to his right.

Decker took a step back, his head snapping up in the direction of the shot. He saw a figure on the hangar roof. The sniper placed there as a last option if Colum failed. Now he was scrabbling backwards, the gun falling from his hands and clattering onto the metal roof before sliding off and landing in the alley with a thud.

The man reached the edge of the roof where he teetered precariously, caught between a sheer drop and a prowling, catlike shape that advanced on him with slow determination.

Shoot it, Colum, Decker thought. *For the love of God, put it down. Now.*

But even as the thought passed through his mind, Decker knew the Irishman didn't have a clear line of sight with the stricken sniper between him and his target. And there was no room for error. With only four projectiles, any wasted shot would make their chance of success that much lower.

Then, as if deciding there was nowhere else to go, the sniper made one last flailing step, and dropped backwards into the gulf between the buildings with a scream soon cut short as he hit the ground.

Decker stood frozen, caught in a rare moment of indecision. The soldier wasn't moving. In all likelihood, the fall had broken his neck. But the urge to help was overwhelming. At least, until a dark shape dropped into the alley on all fours and raised its head to fix Decker with a pair of eyes that burned with pale blue fire.

Like it or not, the Smilodon had arrived.

FIFTY-NINE

THE CREATURE TOOK A SLOW, determined step toward Decker. It moved low on its haunches; mouth open wide to reveal the trademark curved impossibly long upper canines capable of ripping the throat from its prey with one swift bite.

"Decker, run." Colum was already repositioning himself and angling the rifle downward.

Decker needed no urging. He turned and bolted for the front of the buildings, all too aware of the beast's staggering speed.

From above, he heard the pop of a rifle as Colum fired the first of their four tranquilizer darts. He didn't dare turn and see if the dart found its mark, but the curse that soon escaped the Irishman's lips told him it hadn't.

"Look out," Colum shouted as Decker reached the end of the hangars. Instinct took over, and he threw himself sideways, hitting the ground and rolling just as a flash of fur and muscle tore past him with a frustrated shriek.

Colum was running along the roofline, doing his best not to fall off as he leveled the gun for another shot.

The creature came to a skidding halt, breathing heavily, nostrils flaring. It turned back to face Decker just as a second dart whizzed through the air and caught its front quarter a glancing blow. But instead of burying itself into the Smilodon's hide, the needle bounced off and landed harmlessly on the ground a few feet away.

Colum swore again and fumbled to reload. Two down, two darts to go.

Decker risked a glance upward, saw the Irishman perched precariously on the edge of the roof with no way to get closer. He wondered if the dart had failed to break the creature's skin because the distance was too great. Rory's makeshift projectiles were much heavier than a regular bullet and would encounter a lot more drag traveling through the gun's barrel. He needed to give Colum a closer shot.

The saber-toothed cat stood some twenty feet distant, observing him with wary eyes. Did it know what they were trying to do? Decker couldn't see how, but the creature's hesitancy suggested otherwise.

Decker climbed to his feet. His right shoulder throbbed with pain where he landed too hard but was relieved to find he could still move it.

Come on, thought Decker, meeting the beast's stare. *What are you waiting for?*

The Smilodon took a tentative step forward, sniffed the air. Then it pounced straight toward him with frightening speed.

Decker took off running along the front of the hangars. Behind him, the Smilodon changed direction, and in doing so presented its flank to Colum, who was still on the roof.

A third pop.

Decker didn't dare look back to see if Colum hit the beast, or if the dart had stuck this time. Either way, Colum would need to deliver the last shot if they had any hope of bringing the creature down. And Decker was now leading it back out of range. He dug his heel into the ground, made a hard right turn, and raced toward the airstrip. If he could lead the creature all the way around, then back toward Colum, the Irishman could take the fourth and final shot. After that, it was out of their hands. The creature would either succumb to sedation, or it wouldn't. Decker didn't want to think what would happen if it were the latter.

He changed course again, tearing along the side of the runway. Ahead of him were the five Navy TBM Avenger torpedo bombers. He reached the first one and ducked sideways, weaving between it and the next plane.

"Decker, it's catching up with you," Colum shouted, abandoning all pretense of stealth. The creature surely knew where he was by now anyway, so Colum had nothing to lose. "You can't outrun it."

Decker had already come to that conclusion. He could hear the Smilodon right behind him now. To make matters worse, the ground was soft and slippery. Only the runway was paved. The surrounding area was nothing but hard-packed dirt, now turning to mud under his feet. It tried to slow him down, sucking at his boots and making it hard to keep going. At one point, he slipped and almost tumbled, but he put a steadying hand on the side of an avenger and kept himself upright. But it was a losing battle. Another few seconds, and the big cat would be upon him. There was no time to lead it back toward Colum, and no way the Irishman could take a shot from this far away, even if he could get a bead on the fast-moving beast.

Decker came out from between the planes onto the runway, grateful for a few moments on a hard surface. But anything that benefited him also benefited his pursuer. His only chance of survival was to find a safe haven.

He could think of only one place to go.

Decker ducked back between two of the aircraft, raced between them. The TBM Avenger had a unique ability developed for easy storage on the hangar deck of carriers. Its wings folded vertically upward and back when parked. This might provide him with some much-needed shelter. He ducked under the nearest plane and emerged on the other side near the tail. With no time to lose, he turned and found a step-down on the plane's lower fuselage. He put a foot inside and grabbed a circular hand hold inset higher on the body. The aircraft's steel skin was slick with rain, but he managed to pull himself up onto the horizontal section of the Avenger's wing near the cockpit and crouch next to the folded section.

The creature was momentarily confused by this sudden change of tack. It followed Decker under the fuselage, then came to a skidding halt when it realized he was no longer there.

The beast looked around, turning his head from side to side. It let out an angry bellow and stomped the ground with a meaty paw. Then its gaze shifted upward toward Decker sheltering on the wing.

Dammit, Decker thought. *Why couldn't the creature be dumb, just this once.*

But they never were. From Grendel in Ireland to the Cyclops deep in the Amazonian jungle, everything Decker faced appeared to have an unerring ability to sniff him out in short order.

He weighed his options, multiple scenarios running through his head in the blink of an eye. If he jumped out of the wing, he wouldn't make it more than a few steps before the creature tore him to shreds. But if he stayed where he was, it would simply jump up there and do the same thing. After all, it was basically a huge mean-spirited house cat with enormous razor-sharp teeth.

There was only one place left to go. As the Smilodon

stepped a few paces back and hunkered down ready to leap up onto the wing, Decker heaved the aircraft's hinged glass canopy up and leaped inside, sinking down into the seat a split second before the saber-toothed cat landed on the wing next to him with a triumphant roar.

SIXTY

DECKER SLAMMED the TBM's canopy down at the same moment the Smilodon lunged toward him. The creature smacked into the glass with a thud, but the canopy held. For now. The beast adjusted its footing on the slippery wing and lunged again. This time, a crack appeared in the glass and Decker realized his mistake. Rather than putting himself out of the Smilodon's reach, he had merely delayed the inevitable. Decker took stock of his situation. The avenger's cockpit had two seats, with a third seat housed inside a separate dorsal ball turret at the rear. In his haste to escape the saber-tooth, Decker had jumped into the second cockpit seat in between the pilot's position and the gun turret. He was now trapped.

The beast made a third attempt to break into the cockpit, slamming against the canopy and causing more hairline cracks to radiate outward from the point of impact. One more hit like that, and the glass would shatter. But the creature was also unsteady on its feet. Decker watched as it backed up for another attempt, stumbling and almost sliding off the wing.

Then he saw the tranquilizer dart still buried in its right flank. Colum had scored a hit, after all. Decker wondered if this was the only reason he was still alive. Doctor Padian's sedative had slowed it down just enough for him to stay one step ahead. But it had not felled the powerful animal. It would require more sedative to do that, and Colum was, presumably, still on the aircraft hangar roof with the last tranquilizer dart. Even if the Irishman came to his aid, there was no room for error. If Colum missed on his last shot, the creature would probably tear them both to shreds. And then there was another problem. Even with a second dose of sedative, the creature would not succumb immediately. That could take anything from a few seconds to a few minutes. He wondered if his desire to capture the beast alive was misplaced. Maybe shooting it would have been safer if less humane. Not that it mattered. He'd already made his decision and would do the same thing again, given the opportunity. After all, he'd put snipers in place to prevent the exact scenario he was now experiencing. Which raised another question. Where were those snipers? He knew the one on the roof opposite Colum was dead. He had witnessed the creature force the man off the roof and kill him. But there should be two more guns out there somewhere. Had the Smilodon dispatched those men, too? Had it snuck up on them unnoticed before anyone even knew the beast was there? If so, Decker was completely defenseless.

And now the creature was about to make another run at the cockpit canopy. Decker held his breath, waited for the creature's final assault that would shatter the cockpit, and deliver him to those sharp, curved fangs. As he sat there and waited to die, an image of Nancy entered his head. A picture of his bride in her wedding dress, walking down the aisle toward him. It was only two days ago but felt like an eternity.

Maybe it was the expanse of years that currently separated them, or the events of the past few days, but he had never felt so far away from her. He lowered his head and wiped away a tear. He looked up again just as the creature slammed into the canopy with a triumphant roar, sending shards of glass spraying inward toward him and sealing his fate.

SIXTY-ONE

DECKER TURNED AWAY and flinched backward. He raised his arms, waiting for the creature to tear into him. Its breath was warm upon his neck. The pungent odor of rotten meat wafted into the canopy each time the creature exhaled. He closed his eyes and focused on an image of Nancy, wanting that to be the last thing he ever saw. Then, just when he thought all was lost, a shout went up from somewhere beyond the row of planes.

"Hey! You ugly brute. Over here."

Decker opened his eyes and saw Colum standing beyond the row of planes, rifle in hand.

The beast hesitated, turned its head away from the shattered cockpit canopy. Then it jumped down and padded slowly toward the Irishman.

What are you doing? Decker thought. *You'll never get that shot off before it kills you.*

But Colum wasn't backing down. He raised the rifle, aimed at the advancing beast.

Decker knew what would happen if he didn't do something. The creature was too fast and too powerful, even if

Colum scored a hit with the last dart. He needed to buy his friend time, just as Colum had done for him. Decker turned his attention to the canopy. He tried to disengage the master bolt that held the canopy closed, but the beast's incessant pounding had bent the frame and the bolt would not draw back. The canopy was locked in position and no amount of tugging on the bolt would move it. The glass pane broken by the Smilodon's attack might have provided a way out, but shards of glass still ringed the metal framework and would lacerate him even if he could squeeze through the opening. Decker looked around, frantic. He didn't have much time. The beast was woozy from its single shot of tranquilizer, but still a force to be reckoned with. And it was slinking toward Colum like a house cat might toy with a mouse. Before long, it would abandon caution and attack.

Decker pounded on the canopy lid, hoping to jar the bolt free or push out another pane of glass, but all he did was bruise the palms of his hands. Then he looked down and saw the opening to his right next to the seat. It was a small square hatch that led into the belly of the plane. Without hesitation, he slid off the seat and dropped into it.

It was cramped in the space beneath the cockpit. To his right was a bulkhead, behind which the aircraft's powerful engine was housed. To his left, he saw a narrow crawlspace that led under the gun turret. This must be how the tail gunner got into position. Decker flattened himself and crawled through the narrow opening until he came to a wider compartment with two portholes on each side and another seat. The equipment next to the seat gave Decker a clue regarding the occupant's job. He was a radioman and navigator. But Decker wasn't here to sightsee in the belly of a warplane. There must be another way out of the aircraft. He looked around and soon found it. A small hatch in the fuselage behind the wing. He unlatched it and pushed the hatch open, then climbed through and dropped onto the soft earth.

Now it was his turn to save Colum. He ducked under the wing and saw the creature dead ahead. Colum still had the gun leveled upon it but hadn't yet fired, no doubt waiting for a clean shot. That would not happen unless the creature bared its flank to him once again. Decker decided to make sure Colum got his chance.

He backed up, retracing his steps between the aircraft, and circled around until he reached the last Avenger in line. Now he moved along its side, past the folded wing to the tail of the plane. He could see Colum and the creature standing thirty feet away separated by an expanse of muddy ground. The beast was still slinking forward and matching Colum as he backpedaled to maintain a distance between them. That tactic would only work for so long. Soon the beast would lunge forward, and his friend would be dead regardless of if he fired the rifle.

Unless Decker provided a distraction.

He sucked in a mighty breath, tensed himself to run, and shouted at the beast.

The Smilodon stopped in mid-stride. It turned its head in a lazy arc toward him, looked Decker up and down. Then it turned back toward Colum.

"No." Decker felt the breath catch in his throat. He needed a better way to get attention. His eyes fell to the wooden chocks under the wheels of the closest plane-two triangular-shaped wedges that sat on each side of the wheel attached by a piece of rope. He ducked under the wing and yanked the chocks free, then raced forward holding the rope and swinging them back at the same time. He brought his arm forward and let go, letting the chocks tumble end over end through the air until they smacked into the beast's side.

The saber-toothed cat didn't ignore him this time. It swiveled with an angry roar and raced toward him.

Decker turned to run, his foot slipping on the wet ground. He stumbled forward, regained his balance, and sprinted across the airfield. Somewhere off to his right, as a peal of thunder rumbled across the sky, he heard the pop of a rifle. Colum had taken the shot. Now Decker just needed to stay ahead of the creature long enough for the second dose of sedative to take effect. Assuming the Irishman hadn't missed, and Decker wasn't about to look back and see. It didn't matter, anyway. There were no more darts, which meant they were now at the mercy of Colum's aim and Padian's drugs.

SIXTY-TWO

OVER HERE, BOTH OF YOU."

Decker was in mid-flight when he heard Mina calling over the unrelenting wind. He looked to see her standing in front of the aircraft hangar. The large, cantilevered doors stood cracked open behind her. She was waving with her arms above her head, trying to get his and Colum's attention.

Decker changed direction, almost slipping again, and ran toward the hangar with all the energy he could muster. He felt a stitch crease his side. His lungs burned.

From the corner of his eye, he saw Colum racing in the same direction. But he also saw something else.

The Smilodon.

It had gained on them and now occupied a space in between the two running men. Decker thought it looked slower, a little more sluggish, but not enough to make a difference. Doctor Padian had said it could take a few minutes for the drug to work. Minutes they did not have. Any moment now, the creature would decide which of them to kill first and veer in that direction.

Which is exactly what the creature did, changing course with a grace that belied its weight, and zeroing in on Decker.

At least until a slug slammed into the ground ahead of it, thanks to Adam Hunt who had exited the hangar and was now standing next to Mina, rifle in hand.

The creature pulled up short as a second slug followed behind, kicking up mud and making a small crater mere feet from the angry beast. Hunt wasn't trying to kill the animal, Decker realized. He wanted to slow it down and give them a fighting chance to reach the hangar.

"Keep running, man," Colum shouted, as he gave the beast a wide berth. "We're almost there."

Decker put on a spurt of raw speed despite his aching muscles and lungs that screamed for oxygen.

Hunt squeezed off another shot, eliciting another angry bellow.

Decker risked a glance sideways toward the beast. It was glaring at him with those cold blue eyes as it tried to close the gap between them, but it was unsteady on its feet now. That didn't mean it was giving up. The creature swayed, shook its head as if trying to clear a mind fog, and kept advancing, albeit at a slower pace.

"Hurry up," Mina screamed, running out to meet Decker and Colum as they sprinted the last small distance to the hangar. Hunt turned and retreated inside.

Decker ushered Mina forward through the gap between the doors, then slowed to let Colum enter the hangar first. He sensed the creature right behind him, tensed in anticipation of its attack. He hurled himself past the doors into the hangar and turned around, ready to help pull the doors closed, but there was no need.

The creature lay slumped mere feet from the hangar, his chest rising and falling rhythmically, eyes rolled up into his head. A dart was still buried in the beast's calf. Decker didn't know if it was the first or second hit Colum had scored, but he didn't care.

He slumped against the hangar wall, panting.

From deeper inside the building, four soldiers moved forward, wheeling a large crate on a dolly. Padian followed behind. As he passed Decker, the doctor nodded and mumbled a brief compliment. "Good job."

Decker couldn't find the breath to reply. He watched the five men exit the hangar and get to work securing the beast. When he looked away, Rory was approaching him.

"I've been talking with Hunt," the archaeologist said. "I think we can use the storm to get home, but we don't have a lot of time."

"How? You said it would be almost impossible to predict where the lightning would strike or get close enough to take advantage of it without being killed."

"I did." Rory nodded. He looked between Decker and Colum. "But while the two of you were running around playing hide and seek with that saber-toothed cat, we came up with a plan that just might work."

Decker felt a surge of hope. Maybe he would get back to Nancy after all. He pushed himself away from the wall and folded his arms. "All right, tell me what you have in mind."

SIXTY-THREE

DECKER BURST into Colonel Spear's office, fending off the protests of his secretary, who stood helplessly in the doorway as he approached the base commander. "We fulfilled our part of the bargain. The creature has been contained and is on its way to the menagerie. Now I need you to fulfill yours."

"It's okay, Bert," Spear said, waving the anxious secretary back into his own office. He turned to Decker. "What is it you need?"

"I want that Lockheed Electra you've got stashed in a hangar near the runway. I need it. Ready to go as quickly as possible."

"And a pilot?"

"We have our own pilot."

"Ah, yes. The Irishman who showed such interest in it earlier. My men told me about your little stunt separating them so that you could examine the aircraft. I had assumed you were plotting to steal it in order to avoid being locked up here for the rest of your lives if things went south."

"We were," Decker said. "The plan changed."

"Did it, indeed?" Spear turned away from Decker and stood looking out of the window toward the airstrip. "The storm is getting worse."

Decker joined him at the window. He looked out as a shaft of lightning lanced down and hit somewhere beyond the fence in the forest. The rain was coming down in sheets, blown almost sideways by a fierce wind. Thunder rumbled overhead. "The storm could be our way home."

"I'd love to know what you plan to do with my airplane." Spear glanced sideways. "Do tell."

"Rory says we need to be in proximity to the lightning when the conditions are right to rip a hole between your time and our own."

"What if it sends you somewhere else instead?"

"He doesn't think that's likely. Something about swimming upstream and then letting the current carry us back . . . The short answer is that he thinks we're more likely to return from where we came than end up somewhere new."

"I see. You still haven't said where the Electra comes into this."

"The only way we can be sure of getting close to a lightning strike is to fly through the heart of the storm."

"Sounds dangerous. What if the lightning doesn't send you home?" Spear asked. "You said the conditions have to be just right."

"They do. But if nothing happens and we end up stuck here, the plane's fuselage should act like a Faraday cage."

"Sounds reasonable." Spear narrowed his eyes. "How do I know I can trust you?"

"What do you mean?" Decker asked.

"Well, you've already admitted you were plotting to steal the plane and make your escape. If the lightning doesn't play nice and send you home, what's stopping you from flying off into the sunset instead of coming back?"

"Nothing, I guess." Decker shrugged. "But you gave me your word, and I'm relying upon you to be a man of honor."

"Honor."

"Yes."

Spear remained silent for a moment. He pressed his lips together, then nodded. "Okay. You may have the plane. I'll make sure it's fueled up immediately."

"Thank you." Decker felt a rush of relief.

"Don't thank me yet. I will instruct my men to fuel the plane just enough for the task you wish to accomplish. But not enough to get you anywhere useful should your plan fail. Naval Air Station Fort Lauderdale is sixty-seven miles from our current location. I'll give you the fuel to go thirty."

"That's very magnanimous of you." Decker turned away from the window. "We could just land on another island."

"Are you trying to talk yourself out of this deal?"

"No. Just pointing out the obvious. I know you've already thought of that scenario and I want to hear your take on it."

"Very well. As I'm sure you know, the Bahamas are a British colony."

"Which is why you could put this base here."

"Exactly. It also means that we have a strong working relationship with the local powers that be. There are only two airfields big enough to land a Lockheed Electra outside of Singer Cay. Oakes Field and Harbour Island. They are both controlled by the Royal Air Force. If you land at either of them, your plane will be impounded immediately, and you will be taken into custody."

"So, if we fail to get home, our choices are returning here to be locked up, landing at another airfield in the Bahamas only to be locked up, or crashing into the ocean."

"That about sums it up."

"And the other part of our deal?" Decker asked. "The TBM Avenger crews?"

"They take their planes up with you under the same restrictions. Either you will all go home where you belong, or you'll come back here." Spear rubbed the back of his neck and grimaced. "Honestly, I'm rooting for you to get home."

"And save you the hassle of dealing with us."

"No. To tell the truth, it might be useful to have members of CUSP from eighty years in the future available. You've already proven yourselves capable."

"Does that mean you're not going to lock us up?"

Spear smiled. "We'll have that conversation if and when it's necessary. In the meantime, get those planes in the air."

Decker nodded and crossed the room, but before he could step out of the office, the base commander spoke again.

"Decker."

"Yes?" Decker looked back.

"Don't take this the wrong way, but I sincerely hope I see none of you ever again."

Decker paused, a thin smile playing on his lips, then he continued on through the outer office on his way to the hangar where the Lockheed Electra waited.

SIXTY-FOUR

DECKER RAN BACK across the airfield, bent low to shield himself against the torrential rain. The storm was overhead now; the lightning coming thick and fast, accompanied by booms of thunder that felt more like one long rumble than individual claps. When he arrived at the hangar containing the shiny aluminum skinned Electra, the others had already gathered there.

Colum was circling the aircraft, inspecting it. When Decker entered, he looked around. "Did he agree to let us go up?"

"He did." Decker shook water from his clothing, wiped his face. "He's only giving us enough fuel to make a couple of runs through the storm, though. We won't be able to make it to the mainland if we fail."

"Exactly how much fuel are we talking, here?"

"Enough to get us thirty miles."

"Are you kidding me? This aircraft has a range of over seven hundred. What's he using to fuel it, a coffee cup?" Colum huffed in annoyance.

Decker shrugged. "I did the best I could."

"Then we'd better not mess this up," Hunt said. "I don't want to spend the rest of my life held on a mosquito infested tropical island being looked after by a bunch of people who haven't even seen a single episode of I Love Lucy yet."

Decker exchanged a puzzled glance with Mina.

"What? It was the best I could come up with." Hunt looked out through the open hangar doors toward the row of Avengers. "What about those guys?"

"They're coming with us."

"What happens if we get home and find ourselves stuck with a bunch of aviators from the 1940s?" Hunt didn't look pleased.

"I don't think that will happen," said Rory. "Like I said, I think the time stream will carry us back to our own places in history. Those airmen should end up back in 1945."

"I hope you're right." Hunt folded his arms. "For all our sakes."

———

An hour later, the planes were fueled and ready to make the perilous flight up into the thunderstorm, which had shown no signs of abating.

Decker was uneasy. There were too many things that could go wrong. What if they got hit by lightning and crashed instead of returning to their own time? His mind wandered back to the wrecked aircraft they had seen a few days before when they were driving across the island. It looked suspiciously like the one they were about to climb into. Had they driven past their own gravesite without even realizing it? He shuddered and pushed the thought aside.

Out on the airfield, a line of men wearing flight suits were trudging toward the TBM Avengers. Fourteen of them in all. When the airmen reached the planes, they broke into groups and climbed aboard. Decker resisted the urge to go outside and meet the aviators who flew one of the most famous Avenger squadrons in history. He wouldn't know what to say, and besides, there was no time.

Hunt came up beside him. "Did anyone bother to brief those men on what they're about to do?"

"I hope so. Commander Spear thought it would be best if we didn't interact with them, for the sake of the timeline. He promised to fill them in on what we are about to attempt. They have orders to follow us up and stay in tight formation behind the Electra."

"That's good." Rory was standing a little way distant, listening. Now he joined the conversation. "If we attract lightning that opens a portal through time, the resulting rift should be big enough for everyone to fly through."

"Come along you guys," Colum called. He was standing next to a door in the plane's fuselage between the wing and the tail.

"I guess that's our cue," Decker said, starting toward the aircraft. He looked at Mina. "You ready for this?"

"No." The color drained from Mina's face. "I hate flying at the best of times, and that plane doesn't look very sturdy."

"She'll be fine," Colum said, helping Mina up into the cabin. He waited for the others to climb aboard, then followed behind, pulling the cabin door closed behind him and latching it. After everyone settled into their seats, he made his way to the cockpit, but before he sat down, he turned back to address them. "I just want everyone to know ahead of time. It's going to be a bumpy ride up there and if we get in trouble, there's going to be nowhere to go other than down."

"Aren't you a barrel of laughs." Hunt said.

"If the worst happens, can't we just fly up above the storm?" Mina asked.

Colum shook his head. "This plane has an altitude ceiling of 22,000 feet. But a powerful storm like this might extend well into the upper atmosphere as high as 60,000 feet. Not even a modern jetliner could fly above that."

"I think that's enough talking," Hunt said. "Get this bird in the sky. I want to go home."

"Right-ho, boss." Colum opened the cockpit door and ducked inside, closing it behind him.

A silence descended upon the cabin. The air was thick with tension. After a few minutes, the plane's powerful engines rumbled to life and the propellers started to turn, and the Electra taxied out of the hangar. A few minutes after that, they were lined up and ready for take-off on the dark and rain-slicked runway . . .

SIXTY-FIVE

DECKER SAT in the Lockheed Electra's cabin with Mina next to him across the aisle. Adam Hunt and Rory occupied the seats in front of them. Out of the cabin window, Decker could see the five Navy TBM Avengers taxiing into a line behind them, ready for takeoff.

The Electra shuddered and strained as if it were bored with waiting and wanted to get airborne.

From the cockpit, Colum's voice drifted back. "Hold on tight, here we go."

The aircraft gave one more shudder, then started down the runway, picking up speed as it went. A strong crosswind buffeted the plane and Decker tensed when the tail slipped sideways, but Colum quickly brought them back under control.

The engine noise was deafening. A throaty rumble interlaced with a high-pitched whine. It filled the cabin as the aircraft reached rotation speed, the point at which the pilot angled the plane's nose up at the same moment their forward momentum provided the lift to get them into the air.

With all the grace of a lumbering giant, the Electra clawed its way up through the foul weather. The crosswinds, bad enough on the ground, now felt like an invisible fist punching the side of the plane. The fuselage rattled and jerked. Something came loose behind them in the cargo area and fell with a metallic clank.

Mina let out a small whimper and reached across the aisle to Decker. "Are you sure this is a good idea?"

"We don't have much choice now," Decker said, taking her hand and giving it a reassuring squeeze. "Besides, if we don't do this, we'll never get home."

Rory shouted over the engine's throbbing roar. "I'll never complain about CUSP's Learjet again. Assuming we live long enough."

"Amen to that," Decker replied as they bounced down into a pocket of turbulence that momentarily lifted him off his seat.

Mina gripped his hand even tighter. "How high do you think we need to get?"

"Beats me." Decker glanced at the window as a flicker of lightning lit up the sky. He saw the tops of trees flashing past underneath them way too close before the landscape plunged into darkness again.

Colum pushed the cockpit door open. It banged back against the bulkhead. Decker glimpsed the plane's windshield bombarded by slashing rain. Beyond this, there was nothing but inky blackness.

Colum glanced backward briefly into the cabin. "I'm going to take us out over the ocean, then double back and fly through the heart of the storm. We have all five Avengers behind us flying in a tight V formation. I've made radio contact with their squadron commander. He will follow our lead."

"Just make sure we have enough fuel to land again if

things go south," Decker shouted over the storm and engine noise.

"Roger that," Colum said as he took them into a steep rightward bank that made Decker's stomach lurch. "Although I'm rather hoping we don't need to land again. That runway would be bad enough in broad daylight, let alone at night in the middle of a thunderstorm. We'd probably end up crashing into the forest instead."

Mina's hand tightened further over Decker's. Her breathing was coming in short-ragged gasps. When Decker looked sideways, her eyes were scrunched tightly closed.

He leaned across the aisle. "Hey, it'll be okay."

"You've always been right before," Mina said in a small voice. "Please God, don't let this be the time you get it wrong."

"I'll do my best," Decker said as the plane's nose dropped, sending the cockpit door slamming back on its hinges as Colum fought to keep them under control.

More items fell to their rear. Something large hit the deck with a thud. Another object rolled back and forth, but Decker didn't turn to look. He kept his gaze fixed firmly forward as Colum brought the plane around to make his run through the center of the storm as it churned over the island. The clouds ahead of them were like towering walls of roiling blackness flickering with enough electricity to power a city. Flashes of lightning tore through the clouds like spidery cracks that crackled earthward, looking for ground.

Decker's chest tightened. What they were about to do was either a brilliant solution to their problem or insanely stupid, depending on the outcome. But there was no going back now. They were committed.

As if to confirm this, Colum's voice drifted back from the cockpit. "Grab whatever you can, boys and girls. If you thought this was a bumpy ride, it's about to get a whole lot worse."

Decker checked the lap belt strung around his waist, even though it felt like a puny attempt to keep him safe, given the circumstances. He gave Mina's hand another reassuring squeeze.

The Electra bounced and lurched its way toward the center of the storm, dropping and rising on the uneven air beneath it with more ferocity than the worst roller coaster.

In the seat ahead of him, he heard Rory groan.

Hunt cursed loudly when an air pocket lifted him out of his seat and dropped him back down hard.

The cockpit door slammed shut, isolating Colum and cutting off Decker's view through the plane's windshield. Not that he needed to see what was happening up ahead. The view from his cabin window was enough to convince Decker that they had metaphorically stuck their heads into the jaws of an angry tiger. The sky around them burst with energy. Bright flashes lit up the cabin in an uneven staccato beat. He couldn't tell where the engine noise stopped, and the thunder began. All he could hear was a cacophony of raging sound all around them.

The plane made one more violent lurch that made Decker's stomach drop, before a bright finger of lightning pierced the clouds and slammed into the aircraft with an earsplitting crack that sent the Electra into a spiraling, sickening freefall.

SIXTY-SIX

THE PLANE TWISTED and bucked as it fell through the darkness in an uncontrolled descent toward oblivion.

Mina cried out. She was still holding Decker's hand and now she gripped it so tight he thought she would cut off his circulation.

Hunt pressed his fingers into his seat rests, knuckles white, body stiff. Rory let out a pained yell.

In the cockpit, they could hear Colum cursing as he fought to regain control of the stricken aircraft.

There was no way to tell what was going on with the five TBM Avengers flying on their tail, but something was happening to their own airplane. Instead of dissipating back into the ether, the lightning had latched on to them, sending tendrils of arcing electricity across the Electra's fuselage and wings. It danced across the skin of the plane as they dropped through the darkness.

Decker mouthed a silent prayer. He'd already faced death once that day and survived. The second time, it appeared, he would not be so lucky. He could run from the Smilodon, but there was nowhere he could go to avoid this grim fate. He was trapped in a three-ton metal tube that was about to slam into the ground and kill them all.

Except something had changed.

The electricity surrounding their plane was growing brighter. It pulsed and hummed with an ethereal brilliance that hurt Decker's eyes. He squinted and turned away from the cabin window in time to see the air around them pop with flashes of searing energy.

Mina whimpered.

Decker glanced toward her, saw the look of terror on her face, a moment before the sparkling flashes of energy that had invaded the cabin exploded around them.

The plane seemed to melt away like the last lingering remnants of a half-forgotten dream, and Decker felt himself dropping through an endless void with Mina next to him, their hands clasped together. Below him, Decker glimpsed Rory and Hunt in their own freefall, and even further away, the dark silhouette of his friend, Colum.

Then a second bright flash ripped through the void and Mina's hand was wrenched from his own. The brightness faded away to be replaced by a blinding pit of blackness. He felt himself buffeted by forces he could not see, turned end over end with such violence that he thought his limbs would be torn from his body.

He was dying. He was sure of it.

The last thing he heard as the darkness closed in and his consciousness faded was Mina's shrill, terrified scream.

SIXTY-SEVEN

SINGER CAY—TWO DAYS AFTER THE WEDDING

NANCY STOOD under La Casa de Playa's front portico and paced back and forth, waiting for the men to return. It had been a full twenty-four hours since Colum, Rory, and Hunt had arrived back at the hotel, wet, bedraggled, and exhausted. Decker and Mina had not been with them.

The story they told was hard to believe, but since Celine Rothman—a woman born when Queen Victoria was still on the throne—occupied a room on the hotel's second floor, what choice did she have?

Now, after a full day of searching the forest and ruined airbase in the middle of the island, she was forced to accept a new reality. Both Mina and the man she came here to marry were dead. Killed during their attempt to travel forward through time and return home. She had overheard Rory that very morning when he thought she was out of earshot, theorizing on Decker and Mina's fate. He wondered if they had become trapped in the void, never emerging from the time stream as their essence was spread across eternity. Or perhaps they reemerged back in the doomed Lockheed Electra as it plunged to earth and died in a fiery crash. The only ray of hope was that they might have ended up in a parallel universe created by their time travel. Rory backed this theory up by citing the five TBM Avengers. In their reality flight 19 was still missing which meant that either the airmen didn't make it and were killed along with Decker and Mina, or their return to 1945 caused a fork that created a new reality where they never disappeared, although he stressed this was purely speculative and he had no proof. There was no way to know which scenario was correct. The only certainty was that Decker and Mina had not made it back home.

She choked back a sob and looked up as a Humvee made its way up the driveway and pulled up under the portico. The back door opened, and Hunt stepped out, soon followed by Rory. Colum exited the driver's door.

She stepped forward, eager to hear their news, but Colum shook his head.

"We searched the wreck of the Electra," he said, referring to the decades-old crashed plane they had passed on their way to the Grand Fairmont Hotel several days before. "I can't be sure it's the same one we flew into the storm, but we only saw one such plane back in 1942, and it would have been pilotless after we returned to the twenty-first century."

"Did you find any human remains?" Nancy's heart was in her throat. "Were they there?"

"We couldn't find any evidence that John and Mina went down with the Electra."

Nancy felt a rush of relief, albeit short-lived. This didn't prove anything either way.

Colum soon reiterated that point. "Keep in mind, it doesn't mean they weren't on the plane when it crashed. It just means they aren't there now."

"But if it's any consolation," Hunt said. "I saw them

briefly as we were swept forward through time. I saw them tumbling behind me in the void before I passed out. They could still be out there somewhere. You shouldn't give up hope."

Nancy nodded mutely. "Or they could be dead. I might never see John again."

"That is also a possibility." Hunt stepped forward and put his arm around her in an uncharacteristic show of empathy.

Nancy sniffed and looked up at him. "What do I do now? Where do I go from here?"

"You keep going," Hunt said, holding her tighter. "And we never stop looking."

Nancy nodded again, and buried her head in Hunt's chest, and then she began to cry.

SIXTY-EIGHT

AN HOUR after returning from the forest, Colum O'Shea strode down the hotel corridor and stopped outside a second-floor room. He knocked twice, then waited until a female voice answered.

"Come in." Celine Rothman was sitting in a chair near the window, looking out over the lush hotel grounds toward the ocean beyond. When she saw Colum a smile spread across her face. "The charming Irishman, come to check up on me."

"That isn't why I'm here."

"Really?" Celine was dressed in a pair of blue jeans and a tee borrowed from Nancy. Her dark hair fell lose across her shoulders in a shimmering cascade. She looked every bit as though she belonged in the twenty-first century.

"Really." Colum stepped further into the room, noticing a paperback novel lying open on the bed, face down with the spine bent back. "I see you've been keeping yourself entertained."

"I've always loved reading," Celine replied. "There's a whole world of literature out there to be discovered. Eighty years of it just waiting for me."

"I'd hardly call that literature," Colum said, eyeing the book, a well-known spy novel from the fifties. He'd read it himself many years before. "But it's entertaining."

"It is, indeed."

"Well, if you want some recommendations when you finish that one, let me know."

"Am I going to be staying that long?"

"That's why I'm here." Colum had volunteered to have this talk with Celine, but he wasn't looking forward to it. "We're not sure there's a safe way to get you home."

"Because of what happened to your colleagues?" Celine stood and walked toward Colum. "I know I'm supposed to be in seclusion lest I see or hear something that I could use to change the future if I ever get home, but I'm not blind and deaf. Two of your group never made it back from the Grand Fairmont."

"That's correct." Colum felt his throat tighten. "We're still looking for them. But that isn't the only reason we don't think it's safe to try and return you to 1912."

"Then tell me."

"We need a lightning storm in order to send you back. You would have to be in the immediate vicinity of a lightning strike during a time when the conditions are exactly right."

"And if the conditions are not right?"

"You would end up electrocuted, instead." Colum watched Celine's face for any sign of distress, but she kept her face expressionless. "It would kill you."

"I see." Celine nodded. "What are my odds should we try this?"

"Not good. Even assuming we could get you in the right location—and it's a long shot—Rory thinks there's a one in a hundred chance of success."

"Yet you were able to do it." Celine folded her arms. "I

overheard Nancy talking. You were trapped in the past and most of you got home."

"We almost didn't. And like you said, we lost two people. For all we know, they are dead." Colum sighed. "Look, I'm not saying it can't be done, but the risk is high. It would also put others at risk." The best chance of getting Celine home, Colum knew, was to fly up into a storm the same way they had back in 1942, but that would mean whoever flew the plane would either end up in the past, or worse, they would be killed.

"I wouldn't want to be the cause of more tragedy. You've already lost two people, and the guilt of that weighs heavy on me."

"John and Mina knew the risks."

"And Nancy is now without a husband."

"Maybe. I haven't given up hope yet." Colum wished he could tell her it would be alright, that Decker and Mina would reappear a day or a week in the future. After all, they had arrived days apart in 1942. But deep down he felt this was different. Something had gone horribly wrong when they were up in that Electra flying through the storm. He could sense it.

"It's admirable of you to try and make me feel better." Celine paused for a moment, as if she were thinking. "I won't allow anyone else to get hurt because of me. It would be best for all involved if I stay here in this century."

"I will let Adam Hunt know."

"Good." Celine met Colum's gaze. "Will I be allowed my freedom?"

"Yes." There had already been a discussion about this. Since Celine was from the past, nothing she knew could alter the future. The biggest challenge would be acclimatizing her to a world of technology that didn't exist in 1912, but Colum suspected she would do just fine. "You will be allowed to live your life in peace, with a few caveats, of course."

"Like keeping quiet about where I'm from and what I know?"

Colum nodded.

Celine smiled. "I don't know what people are like in this day and age, but I think that even if I tried to tell my story most would dismiss me as a lunatic."

"Maybe." Colum was impressed by her shrewdness.

"Now we've settled my fate, I think there's only one thing to do," Celine said. She lifted her left hand, took the two bands of gold and jewels adorning her ring finger, and slipped them off. She looked at them for a moment, then put the two rings on the nightstand before glancing up at Colum again with a sad look in her eyes. "All done."

"Your wedding ring." Colum eyed the rings sitting on the nightstand. "Don't you want to wear it?"

"My husband is long since dead, Mr. O'Shea. I'm no longer married," Celine said. The sadness was replaced by a look of determination. "I will keep them with me always, but if I'm going to stay here, I have to look forward, not back."

"I think that's an admirable sentiment."

"It's a pragmatic one. There is no point in dwelling on what a person cannot change. I married Howard for practical reasons, and although I loved him in my own way, I see no point in wallowing in pity. There's a whole new world out there, after all"

"That's true."

"The only question is what I will do now. My money is behind me. My class. Social status. I am utterly alone."

"I have a feeling you'll get by."

"I always do."

"Of that, I'm sure." Colum observed Celine for a moment, then moved toward the door. "I'll take my leave for now."

"Come back soon?" Celine took a step toward Colum, stopped as if thinking better of it. "I would appreciate the company."

"I'll drop by later, I promise." Colum stepped out into the corridor. He turned back toward her. "Maybe I'll bring you a few more books."

"I'd like that." Celine met Colum's gaze. "I hope you find your missing friends."

"Me too," Colum said in a quiet voice, then made his way back along the corridor toward the elevators. When he glanced back, Celine's door was already closed.

SIXTY-NINE

OH MY, I think he might be dead."

"Dead or not, what is he wearing? Looks like some sort of a soldier."

"He ain't dead. He's passed out drunk. That's what he is. Must have snuck out of the barracks over on Carriage Road."

Decker registered the voices before he was even fully conscious. Two men and a woman with thick accents he didn't recognize.

"He's wakin' up, look." This was the woman. "Told you he wasn't a goner."

Decker opened his eyes. He saw feet wearing scuffed leather boots with frayed laces. Beyond this, a cobblestone street. It was dark. And freezing cold. He could feel the bitter chill through his thin shirt.

"Come on then, let's get you on yer way."

A hand appeared and gripped Decker's arm. He felt another hand on his shoulder. Together they lifted him up and held on until he regained his feet. When the hands released him, Decker stumbled and almost fell again.

"Easy there, mate," one of the men said, steadying him. "Take it slow now."

"Where am I?" Decker looked around. He was standing in a narrow alleyway. A gas lamp burned nearby on a pole, casting a pool of yellow light into the darkness. The memories were coming back now. The Electra plunging through the storm. The lightning that wrenched them through time. He wasn't on Singer Cay, and this was not the twenty-first century. There was no sign of Mina, either. He looked at the three figures clustered around him. The men, both in their fifties, wore heavy jackets and dark trousers. One had a flat cap on his head. The woman—who looked younger than her companions—hugged a woolen shawl around her ample frame. All three looked like they had led hard lives. "I was with a girl. Early twenties. Have you seen her?"

"A girl, eh?" One of the men chuckled. "Out for some easy fun, were you?"

At first, Decker didn't understand what the man was insinuating, but then it dawned on him. "No. It isn't like that. I'm not . . . She's my . . . companion."

"Right. Whatever you say, fella." The woman didn't sound like she believed him. "Looks like your *companion* scarpered."

"Probably whacked him over the head and robbed him," one of the men said. "That's why he was out for the count."

"What date is this?" Decker asked, growing frustrated by the conversation. "What year?"

"She must have hit you hard if you don't even know that." The woman reached for his arm. "Come on. We'll take you over to the King's Head. Get you warmed up."

"No. I'm fine." Decker pulled away. He stumbled past them, still unsteady on his legs, and made his way along the alley.

"That's gratitude for you," the woman called after him. "Well, if you don't want no help, I'm off."

Decker ignored the woman. He could see an open expanse ahead and beyond that the lights of a city. He reached the end of the alley and came out onto a wide walking path bordered by a stone wall. Next to this, a river ran off into the distance, cutting the city in half.

Decker stopped under a flickering gas lamp, unsure what to do next. There was still no sign of Mina. Had she made it back to their own time? He hoped so.

He was about to start walking again when he saw something fluttering in the breeze on a bench several feet away. A newspaper. He hurried over and snatched the paper up, looked at the masthead, shocked to see where he was. Then his eyes slid lower to the date.

November 3rd, 1911.

He read the date again, the breath catching in his throat, just as a somber bell tolled across the city. Decker looked up, saw the source of those chimes sitting further along the river. A tall square tower with clock faces on each side next to a long gothic building that dominated the skyline. And inside that tower, the mighty bell known as Big Ben striking the hour. How it happened, he didn't know, but John Decker was in the city of London—alone and stranded, over a hundred years in the past.

READY FOR MORE JOHN DECKER?

The next book in the John Decker Series
DARK FORCE

Alone in the year 1911 and stranded in London, John Decker seeks out the precursor to CUSP, an organization known as the Knights of St. George, hoping they can help him get home. But when he locates them he ends up with more questions than answers.

Meanwhile, in a village on the outskirts of the city, something terrifying has been released. A supernatural force that drives people to murder.

Agreeing to help the Order, Decker arrives in the small hamlet of Mavendale to investigate, where he finds an abandoned workhouse shuttered decades before, a history soaked in blood, and a malevolent entity looking for victims…
Pre-order now

Printed in Great Britain
by Amazon